I0724776

KINGS OF EDEN

MILA YOUNG

HARPER A. BROOKS

Kings of Eden © Copyright 2022 Mila Young & Harper A. Brooks

Cover Design by Maria Spada, Book Cover Design
Editing by Briann Graziano and Proofreading and other Author Services
by Renea
Proofreading by Nic Page and Robyn Mather

Visit our books at
www.milayoungbooks.com
https://harperabrooks.com

All rights reserved under the International and Pan-American Copyright
Conventions. No part of this book may be reproduced or transmitted in
any form or by any means, electronic or mechanical, including
photocopying, recording, or by any information storage and retrieval
system, without permission in writing from the publisher/author.

This is a work of fiction. Names, places, characters and incidents are either
the product of the author's imagination or are used fictitiously, and any
resemblance to any actual persons, living or dead, organizations, events or
locales is entirely coincidental.

Warning: the unauthorized reproduction or distribution of this
copyrighted work is illegal. Criminal copyright infringement, including
infringement without monetary gain, is investigated by the FBI and is
punishable by up to 5 years in prison and a fine of $250,000.

DEDICATION

To our two mysterious men... Edwin and Adf

You know who you are!

Mila and Harper

CONTENTS

KINGS OF EDEN SERIES

Kings of Eden

Stolen Paradise

Ruthless Lies

More coming...

KINGS OF EDEN

I'll never fall to my knees... even if that's exactly where they want me.

My life's never exactly been the easiest. Or the most godly. I've danced for powerful men. *Deadly* men. And when one wants to take things too far, I barely escape with my life. What I didn't know is that someone else was watching me from the shadows.

Someone deadlier… Someone scarier.

Now the Kings of Eden are after me.

They say I have something they want, and because of it, they've made me their captive.

Now, I'm swept up into their deadly world of gang wars and destructive magic. Dracon, Cassius, Knox - they're criminals, murderers, monsters… But I can't resist.

The chaotic power inside me craves the chaos they give.

But even with so much at stake, losing my heart scares me the most.

CHAPTER ONE

EVE

The lights on stage dim and then change to blood red. As I spin around the pole, a dark silhouette against the backdrop, the crowd whistles and cheers. They know what's coming. My big finish.

I may have strolled out in a white robe, feathery wings, and a faux halo, but this is when I make my transformation from an innocent angel to a hotter-than-hell devil. Fully attired in a red lace thong, pasties, leather harness, and yes, even horns.

The crowd *loves* it. It's always my most popular and highest paying set at Kat's Kradle. So sure, I'll be a corrupted angel as I do my splits and twirl around. I bend over in front of them, gripping the pole, as that move always pays so well. Doesn't bother me any. It's money, at the end of the day. A job to pay my bills and keep me off the streets.

Back on the pole, instinct and memory kick in, and I climb. The crowd goes absolutely wild. When I do my last spin on the pole, Mack gets the old fog machine going, and the black lights turn on to illuminate the painted flames on my arms, chest, and thighs. The men watching at the tables cheer with their approval, begging me for more, every single one of their faces reflecting the same hunger to have what they can't touch. Their lustful stares only fuel my ego and power. I enjoy making men bend to my whim–and we get all kinds of influential men here. CEOs, doctors, business tycoons. Kat's Kradle isn't like one of those sleazy gentlemen's clubs in the sketchy part of town. No, the owner, Kat, is one smart cookie. She set her business right in the heart of Andover City, where the money is. And I was lucky enough to score a job here.

As I toss my long blonde hair over my shoulders, money flutters all around me, and when I look up, my gaze locks on an unfamiliar face seated right at the front of the stage. Of course, we get strangers in the club as well as regulars, but I remember every person who stays for my set, which is always at the very end of the main show. Especially men as massive and intimidating as this guy.

His shoulders are as wide as two football linebackers, and even though he's sitting, he's taller than most of the men in the place. He has to be close to seven feet, if I were to guess–a wall of a man with a shiny bald head and permanent scowl on his face. I would've definitely remembered him.

He doesn't throw money like the others. He only stares, holding a burning cigar between his fingers. But he never puts it to his lips, only fiddles with the one end and lets it smolder.

What's even more surprising is that I can't sense an ounce of magic on him. Not even a tingle. One of the few perks of having such strong magic flowing through my own veins is that I can sense it in others, and Mr. Mountain is as dry as the desert.

Human...

Huh. That's surprising. Most at the club are some kind of supe.

The music stops, and the audience applauds. All except Mr. Mountain. He only stares at me with those serious, dark eyes.

A different feeling rakes over me. Fear.

I don't know what it is about this stranger, but he unnerves me. And I want to be as far from him as possible.

Instead of staying through the applause like I usually do, I quickly gather up the stacks of cash and walk off the stage, goosebumps rising on my skin. I glance over my shoulder to see that he's still watching me with those haunting eyes. The moment I pass through the thick red curtain, Mercy's there with my fuzzy robe and her trademark sweeter-than-sugar smile. Mack's there too, the club's custodian and Kat's long time friend, with a broom in hand. He's ready for the crowd to quiet and the lights to fade out to clean up.

Mercy drapes the robe around my shoulders, and I almost moan out loud at how soft and plush it feels. "You were great," she says, green eyes shining. "As always."

Why a little southern belle like Mercy came north and got into dancing, I don't know. I've never asked, but like everyone else, I have my suspicions from the small bits she's told me. Like maybe it's that she's part fae, and the magic inside her calls to other supernaturals. Revs up their engines, if you know what I mean. Or it could be she had a traumatic experience with a blood merchant growing up since many buy fae blood on the black market. But I don't pry too much. I can wait until she's ready to talk.

Being one of the newest girls here, Mercy's still on the shy side, but she doesn't have to do much to have men begging to take her home. Adding her to our lineup really helped make it a full house every night.

I slip my arms through the robe and wrap the ties around my middle. "Thanks, love."

"Are you going straight upstairs after closing?" she asks, still dressed in the school girl outfit from her dance, a plaid skirt, see-through white blouse, and fake glasses. With her shortness, heart-shaped face, and curly brown hair, she fits the innocent sexy stereotype very well.

I wink. "Maybe. Or maybe I'll get into some more trouble tonight. Who knows?"

You'd think a girl like her would get chewed up and spit out in a cruel city like Andover, but she's been hanging in just fine so far.

Surviving.

Like the rest of us.

Don't misunderstand me—I love what I do. I was never the "sit behind a desk" type. Against common belief, I have my college degree in mathematics and could probably get a job easily with a 401k and all that fancy shit if I wanted to.

But the thing is, I don't want to.

Where's the excitement in working nine to five in a stuffy office for just enough money to live on? No, thank you. I make thousands a set. Since I have seniority at Kat's, I make my own hours, my own dances, and every night, there's always something new happening and that way, I'm never bored.

Man, my mother would have a heart attack if she were here, watching me.

Good. The bitch.

"How about you?" I ask Mercy. "I know Demi was going to grab some food at Buck's."

She shivers, visually creeped out. "I don't like vampires. Too… grabby. And bitey."

And since Buck's is a vampire-owned bar just down the street from Kat's Kradle and she can't help the magnetism she has with the opposite sex, I can see that being a problem.

"Besides, it's my turn to help Mack clean the dressing rooms," she goes on and then shivers for a different reason.

"You poor soul," I chuckle.

"Eve! Eve! Eve!"

Mercy and I spin to see Demi racing down the back hall toward us. She's already in her yoga pants and t-shirt, with her chestnut curled hair pulled back in her typical "fuck it" ponytail, as she calls it.

"Speak of the devil," I say. "We were just talking about you."

That's when I realize her eyes are wide, and she's flush with panic.

My stomach tightens. "What is it? What's wrong?" Don't tell me it's her fuckwit of an ex again. I threatened him last time. This time, I'll stab his ass.

Demi glances at Mercy, wondering if it's okay to say the next part in front of her.

"Fuck, Dem, out with it."

"Okay, okay." She sucks in a deep breath. "Did you see who was in the audience tonight? Right in front?"

My thoughts instantly fly to Mr. Mountain in the flashy white suit and piercing dark eyes, but I play dumb. "Who?"

"Big guy. Bald head. Cigar." Then she lowers her voice to a harsh whisper. "Do you have any idea who he is?"

Mercy and I both shake our heads.

"That's Xavier Franco. The head of the Black Spades."

Every muscle in my body tightens, and nausea rolls

through me. Oh, no... I knew he was bad news, but one of the biggest kingpins in the city? In Kat's Kradle? I definitely didn't expect that.

Anyone alive knows of the three gangs who run this city: The Black Spades, the Lords of Night, and the Kings of Eden. They have their hands in every trade, every powerful back pocket, and damn near every government official from this state to Washington, DC. Death follows them wherever they go.

I've lived my entire life in Andover and I've never seen Franco, the vampire Lord brothers, or the three supernatural Kings in this joint. I was hoping I never would. They're all deadly in their own right. I've heard rumors that to see them is like a premonition of death.

Franco, being here, can't be a good sign.

"Kat's back there losing her damn mind," Demi goes on breathlessly. "She wants to kick him out. You know how she is."

I sure do. She's worked long and hard to keep her club clean of their underhanded dealings. But kicking out the head of the Black Spades will have consequences too.

Mercy's brow knits in confusion. "I don't understand. Black Spa–"

"Shhh! Don't even say their name." Demi waves her hands to cut her off. "It's safer if we keep it out of our mouths altogether."

Mercy's voice rises in worry. "What do we do?"

"Kat wants us all to go home. Now. She wants us to clear out. She's going to close early."

Wow. Kat never closes early for anything. She must be really scared.

"I think you guys should come to my place. It'll be safer," she adds.

She's probably right. Mercy and I live in the apartments above the club, while Demi lives closer to the harbor and closer to her younger sister's high school. We'll be better off staying as far away from Franco as possible, just in case something goes down. The man doesn't do anything without a purpose, including his visit to the club.

"Let me just put some clothes on and we can sneak out the back door," I say and clutch the robe tighter around myself.

"I'm not even going to get changed. Let me just grab my coat. I'll meet you there." Mercy turns and hurries off toward the lockers.

She could do that with her outfit, but I had nothing except my thong and pasties on under my robe. I needed to throw *something* on, or risk being arrested for public nudity.

"Five seconds," I say. Demi nods and I speed walk down the hall, past the storage rooms, the boiler, and kitchen, and notice how eerily quiet it is. The cook and kitchen staff must have already taken Kat's advice and ran home.

My heart beats a little faster as I walk faster to the dressing room Demi, Mercy, and I share. I pass a few other girls along the way, but none even look at me as they rush for the exit in the opposite direction.

Maybe I should've just braved it in my fuzzy robe.

In the frigid late-winter weather outside? Yeah, I don't think so.

I'm about to step into the dressing room when a strong hand clamps around the top of my arm, stopping me dead in my tracks.

My scream lodges in my throat, and as I look up, I find a tall man dressed in all black with sunglasses on and an earpiece in his ear. Like the president's goddamn secret service.

I try to yank myself free, but his fingers bite in to hold me in place. Even though he's practically twice my size, I muster up all my courage and glare at him. "I'm going to need you to let go of me."

His chin tilts down, and he peers at me from over his sunglasses. "I'm afraid I can't do that, Miss Dalton."

He knows my last name?

Anxiety growing, I grab his hand and attempt to pry his grip off me. "Get your meaty paws the fuck off me. Now."

"Xavier Franco requests an audience with you," he says, unfazed. His voice is gruff, like his attitude.

At the mention of his name, my entire body ices over. My mouth opens, but I'm unable to form words. I've been completely taken over by fear.

One of the biggest kingpins in the city wants to meet...*me?*

And that means this guy who's been sent to fetch me must be part of his security detail. When I glance down, I see the handgun strapped to his hip.

Oh, fuck... I'm in deep shit.

"I–I–I don't think so," I manage to stammer out, but he ignores me and holds up a white clothing gift box instead. I hadn't even noticed he had the thing. Too distracted by– oh, you know–the deadly weapon inches away.

"He wants you to wear this," the guard says and pushes the box into my arms. I fumble with it, causing a black slinky piece of cloth to fall out. I'm able to snatch it before it hits the ground and when I hold it up, I realize it's a spaghetti strapped dress that shimmers iridescently, even in the hallway's low lighting. I gasp. The fabric feels like water in my hands. Designer. Expensive.

Part of me wants to throw the thing at the stranger and tell him to shove it where the sun don't shine—what does Franco think I am? An escort?

But at the same time, if it's a gift, refusing it would be an insult, wouldn't it?

It's a *nice* dress, and I deserve nice things too.

There's also the little fact that saying no to Franco could have other, more deadly, consequences.

I don't have time to debate it though. The guard gives me a firm shove into the dressing room, making me nearly trip over my feet. "Five minutes," he says and reaches in to grab the door handle. "I'll be right here."

Then he slams it shut before I can refuse.

Still, a bit stunned by it all, I just stand there, staring at the door, blinking like a fool. This is happening so fast, and I have so many questions swirling around in my head that I can't seem to move.

Not until the guard's voice comes from the other side of the door.

"Four minutes."

Oh shit. Is he really counting down?

Heart racing, I glance around the dressing room. Three vanities, mirrors, costumes thrown every which way, and makeup and shoes all over the place. But not the one thing I need right now. No exit door.

Trapped.

"And if I had other plans for the night?" I call out, hearing the shake in my voice and hating it.

"They're canceled," is all he says.

I glance down at the box in my arms.

Franco, head of the Black Spades, one of the biggest drug cartels and black-market dealers on the east coast, wants to spend an evening with me.

This is how I end up on an episode of *Unsolved Mysteries*.

"Three minutes," he continues to count down, and dread twists up my spine. There's no way the time is really passing by that fast. "Mr. Franco doesn't like being kept waiting."

I really don't want to do this, but it looks like I'll be dead either way.

I quickly drop my robe and pull on the dress, not even bothering to take off my devil getup from underneath. No time anyway. It fits like a dream, gliding over my curves and hugging me in all the right places. And that's saying something for me. Girls like me with wide hips, thicker thighs, and a tiny waist have a hard time finding formal clothes that actually fit, but somehow, this stranger nailed it on the first try.

I'm not even sure I want to know how he found out these things... First my last name, my work, and now my dress size. Things are getting creepier by the second.

The door opens suddenly, and I leap back with a small scream. He didn't even finish counting; the bastard.

The guard's gaze narrows on me. "The limo's out front."

Stepping out of the room, I glance up and down the hall, hoping–praying–someone else will be around to see me leave with this man. But, as luck would have it, we're alone. And my purse and cell phone are in the lockers behind the stage.

Somehow, he's behind me, pushing me forward again. I'm lucky I'm a pro at wearing stiletto heels, otherwise, I would have gone down and broken something by now with all this manhandling. I can't sense a lick of magic in him, but he's fast and strong like a supe. I guess with that much muscle and height, he can be.

As I walk silently toward the front of the club with the guard close to my heels, I spot another man dressed in all black, wearing sunglasses, holding open the front door. The entire club has been cleared out. It's the eeriest thing I've ever seen. The club is *always* bustling, even when closed. I don't even see Kat, which has my stomach in knots. I hope they don't have her tied up somewhere, or worse.

As expected, I'm led past guard number two and into the arctic night. I instantly wrap my arms around myself, shivering against the bitter wind. When my gaze falls upon the white stretch limo parked at the curb, my veins ice over too.

Guard number two rushes over to open the back door, and that's when I see the same man from the front row of my show now lounging across the leather seat. The man, the crime lord himself.

Xavier Franco.

CHAPTER TWO

EVE

"Evelyn Dalton." Franco's voice washes over me and makes me quiver in my spot. All he's done is say my name, my full *real* name. It may seem innocent on the surface, but with it, he's revealed so much more.

No one knows me as Evelyn. *No one.* I haven't used that name since I left my childhood home at sixteen and was thrust into growing up too early. I shortened it when I shed myself of my mother's overbearing lifestyle when she threw me out of her home and I became my own person. I've been Eve ever since.

Him knowing my birth name tells me what I've been dreading. He's done research on me, studied me.

But why?

"Please." He waves for me to join him inside the limo. "It's cold out there. Come in."

I hesitate and glance back at Kat's Kradle and then down the empty sidewalk. Could I make a run for it?

Did I want a bullet in my back?

No, not particularly.

He must see the thoughts tumbling through my head

because he gives his guard the subtlest of nods and his meaty hand is back around my arm and I'm being shoved into the back seat. My ass hits the leather at the same time the car door slams behind me.

My gaze swings to Franco, who almost takes up the entire side seat of the limo across from me. At least he hasn't made any moves to get closer. Not like there's much space in here with his monstrous size, but I'll take every inch I can get.

A smile slowly lifts his lips. "You're wearing the dress," he says. As if I had a choice in the matter. "It looks great on you."

"Thanks," I reply, my throat tight. I've never been shy about my body, but I cross my arms over my chest, feeling naked in the limo's low lighting.

The engine rumbles and we're jerked forward as we start to drive. Franco stares at me for a while, and my skin crawls. I don't know what's worse—knowing what he has in store for me or sitting here in silence and letting my mind wander. Both are tortuous.

After a few grueling minutes, I make the decision to know if my death is coming. At least, then I won't be surprised and can fight if I have to.

Readjusting the low hem of the dress to cover more of my thighs, I clear my throat. "So, Mr–"

"Xavier," he cuts me off, then reaches for a glass at the minibar and a bottle of what looks like scotch. He pours himself some and then a second, which he holds out for me.

I want to refuse it, but again, the fear of what might happen if I say no takes over and I take it instead.

Pleased, Franco leans back and takes a sip. I only hold mine in my lap.

"Uh, Xavier, then…" God, his name tastes bitter on my tongue. "Can I ask why I'm here?"

To my surprise, his eyes widen. "Colton didn't tell you?"

Colton? Oh, he means the guard with the rough voice who can't count.

When I shake my head, he grunts in annoyance. "Oh, well, let me apologize. This all must be rather confusing to you then."

I don't say anything. I only wait for him to go on.

"I must confess, I was a bit mesmerized by your performance tonight on stage," he says. "It…spoke to me, you could say."

Is he trying to be poetic? How could swinging around a pole dressed as a sexy devil *speak* to him? What is this guy getting at?

"With me being the man I am, you can imagine it's hard walking out the door without being recognized… So, I thought to myself, maybe this time, why not maybe get a little food and actually enjoy the company I'm with?"

Wait a fucking minute. Is he–is he suggesting that all the mess at the club, the surprise dress, and this impromptu limo ride is because he wants to take me to dinner? Like on a date?

Every red flag is waving in my face right now. I mean, I'm sitting in a limo with one of the deadliest men alive. He's researched me, he's sought me out, and all because he wants to *enjoy my company?*

I don't think so.

His head tilts to the side as he studies me. "What do you say?"

He's acting like I have a choice.

My hands shake, causing the glass in my lap to come

too close to spilling. When Franco reaches over and takes it to set it aside, I flinch.

"I have a reservation for us at Barlton D's downtown. Have you ever been there?" he asks.

My eyes widen. Barlton's is one of the most expensive steakhouses on the east coast. Certainly, the ritziest in the state. Celebrities go there. Only the crème de la crème are even allowed to walk in.

So, have I been there? In my dreams.

I shake my head to answer his question, still worried I might say the wrong thing and end up in a ditch somewhere for the buzzards to feast on.

He smiles, showing off perfectly straight teeth. "Tonight will be an experience then."

"I…I was supposed to meet my friends…" I begin carefully. "They might get worried when I don't show up."

"I'm sure they can do without you for one night." His response is quick and sharp, and his stare hardens on me, making me snap my mouth shut.

"Besides…" he drifts off and taps the tinted window between us and the driver. The limo makes a sharp right and I slide across the leather to the window. Glancing outside, I see buildings and streets passing by. It takes me a moment to realize where we are, and my stomach sinks.

Not only are we traveling farther away from Kat's Kradle, but we're nowhere near downtown.

My anxiousness triples. Where is he taking me?

I glance down at the door handle to find there isn't one. None.

Oh my God.

My pulse hits an all-time high.

When my gaze swings back to Franco, his expression has turned unreadable.

Just then, the car jerks to a stop, tossing me forward, then back, and then the engine cuts off. Again, I look out the dark window to see a single light in the darkness. It's in a gazebo and beyond it, a long stretch of black waves.

The harbor? He's taken me to the harbor?

My previous fears about being tied up and dumped into the water, never to be heard from, come rushing forward again.

"A little detour first," he says, his voice still rumbling with friendliness, but his expression tells a different story. Reading with his truer, darker intentions. "Don't worry, it won't be too long."

My throat tightens and I can barely draw in my next breath. He moves over to the back seat to sit beside me, but with his massive size, he's practically on top of me. I do everything I can to make more space between us, but I'm already firmly pressed up against the window with nowhere else to go.

His giant hand comes down on my knee, and I freeze.

"Mr. Franco–"

"Xavier," he corrects me again, a bit firmer this time.

"I'm not quite sure why we're here," I begin. "Why *I'm* here."

"As I said before, I just wanted your company. A little of your time..." His hand glides farther up my leg, pushing up the dress with it and revealing more of my bare thigh underneath.

Instinctively, I slap my hand down on his to stop him, but he only glances at me instead. His perfect grin has turned into a wolfish one now, and the tone of this trip has quickly turned from a strange excuse for a dinner date to something more sinister. Sexual.

A warning zips up my spine. It doesn't take a rocket

scientist–or a stripper–to know what Franco really wants here. But I'm not that type of lady. I'm strictly a look, don't touch kinda gal. No judgment, just not my thing.

But he doesn't seem to be getting the hint. Even with my hand gripping his, he still moves it further up my leg.

"I'm sorry," I say, squeezing his hand harder. My annoyance is quickly overpowering the fear, but I try to mask both in my voice. "I think you're mistaken. I'm just a dancer. My services don't..." *How to put this...?* "Don't extend past the stage."

That makes him pause.

Okay, I can see where he might get confused. Some of the girls at Kat's take it a step further with some clients outside work hours, so I'm not offended if he thought I may be one of them.

"If you want, I can introduce you to some of the girls I know who–"

"I got you that dress."

His words take me off guard. "W-What?"

"The dress," he repeats more aggressively. "The limo. The dinner. You owe me."

Anger prickles across my skin. And here I thought he might have made an honest mistake about me. Wishful thinking on my part.

"I didn't ask for any of those things," I reply. What is it with men who think they need to be rewarded after doing the bare minimum? "So, really, I don't owe you anything."

"I'm afraid you're dead wrong," he says in a menacing voice, and the real Xavier Franco reveals himself. He grabs the hem of the dress in his fist and wrenches, tearing the material easily and exposing my red panties and leather straps from my angel-to-devil dance set. I gasp from the shock of it, but when his fingers clamp around my upper thigh, brushing against my underwear, fury floods me.

"Get off me!" I claw at his arm, trying my damndest to shove him away, but with his size and weight, it's impossible. "Get off!"

I reach over to the other door but find it's missing its handle too. How the fuck am I going to get out of here?

"No one ever says no to me. No one!"

Another loud tearing sound grates across my eardrums. When I look down, I see that he's torn the strap of the dress and most of its side. The expensive fabric falls across my breasts, revealing more of myself to him.

If I let this go on, he'll have me naked in a heartbeat. I pound at the door and window with all my strength, but there's no way out that I can see.

Franco undoes his belt in a flash, but instead of doing so to whip out his dick, he does something even more terrifying with it. He wraps it around my throat and pulls it tight from behind, instantly cutting off my airway. My back slams against his chest. I kick out and sputter, trying desperately to either loosen his hold or suck in a bit more air into my lungs.

Grunting, he jerks me against him, and his hot breath spills over the side of my face. I can't help but think that this is it. This is how I die. I'm done for.

"Miss Dalton, you've made a mistake," he whispers in my ear before tracing his tongue along my earlobe. "We could've had a nice time. I could've treated you like a queen for the night, but instead, you wanted to play hard to get. Now, look at you. Turning bluer by the second."

He's right about one thing. My body is screaming for oxygen and my vision is beginning to darken.

Deep inside me, something is stirring too. My magic

that I've suppressed for years has found an opportunity to rise up again. Problem is, I'd shoved those powers into a box long ago for a very good reason–it can destroy everyone. Including me. Using them now will only kill me faster.

Not that I could use my magic right now if I wanted to. Struggling to breathe, my focus and strength are fading fast. My hand drops and hits something hard and pointed. Next to me on the seat is one of my six-inch heels. It must've flown off during my thrashing and kicking.

Grasping onto the last strands of consciousness, I wrap my fingers around the sole and swing it over my shoulder with all my strength. Franco screams a terrible blood-curdling scream and lets go right away. Finally free, I greedily suck in air to refill my lungs and hurl my shoulder into the door. I throw all my weight into it, and luckily, it pops open.

Pain radiates up and down my arm strong enough to make my eyes water, and I tumble out of the back seat into the night. Behind me, Franco continues to scream, and as I push to my feet, I catch a glimpse into the back of the limo and see why.

The heel of my stiletto is embedded in his left eye. Blood runs down his face and coats his white suit and the white leather interior of the car. Touching the side of my face, my fingers come back covered in blood too. His blood.

Fuck!

I find my other abandoned high heel on the gravel and grab it before sprinting across the dark parking lot, not feeling the cold winter air as the adrenaline pumps through my veins. The rocks underneath my bare feet hurt like hell, my neck aches, and I can't even lift my one arm–

I'm sure my shoulder is dislocated–but it's nothing compared to what would've happened if I would have stayed in the back seat a few moments longer. I'll take it all over almost being raped and murdered by the deranged Xavier Franco.

Clutching my shoe as if it's a deadly weapon, which I guess it was, I race up the street, the entire time listening for the unforgettable roar of his limo's engine behind me.

I might have escaped tonight, but I'd just signed my own death warrant. There aren't many people who've confronted a member of the Black Spades gang and lived.

And I had just possibly killed their leader.

CHAPTER THREE

EVE

My hands shake uncontrollably as I shove my clothes into the duffle bag.

I've been working at Kat's Kradle for years now and I've never felt afraid for my life. Sure, there've been jerks who wait for me at the back of the club, hoping to catch me alone, or the times a creep leaped onto the stage and groped me. Those are threats that come with my job, and it's something I've accepted. That's why Kat has guards positioned near the stage to protect her girls.

But now, the head of Black Spades wants my blood. And this is a completely different ball game. A terrifying one.

It's been two days since the bastard kidnapped me, and I drove my stiletto heel into his eyeball. Two days of waiting to hear whether he's alive or dead. Two days of excruciating panic as I stayed hidden at Demi's place, because Franco is the kind of monster who thrives on retribution against anyone who's wronged him.

And fuck me, but I did a great job of that.

Franco deserved that, and so much worse. But the price came at a risk to my life.

The incident left me shaken. The two nights I slept at Demi's, she had to hold me for hours after I woke up screaming and sweating. Ever since Mom tossed me out of the family home, night terrors have plagued me. When I'm stressed, they wreak havoc. And recently, I've been beyond stressed, a complete mess.

I blink away all thoughts, staring at the bag. I can't believe I'm doing this. Even with no signs of the Black Spades, I made the call this morning that I had to get out of town. I can't live like this, not knowing. Living in fear and with the ridiculous hope that Franco will forget me. Part of me hopes my attack was enough to kill him, that he'd bleed to death or something, but I'm just not that lucky.

I've never been the lucky girl. My mom kicked me out at sixteen because she couldn't handle me, apparently. I'm not saying I'm the easiest to get along with, but I never expected her to toss me out on my ass. She's my mom for fuck's sake, and with that, memories flash through my mind.

"Get out," the cop barks, his flashlight pointed at me, blinding me momentarily as I shuffle out of the back seat of his car.

Another officer is talking to Mom in the driveway, and dread weighs down on me. She's nodding, her brow pulled into a deep frown. Dressed in a white bathrobe, it's obvious she's been dragged out of bed. She has her arms folded across her chest, and she's angry.

I know the pulsing blue and red lights will wake the whole neighborhood soon. It's past two in the morning, and the neighbor's front porch light flicks on.

I'll be grounded forever, maybe even longer.

The thing about my mom is that she's a beautiful woman,

utterly stunning, with blonde hair flowing past her shoulders and ice-blue eyes. She likes to give her opinion, even when it's not needed, and tends to look down on others. Me included. Her intense involvement in the church hasn't helped any. She uses it to justify her judgmental, unsympathetic nature. On top of that, she has a furious temper and hates to look bad in front of others.

That's where I come in. Her greatest disappointment.

I follow the police officer over to her, and before she can even look at me, I whisper, "I'm sorry."

"What have you done this time?" Her scolding stings, especially under the scrutiny of the two officers watching me. I scrunch up my toes in my boots.

"Amanda and I went for a joyride after the movies. She just got her license. No one was hurt."

Her eyes pierce into me, their usual light blue now dark like hundreds of crashing waves during a storm. I'm never going to hear the end of this.

"Ma'am, your daughter's friend took her father's car without permission and was caught speeding in a residential area. We also found a stolen puppy in the back seat, which has been returned to its rightful owner."

"Jack's running a puppy mill," I blurt to the cop, wishing they'd listen. "They're kept in cages in the basement. Why aren't you arresting him for animal abuse? We were saving the poor puppy."

"Evelyn," Mom warns with a stern voice.

The fat cop stares down at me. "You will be lucky if there aren't charges pressed for trespassing and theft."

Mom makes a gasping sound, clutching her bathrobe around her throat. There's not an ounce of pity on her face and she looks ready to lock me up for eternity for daring to embarrass her. I shiver at the thought, half-convinced she'd do it.

Desperation coils around me when I look at her pale face.

"Get in the house, now!" she bellows at me.

With a loud exhale, I drag myself toward our two-story house while she's exchanging information with the police officer. I still can't believe she instantly blames me when I try to do the right thing.

By the time Mom comes inside, I know I'm in deep shit by how hard she bangs the front door shut.

"I've had enough, Evelyn," she says in a low voice as she walks into the living room. The walls are trembling as she clenches her hands at her sides, and she just stares at me. I'm not sure if she's going to pass out or have a stroke from how strained she looks.

Next thing I know, she's marching upstairs, and I hurry after her because I've never seen her like this. Normally, she screams at me, throws things around, wacks me with whatever she can grab. But this... it scares me.

In my bedroom, she grabs my backpack and starts stuffing it with random clothes I have thrown on the floor.

"W-what are you doing?" Panic claws at my chest. "Mom! Please, I said I'm sorry. We were trying to help–."

"No," she snaps and turns to face me, shadows dancing across her darkening features. "You are selfish and don't know the trouble you've caused me. The unnecessary attention you bring to us. Do you know how long I've worked to ensure no one knows what you are? An abomination. A freak. But you make it a hundred times harder."

"That's not fair." Unsavory words race through my mind and bubble up my throat. But I need to control my emotions, otherwise, things will get bad very quickly.

Her scowl deepens. "You're not fair," she hollers back. "I'm exhausted from dealing with your mistakes. Every week it's something different with you. The police, the teachers after you accidentally burned down the restroom, the neighbors, random strangers, all come to my doorstep because of something you've done. And I've had enough."

"Mistakes?" I'm a fucking mistake to her. My throat constricts at how hard it's been living under her oppressive rules.

"You're bound for Hell," she whispers harshly. "I've tried but even I can't save you. And I refuse to let you drag me down into the fire with you."

With a sigh, she pushes the bag into my arms, and panic closes in around me. "Finish packing. I want you out of my house in the morning. I can't do this any longer."

My eyes widen, and I feel like I'm going to throw up. "Wait, what? You're kicking me out? Are you fucking kidding me?" Had I heard right?

Her gaze is full of rage. "I've had enough. I told you before, one more incident and I'm done with you." She shakes her head, her brow furrowing as she murmurs, "Maybe I'm not cut out for this." She sounds defeated, then abruptly storms out of my room, shutting the door with a bang.

"Mom?" My voice trembles.

No, no, no...

Tears well in my eyes, and I collapse to my knees. What the hell just happened? Fear pounds through me as confusion tilts the world around me.

"You're leaving?" Mercy's strangled voice cuts through my thoughts and rips me back to reality. I blink away the memory swirling in my mind.

I raise my head to find Mercy stumbling into my room, her chin trembling. Dammit, she must have found out I'm leaving for a while. I turn and pull her into an embrace. She wraps her arms around my middle, and I know she's scared. We all are.

After I told Kat and the others at the club what happened, Kat shut the place down for a few days. She put a sign up on the front door that we're being renovated, a convenient lie. But in reality, she's waiting for the dust to settle.

That's another reason I need to go. To steer the danger away from her and my friends who work here.

"It's going to be okay," I say to Mercy, then pull back as she wipes away a loose tear. Her brown hair hangs loosely over her shoulders, and she keeps pushing it behind her ears. Her eyes glisten with tears.

"I'm the one who's supposed to be saying that to you," she answers. She gives me a lopsided grin, but she's doing a terrible job of convincing me she's okay. Everyone's shaken by my attack.

"So, any space for a friend on your journey?" she teases, and I look at the girl who I think of as a little sister. The girl I've protected since the first night she started working at Kat's Kradle. Who I taught my sexiest moves on the dance pole, and who in turn introduced me to taro cake. Now, I'm obsessed with the delicious purple treat. Which is obvious by my thick thighs. But men love my body on stage, and so do I.

"You can't leave me behind. And no way will this place be the same without you, Eve."

"It will be safer with me gone, and we all know it. But I promise things will settle down and I'll be back."

She pouts. "So, that's a no then to me inviting myself?"

I half-laugh, surprised I can still experience any level of joy when I feel like crawling under a rock for eternity. I'm not a person who normally runs from danger. But what can I do against the head of a fucking gang?

Yep, leaving is the right decision.

Mercy is giving me her cute puppy-dog eyes, and she's

doing a great job of trying to convince me to let her join. To have someone with me, so I'm not alone.

Wait, no…what am I thinking? As much as I'd love her to come, I can't do that to her. It's too dangerous.

Mercy's twenty-one years old, only four years younger than me, but could easily pass for eighteen. When not performing, she wears no makeup, has her hair messy, and is a wallflower most of the time. Well, except to me and when she's performing on stage.

"I just don't know what I'll do without you here," her voice hitches, and my heart clenches. I'm drowning under the weight of her words, under the kindness she offers me.

For a long time after my mom kicked me out of our home and I lost everything, I believed I didn't deserve happiness. That I must be a horrible person. Mothers are supposed to love their children unconditionally, right? Yet mine didn't even want me.

But when Kat took me in and gave me a job, I started working on myself, on building back my confidence and finding my worth. I enrolled in kickboxing classes, enrolled and graduated college, did whatever I could to give me a life I could be proud of.

I'm not saying I'm anywhere close to being fixed… I'm not sure I can ever stop feeling broken. All I know is that I found myself a new family here at Kat's Kradle, and it kills me to lose them. I love the girls here, especially Mercy and Demi. I'm going to miss them terribly, but I won't let them get hurt because of me.

"You're not coming, hon. I will not risk your life. It'd be too selfish of me. Stay here and help Kat get things back to normal. Besides, I'll be back before you have the chance to even miss me." I give her a wink and go back to packing.

The quicker I get out, the better I'll feel for everyone's safety.

Mercy helps fold the clothes I've tossed on my bed to pack. "What will you do? Do you need cash?"

"You're too sweet. But I think I'm going to be fine. I don't know where I'm going yet, but you'll be the first to know once I'm settled, okay?"

She's nodding, and I already miss her. "Deal."

"Good."

"And if I don't hear from you, I'm going to hunt you down." Her stern voice makes me laugh because she's too adorable to be angry.

Her phone dings and she grabs it from her back pocket. Reading the message, she tilts her head and frowns. "Kat needs some help restocking the bar."

"Go ahead. I can handle this," I say.

She heads for the door with hesitant steps. "Don't you dare leave without me getting another hug, do you hear me?"

"Loud and clear."

She blows me a kiss, then rushes out of the room on bare feet, dressed in daisy dukes and a loose t-shirt.

With Mercy gone, I focus on my task at hand. Packing a small bag has me leaving so much behind, things I bought and worked hard for, but I keep telling myself I'll be back. I'm not really abandoning my things for good.

This can't be a permanent thing.

I head into the bathroom for my toiletries.

A loud bang comes from downstairs in the club, like something big has fallen over… or had it been a gunshot? Seconds later, there's a piercing scream.

The toothpaste and toothbrush in my hands drop onto the sink from how hard I flinch.

The paralyzing fear that Franco has returned for me already shoots through my body. My brain barely registers my movements as I rush to the window in my bedroom, and slowly I slide the curtain aside to look out on the street. I scan for the white limo down below, but everything looks normal. No gang members rushing toward the club or cars crowding the street.

Footsteps sound outside my room, and the door swings up suddenly. For a millisecond, I swear I'm going to find Franco in the doorway with a gun. But it's only Mercy. Her features twisted with terror.

"Eve," she gasps my name like it pains her to say it.

I suck in a shaky breath, and see Kat hurrying inside next, her black curls spilling out of her normally tight bun. Her eyes are wide with fear, and she's twirling her tattooed fingers in the air to hold a conjured spell. The magic sizzles against my skin.

"I can only keep the doors locked for so long! You need to go, now!" she shouts.

Mercy's at my side, grabbing my arm, pulling me out of the room. "Quick!"

I snatch my duffel bag, which is way lighter than it should be and then ask in a rush, "What's going on?"

Kat's already ushering us out of our apartment and through the hallway. "The Black Spades," she answers. "Franco's thugs."

My heart climbs into my throat.

The sorrow and fear on her face shatters me. She's always been so kind to me, took me in, gave me a place to stay, acted more like a mother than my own flesh and blood, and I brought death to her door. "Kat–"

"Shhh! Hurry." She glances over her shoulder. Another thunderous boom comes from downstairs, this time the door to the upper floor apartments being thrown open. Her spell snaps back, too weak to hold, and the sense of magic dies abruptly. Heavy footsteps start up the main steps. "Fuck! Out the back! We'll give you time to get away, but you have to be fast."

I'm going to be sick, but my gaze follows to where Kat's pointing to the fire escape door at the end of the hall. Mercy's wrenching me forward, desperate for me to get ahead of her.

I sprint toward the door. A quick look back, and Kat and Mercy are frantically waving for me to go.

There are so many things I want to say to them, my throat thickening, but the encroaching footsteps steals my chance.

I yank the door open and lunge outside onto the metal fire escape stairs. With my duffle bag over my shoulder, I scan the alley below. It's empty.

Thank you, universe.

Breath racing, I hurry down the wobbly steps, moving with speed in my stilettos to avoid them getting stuck in the steel grating. Thing is, I've worn them so often that I'm convinced I'm faster with them on than barefooted.

My heart thunders in my ears, but I can't freak out.

I have no idea what the hell I'm going to do. All I know is that I'm in deep shit.

My pulse thumps in my temples. I should have left earlier and now I'm paying the price.

Taking wheezing breaths, I hurry down the last few steps and hop down.

I make sure the coast is clear before I sprint down the narrow passage, past the trash cans, the morning sun on my back. My mind's racing, trying to figure out the fastest way to the train station. Once I'm there, I'll breathe easier.

At the end of the alley, a long white limousine pulls out, blocking my exit. My heart jackhammers.

Oh no… That's Franco's limo!

A whoosh of air moves past my ear, and I jump in my skin, shuddering.

Before I can even spin around, something rock-hard locks tight around my throat and shoulders. It takes me seconds to realize I'm in someone's arms. When I turn my gaze, I find the culprit. Franco's asshole guard who can't count backwards to save his life. Colton. He's sneering at me by my shoulder.

"Hello again," he says.

"Fuck you," I spit back, thrashing against the bastard.

Dropping my bag, I jab an elbow into his gut and stomp my heel down on his foot. He groans, and I wrench out of his weakening hold. Then I take off, but another man dressed in a leather jacket pops out of a shadowy hiding spot and snatches me by the arm. I'm wrenched to a stop.

"You have unfinished business with the boss," he rasps like he's inhaled a few too many cigars. His teeth are plated with gold.

I kick out my heel, but the bastard springs out of the way. He's faster than his buddy.

I try to yank myself away, but his knuckles collide with the side of my face. I scream from the excruciating pain zigzagging across my face. Tears rise in my eyes, and my whole body flings backward from the impact.

The pain blinds me; it's all I can focus on. Blood even coats my tongue, so I barely feel myself being lifted off the ground and thrown over the man's shoulder. It's not until his meaty hand slaps across the back of my thighs that the panic hits.

The world is dancing with stars right now, and

somehow I'm screaming louder despite my skull feeling like it's just cracked open from his strike. The pain is unbearable, pulsing like undulating waves.

He's carrying me away from the club, with Colton taking up the rear.

No one's coming for me. I've never believed in being saved by a knight in shining armor and all that bullshit. I've always looked out for myself. But right now, I'd kill for some help.

That's when my eyes lift to a patch of unnatural darkness by the fire escape, one that shouldn't exist from how the sun is hitting. Stranger still? I swear I see two indents or holes, like eyes, watching me be carried away to my doom.

CHAPTER FOUR

KNOX

I stand inside the Black Spades' warehouse in my spirit form, sticking to the shadows, on a personal assignment for the night. The infamous asshole Xavier Franco and his groveling gang took something from me, and I'm here to take it back by any means necessary.

After months of searching and jumping through hoops, I've finally tracked my Mortem Blade to this filthy place. Do they know what they really have, the immense power it possesses? I doubt it. Since the Black Spades are human, they probably just think it's like all the other priceless artifacts they've stolen. Not actually part of Death's scythe. *My* scythe. And one of the most powerful things in all of existence.

My hands are itching to spill blood. I've been without my blade for too long, and knowing it's somewhere in this place, so close, I'm anxious to burst out of my shadow and rip some fucking heads off.

As tempting as that notion is, Dracon's annoying voice replays in the back of my mind.

"Don't you fucking dare start a blood feud right now, Knox. We can't afford any more mistakes."

"Without Saxon, we need this deal to go through, so you have to keep your nose clean, do you hear me?"

"I fucking mean it, Knox."

On and on.

I swear, he loves to hear himself talk.

He's been even more up my ass than usual, but as annoying as it is, I know it's because we lost Saxon.

As a wolf shifter, he was closer to Dracon than me or Cassius, and I think Dracon is holding a great bit of guilt over his death, none of us could've stopped it. When your time on the living plane is up, there's nothing you can do but accept it. As one of the four horsemen–Death incarnate–I know it for a fact. It's inevitable, final, like I used to be when I was at my full power and had my scythe.

Losing Saxon had more of an impact on our empire as well. While we all had our own roles to play as the Kings of Eden, Dracon handled most of the business side of things, and because of his take-no-shit attitude, he's gotten us this far, making us one of the most powerful gangs on the east coast. But Saxon's death created a vulnerability. Not only did it blindside us, but it made us look weak to our enemies.

And they've been practically crawling over each other for an opportunity to take us out.

Hence why Dracon is pushing for a merger with a smaller gang from the next city over.

For me, it's another reason I need my blade.

That's what's led me here.

The warehouse where Franco keeps his stolen shit is dimly lit and mostly filled with wooden crates. Well, except for the two black Maseratis parked near the shut roller doors, shining like they've never been touched.

I watch as one of Franco's henchmen drags the cute blonde from Kat's Kradle across the concrete by her hair.

Her screams echoing in the expansive space.

Poor bitch. I wonder what she's done to get onto the Spades' shit list.

She's a pretty thing with full breasts, a round ass, and long blonde hair, reminding me of some of the girls in those porn movies Cassius's watches on full volume. Except nothing about this one is fake, and I find my fingers twitching at the thought of running my hands along every dip and curve.

Catching myself, I turn my attention to Franco, who's reclining in a chair in the middle of the open space, grinning. The men toss the girl at his feet, and he peers down at her with his one good eye. The other's in an eyepatch, which is a new one,but he holds a cigar between his fat fingers and sneers.

As the girl hits the concrete floor, she lifts her chin to meet his gaze with fire in her eyes.

"Aren't you a sight for sore eyes?" she says.

Holy shit. She didn't really just say that, did she?

Brilliant. Fucking brialliant.

Franco glares daggers at her, but she's grinning sadistically and my little black heart beats a aster. She's got some balls, this one.

When his fingers graze the eyepatch, a thought strikes me. Could it be possible that the little blonde is responsible?

Fuck. I'm cracking up on the inside. Franco isn't a good-looking fucker, so I'd say she did him a favor by taking out one of his eyes. All he needs is a parrot and hat and then he can rule the seven seas...

Unlike us or the Lords of Night, Franco and the Black Spades moved into Andover City fairly recently, but they moved into our territory swiftly and like a goddamn hurricane, swiping a lot of our clients and businesses. Drugs, counterfeit cargo, money laundering–you name it–they stuck their sticky hands into every pot they could get into, making them an immediate threat to us. Even if they are mostly humans.

Dracon, Cassius, Saxon, and I were the Kings in this city, brutal fiends who've been ruling together for over a decade. We'd kill before rolling over for anyone. Even with one man down, we still have a fierce reputation, but our title and status has been rocked. But it's only temporary, especially with Dracon in the lead. Saxon wouldn't want us to give up either.

So, out of the three of us left, Dracon is in charge of the operation and always has total domination on the brain. He is a master at arms and weapons trafficking. And at one time, eons ago, had enough power to bring the entire nation to war.

Cassius is almost as fucked up in the head as me–*almost*–but for different reasons. Even Hell spit him back out, and for a demon, that's saying something. He's uncontrollable. Wild. And a shit ton of fun. So, all the things Dracon isn't, which may be the real reason we get along so well.

We aren't human but we aren't ordinary supernaturals either. We are some of the most dangerous beings in the country–hell, the world. And boy, would I love to just hunt down and kill every last one of our enemies... Nothing would give me more joy than unleashing death on them all, but at the same time, I'm limited on this plane.

I'm even more limited without my blade.

My gut twists at the memories of how I ended up on the living plane, of Aris, but I shut them down fast. I don't have time for all the emotions they stir up.

Instead, I try to come up with what the easiest way to get my Mortem Blade is *without* slaughtering everyone in here and pissing Dracon off. No matter what he and Cassius say, I know it's here. I can feel it in my soul.

Maybe I could use this situation with the blonde to my advantage? To cover me?

I turn back to the show in the center of the warehouse. Franco takes a long draw of his cigar, then blows out a puff of smoke, trying to appear unfazed but his hand shakes.

"We're about to rebalance things." He waves a hand to one of his two armed men, and the dark-haired guy retreats, weaving his way past the stacks of wooden crates.

"You don't scare me," the blonde bravely responds with a confident voice, her resolve strong. If she's afraid of Franco, she doesn't show it. She doesn't waver in his presence, where I've seen grown men fall into a mess of fear.

Franco is a large bastard with a shaved head, and a thick double chin, but he's all muscle and solid as an ox.

I stare back at the blonde. She's a fucking stunning creature. And I watch as she climbs to her feet. Sure, her bravery might be misguided given her situation, but I'll give her points for trying.

My gaze drags over her captivating curves filling those tight jeans and a blue button up shirt, the fabric speckled with blood from her busted lip. She really is a beautiful thing. Which says a lot since I haven't had a woman draw my attention in… well, forever.

What a shame she won't be seeing dawn, since Franco has her. A damn shame.

She surveys the warehouse quickly, her gaze flashing over me in my shadowy corner. Then, she pauses for a second, causing my breath to catch.

Can she see me?

I chuckle to myself. *Don't be a fucking idiot, Knox.*

Impossible. No one should be able to see me in my spirit form.

Her green eyes brim with destructive energy beneath the lights. Suppressed magic. And I'm even more intrigued.

What *is* she? A spellcaster of some kind?

She tears her attention away and turns back to Franco and his henchmen. Her lips thin with anger. The longer I stare at her and the scene unfolding in front of me, the more interested I become. Which is unnerving in itself.

I don't care about her–I don't care about any living souls. I don't. If Dracon and Cassius hadn't formed the Kings of Eden and invited me in, I doubt I would care about them either. Life is a flame, brightly burning for one second and easily snuffed out the next. Yet, I can't keep my eyes off this fiery girl and the immense danger she's in. Her fighting nature tells me she's lived with darkness, and I'm curious to find out how far it's etched into her soul, how long would it take me to break her?

I enjoy breaking things, even if they can never be put back together. Though, I suspect this exquisite thing might already be beyond fixing.

The dark-haired henchman returns, carrying a bundle wrapped in material under his arm, then dumps it on a nearby wooden crate and unravels it. He's got his back to me, but I hear the clatter of metal and know instantly we're dealing with knives.

Oh, good.

Easing my shadow a little closer, I scan the knives on the black fabric. Mostly daggers with leather hilts. If my corporal body wasn't hidden outside the warehouse, I might have stolen a bunch to restock my morgue. I've always had a love for sharp, shiny things.

"Are you ready to have fun, Evelyn?" Franco asks, his voice an echoing boom in the vast space.

Fun, huh? A thread of excitement weaves through me, and I lean closer. Now Franco's speaking my language.

Then I realize he's revealed the blonde's name. Evelyn.

Evelyn, Evelyn, Evelyn.

Hmm… Doesn't really fit her, in my opinion. Sounds too pure for this spitfire of a woman, but what the fuck do I know?

Franco goes on without missing a beat. "Have you ever heard the saying, an eye for an eye?"

"Go shove your head up your ass, cocksucker," she spits in anger.

In an instant, Franco's on his feet, towering over her as he accepts a carving knife from his guard.

There it is… A flicker of fear in her eyes. So subtle and brief, but I see it. And that's all it takes to send ripples of anticipation straight to my groin.

On cue, her fight or flight response triggers, and her attention snaps to one of the metal doors beside the loading dock. Even she must know that she wouldn't make it if she tried.

No, she's going to have to fight before she can flee.

Suddenly, Evelyn drops low and kicks her leg out to

slam her heel right into Franco's knee. The large fuck-muncher doesn't even budge.

Realizing she's fucked, she whirls around and sprints past the men.

The Spades give chase.

Shockingly, she's lighting fast on those pointed shoes, and she whips around the pallets and shelves with ease. When one of the guys gets too close, she clocks him in the face with her fist. The other she kicks in the chest, sending him stumbling back and sputtering to breathe.

Oh, shit! Where's the popcorn? This shit is getting *good.*

The dark haired one rights himself rather quickly, clutching his jaw, but he grabs her from behind and pins her arms at her sides.

"Bring her to me!" Franco bellows, losing his patience. The Spades waste no time dragging her back to him and forcing her back onto her knees before him. Barking a heavy laugh, he points one of the knives at her face, inches from her eye. "Nice try, now my turn."

The air changes suddenly, the energy all around us increasing. The humans don't seem to notice the shift yet, but her body trembles in place. She's the one doing it, but unlike spellcasters who create magic temporarily out of thin air, she's drawing on the forces of the living plane to manifest power.

And that magic is raw, untamed, and even deadlier.

"You're going to regret this," she snarls, and with her words, I feel the crackle and pop of energy being ripped from natural order and thrown into chaos. Because I'm in my spirit form, I'm more sensitive to these things, but even I can see the effects of such power crossing over into the living world. An unknown gust of wind pushes through the building, rocking overhead lights and rustling any plastic and styrofoam packing.

I can't believe what I'm witnessing. This stripper–this *Evelyn*–is doing things some of the most powerful witches and sorcerers could only dream of.

Franco raises the knife, and it's clear he's determined to do more than just take out her eye.

I wait a second for the crescendo, for the taut band of her building power to finally snap and unleash hell on him, but when nothing happens, disappointment seeps in. As does worry.

She's really going to let him kill her? After all that?

She's not going to use her gift and escape? But why?

Something comes over me then. Something so fucking crazy and reckless that I don't even try to make sense of it. As a phantom, I can't do much in this form, so I propel myself forward and rush at Franco as a haze, a fog. It does the trick though and momentarily distracts him, making him jump to his feet and swipe his knife through the air. It slides right through me, unable to do any damage.

"What the fuck?" he shouts. "What was that? Colton, Jimmy, go check it out."

Pulling out their Glocks, the Spades twist around, searching for a foe that can't be seen.

At the same time, Evelyn rams her arm into Franco's knife-wielding hand, shoving it out of her face and causing him to drop it onto the ground. Then she kicks her leg up, right between Franco's legs connecting with his nuts.

His eyes bulge, and a strangled squeak comes from his throat.

In a flash, she's sprinting toward the door.

Fuck yeah! Now he's down an eye and two balls.

Franco groans and collapses into the chair, writhing

and holding his groin, while the other Spades forget about me and leap after her.

She moves fast, ducking and weaving out of reach. Rapid gunshots pop in her direction, but she's able to keep out of their aim.

Just before she reaches the door, the bigger guy catches up to her, grabs her by the hair, and yanks her backward. Screaming, she stumbles and her hand shoots down to her foot, making quick work of the straps. Next thing I know, she's gripping her black stiletto and swinging the heel towards his neck.

He swerves but not fast enough. I can't see where she's hit him, but blood splatters across his white shirt.

Evelyn hurls herself away from him, kicking off her other shoe, while still wielding the bloody one.

Who the fuck is this girl?

Fire bursts in my chest. I'm sliding forward again, mesmerized by the heel-whirling beauty. My cock's getting harder just watching her.

During all the commotion and excitement, no one's noticed Franco lumbering closer with a giant wooden crate lifted over his head.

"Enough of this!" he yells. Face red from holding up such a massive weight, Franco manages to throw it over everyone's heads, screaming out his rage. The crate crashes against the door and busts open, the pieces of wood and packaging straw now blocking her way out.

Then, he stalks toward her.

Cornered and desperate, Evelyn spins and starts shifting through the straw for something to use as a weapon—something better than a shoe. And she's going to need it too. Franco looks like he's done playing around. He wants to snap her in half with his bare hands.

Whipping back around, she now holds an actual weapon in a tight grip. Some kind of shortsword, like a curved blade. It's ancient looking with a bone-shaped hilt. When Evelyn waves the deadly thing back and forth, hundreds of tiny symbols appear on its shiny face, ones that are only visible when the light hits it the right way.

Son of a bitch! That's not just any blade!

My Mortem Blade.

No fucking way.

Even more shocking is that Evelyn is holding it in her hand. A living person, grasping a piece of Death's scythe… something only a horseman has been able to do before. It brings instant death to anyone else who touches it, just like… Just like…

When the skinny man tries to be sneaky and grab her, she swings and nicks him across the torso, which would only be a flesh wound normally. But with the Mortem Blade, his body stiffens from rigor mortis immediately and he topples over. Dead.

Well, just like that actually.

Franco and the remaining Spade stand there shocked.

"What did you do to him?" Franco barks.

"Not a step closer!" she shouts back, pointing the tip between the two of them. Her voice shakes. "Or you'll end up just like your friend here!"

Not wanting to test it, they shift back.

Without wasting another second, Evelyn kicks away the pieces of wood and straw to unblock the door, managing to get it open enough, and slips outside.

With my Mortem Blade!

I zip through the warehouse and through the small crack left in the door. Finding my body where I'd left it behind a cargo container, I snap right back into my corporal form. As usual, I stagger to my feet, slightly disoriented from the sudden shift in weight and space, and my vision spins. My skin feels stretched too tight.

Then the gorgeous blonde sprints right past the container, and my gaze cuts after her. My blade is still in her hand.

She can't be a mere mortal. There's no way.

Only a horseman can hold such power in their hands. Only me, Opia, Brone, or…

Aris.

Icy dread seizes me.

Aris, my brother, and my enemy.

I've been hiding from him since the fall to this realm, knowing that if he found me again, he wouldn't hesitate to use my own blade against me. He'd threatened it so many times, and he's the kind of bastard that likes to keep his word.

The only logical explanation I can find is that she is possessed by him. It would give an answer for the intense power I felt from her too.

Oh fuck… Why hadn't I thought of this sooner? He's been hunting down the Mortem Blade, like me. I'm sure of it.

An ache sharpens in my chest and shivers wrack over me. Not much scares me…but this does. My past now bull-dozes over me, promising to destroy me.

Pathetic.

But what if I catch him first?

Grinding my teeth, I leap over pallets and milk crates after this so-called Evelyn, moving within the shadows.

The moment she feels my presence, she twists her head in my direction and that same spark of fear I'd seen before appears again.

There's no hiding now.

Catching up to her is effortless, and when I do, I slap my large hand across her mouth and nose, smothering her.

She thrashes, raising my blade. I grab her wrist and hold her until she passes out.

It's easier than expected, but this poor girl's been through a lot these past few hours. Even with a horseman inside you, the mortal body can only take so much, so it's not too surprising she goes down without much of a fight.

The idea of finishing her and Aris off now crosses my mind, but where's the fun in that? War and I have a long history together, and after the shit he pulled to get me here, I've been itching to get him back. While in this form, he's trapped. He'll be at my mercy to feel every lick of pain I bestow upon him.

And unfortunately for him and Evelyn, I am feeling a little more generous than usual today.

CHAPTER FIVE

KNOX

I am meant to be alone.

A phantom. A flicker of a flame. A whisper.

I can come suddenly, unexpectedly, or planned.

I am Death. The end. Final and permanent. A horseman in the apocalypse.

So how did I, one of the most powerful beings ever to exist, go from ruling all the spirit realm to hiding like a fucking coward among the living?

Simple answer? Aris, a horseman in the apocalypse. War.

There are only three other creatures besides me who can wield my scythe without being destroyed: Aris, Opia, and Brone. All created from the very fabric of time and space, children of the cosmos.

Aris and I have never seen eye to eye, and the last time we faced off our battle had rocked the universe. We'd been catapulted into the living world, but in the chaos, my scythe suffered a fatal blow. I thought it was destroyed—until a few months ago, when I heard its dark magic buzz across my mind again.

Some underground detective work and I discovered a piece of it had been repurposed into a different weapon and was being bounced between museums as an ancient artifact.

I wonder how many people died handling it before they realized it couldn't be touched with bare hands… But I digress.

While the exhibit was in transit, the shipment was hijacked and all the priceless items were taken. Including the Mortem Blade. The theft stalled my search for a while, but once I found out the Black Spades had part in it, I knew it would only be a waiting game until all the artifacts turned up in Andover's harbor.

And now, after all this time, I have Aris and my blade in my possession again, in *my* morgue. The very place where I've dragged many of the King's enemies and then carried them out in pieces.

I stare at Evelyn, now laid out on the metal autopsy table, her long, blonde curls spilling over the sides. She's covered in bruises and small cuts, but nothing to fill the drains. I'll be fixing that soon, though.

Maybe Aris thought picking an attractive woman to possess would hinder me somehow, but that was foolish on his part. Human or supernatural, all mortals are the same. Insignificant. Misguided. Just a mere fraction of a blip of existence. I'm not tempted by baser things like sex, like most men. Even powerful ones like Cassius and Dracon have urges. Weaknesses. But not me.

Unfortunately for this little mortal gem, her life's going to be cut short. She's unconscious and beaten up, and I can still feel the power radiating off her in waves.

Yeah, Aris is definitely hiding in there.

I whirl the Mortem Blade between my fingers. Holding

my scythe again—even if it's just a piece of it—has energy vibrating over my skin. Power that I missed terribly and even forgot I had. It's like connecting with an old friend, as the mortals say.

I wave it over the length of Evelyn's body. Over her collarbones, the curves of her breasts, her stomach, then along each of her legs. The Mortem Blade sparks blue as it senses Aris's familiar power close by.

"Come out to play, you hot-headed bastard. I know you're in there," I murmur.

On cue, Evelyn's eyes snap open. It only takes her a second to take in her new surroundings—the wall of cold storage lockers, the table of different tools I've chosen for her exorcism beside us, the bright overhead light. She yanks her arms only to find they've been bound by leather straps. Her legs too.

"What's going on?" Then the panic sets in, raising her voice. It's a beautiful thing to behold—the way her pupils dilate, her muscles tense, her mouth opens in a silent scream. She thrashes wildly, but the straps hold her tight. "Let me go, you psycho!"

I ignore that. I've been called too many things over my lifetime to care.

I slam my hands on either side of her, making her jump from the loud noise. Then I climb on top of the table, straddling her. "Come on, Aris. Let's finish this, once and for all."

She throws her head side to side as she struggles to break free. "I don't know who you're talking about! I'm Eve! Eve!" she yells.

Eve, huh? Not Evelyn?

A nickname then.

Doesn't matter.

I lift my blade, and when her eyes find it, a scream rips from her throat. It's like fucking music to my ears. Leaning in close, I press it to her shoulder and draw a nice long red line across her perfect pale flesh. She bucks and kicks more, but it does nothing but heighten my excitement. I'm gonna rip Aris out of this pretty girl's body, even if I have to peel the skin from her layer by layer.

When her blood bubbles up, I dip my head and run my tongue over it, taking in the taste of copper and magic.

Oh, yes! So much power!

It dances across my tongue.

Her entire body freezes, and when I pull back to look at her, something unexpected flashes in her green eyes.

It only lasts a half a second–if I had blinked, I would've missed it–but I would have sworn I'd seen hunger. Hunger for more. And I don't know why, but my cock twitches in my pants.

It's almost as if this woman craves darkness. Like me.

I wipe my mind clean. I have to focus, to remember that this isn't some mortal. This is Aris in a whore's body. That's all.

She uses my moment of distractedness to slam her forehead into my nose. I hear the crack, feel the sharp, shooting pain, taste the warm blood pouring down the back of my throat, and as I jerk upright, my body shocks me again. My cock is rock hard. Painfully so. I've never been aroused like this in… Shit, I don't know how long. I've almost forgotten what desire even feels like.

But as I lick more of the blood on my lips and stare down at Eve, who's strapped helplessly to the table underneath me, now splattered red with my blood, my erection tents my pants, pointing at her like a mother fucking divining rod. Desire is one of few words I can use to describe what I'm feeling right now. Desire and confusion. All because of her.

She glances at my obvious arousal, and her lip curls up in disgust. "Are you fucking getting off from this?" she shoots at me, which only triggers my anger. I don't want to feel anything. I haven't for hundreds of years–maybe more.

Aris's plan to use Eve to agitate me is actually working, and it enrages me. I'm supposed to be better than this. I'm Death, for fuck's sake. I shouldn't be hesitating over Aris in a pair of tits. This was still War.

Furious, I slice my blade blindly. Her scream confirms I've made contact, and when I see another streak of blood appearing across her left breast, the urge to lick that one up too grips me tight.

No. I need to stay focused. The last time Aris and I battled, I'd lost my scythe. I can't fuck up like that again.

"I'm not Aris!" she continues to shriek. The small table beside us shakes, rattling all my surgical tools on it. "I don't know who the fuck you're talking about!"

"Oh, but you are Aris. You can try to be clever, sneaky, slimy, but I know a parasite when I see one," I hissed.

The sound of creaking has my gaze shooting above us where the overhead spotlight is now swinging.

As her blood drips from the Mortem Blade, blue sparks of energy continue to dance along its curved edge. If she was telling the truth, then she'd be dead by now. No one else could be touched by Death's scythe and live. It's impossible.

"Look, I'm just a stripper. I work down at Kat's Kradle," she begins in a breathless rush. "If you work for Franco, I'm sorry. But the guy tried making moves on me the other night and wouldn't take no for an answer. He's a grade-A asshole and..."

I tune out her ramblings, only able to focus on the way her chest rises and falls with every shuddering breath. And how a single bead of her blood is now traveling down her cleavage, toward places unknown.

Without thinking, I stick my blade between the buttons of her blouse and run it up the seam, popping each one off with ease. The material falls away to reveal a flat stomach, black lacy bra, and the perfect mounds of her breasts. My throat tightens.

Fuck. She's even more gorgeous without clothes on.

I can't help myself. I slice across her other tit to give her a matching pair of cuts.

"Let me go!" she keeps screaming, but I'm not listening. My pulse is a thundering presence in my ears as I watch the blood leaving another trail down her cleavage. It's doing something to me, something I can't quite explain.

My hand shakes around the Mortem Blade.

More... I want more.

I need her covered in blood.

Another slice–this time on her forearm. I grab a rag from the instrument table and shove it in her mouth. Tears gather in her eyes, but when she tries to yell again, her voice is muted. Around me, the walls shake. I remember the great power I felt her start to manipulate while in the warehouse but never use fully. Will she now? Will Aris?

The questions fade away easily the more I watch her. Time seems to be slowing down too, and I'm losing track of what's real and what's my imagination. The frantic beating of my heart is the only thing keeping me connected to this plane and out of my spirit form.

More!

I press the blade between her gorgeous breasts and lock eyes with her again.

There it is —that glint of fire in the sea green. It only adds to the storm raging inside me.

More!

CHAPTER SIX

CASSIUS

"Hey, hell bitch!"

The taunt has me jerking my attention away from the sexy babe in front of me on the sidewalk. Away from the round ass, covered in a dress clinging so tight to her that I can easily make out her lace thong and perfect cheeks, moving with each step. Gorgeous.

Instead, I glance down a dingy alley to locate where the voice had come from.

A cluster of Black Spades vermin is hanging out at the side door to Chuck's Diner, which sits ajar. They're easy to spot, the drug-peddling humans with an inked spade to symbolize they are part of a cartel. These idiots have it on their inner arms. And with their bloodshot eyes and sniffling, it's clear who these guys belong to. Franco.

"You talking to me?" I ask, my veins dancing with adrenaline because if they're itching for a fight, I'm game, mostly because I loathe these mongrels. And they are crossing onto turf way too close to my home.

One of them is cracking his knuckles, and aside from one guy built like a barrel, the others are lanky and tall.

"And if we are?" the beefster challenges me.

When a muffled sound comes from behind the dumpster, where two of the men are busy with something…or more likely, someone, my intrigue is piqued. I glance from the open door of the diner to where a female cry sounds from the other side of the bin.

Let's be honest. These pricks are so low on the totem pole, no one will miss them if they are gone. And who said I can't be the good guy occasionally and help someone out? I laugh to myself because I am the furthest thing from a *nice guy*. Still, I crack my neck before pivoting my direction toward the alley.

I count five sons of bitches. Three eying me, and two with the girl. Easy.

"Well, you better let me have a look at what you're hiding back there," I say, strutting closer, rolling the sleeves of my shirt up to my elbows. I had no plans on breaking anyone's face today, which is why I wore my Giorgio Armani dress shirt.

Oops.

Dracon's going to be pissed too.

Double oops.

The veins in my neck pulse when they make a small semi-circle in front of me. They're novices and are going to be sorry.

Curling his hands, fingers branded with brass knuckles, the barrel guy laughs while one of his friends spits on the ground.

"Come closer," he urges, and I laugh at how idiotic he sounds.

Then I suck in a deep breath and blow black churned air into their faces.

They choke on my sulfur, reeling back, and I lunge after them. Being part-demon comes with perks.

They shuffle on either side of me, hurling punches, grabbing at my clothes, kicking me like a pack of wild dogs. Throwing out an arm, I slam one across the face, then I snatch the other by the throat just as the barrel guy charges me.

We clash, and I stumble backward, taken aback by his sheer force. But I'm still holding the scrawny guy who's clawing at my hand, his eyes wide from me strangling him. I tighten my grip, and with one twist of my hand, I snap his neck.

Tossing the fucker aside, I kick the barrel guy in the gut, sending him staggering backwards and howling. He coughs up blood. Then I throat punch the third guy, leaving an imprint of my knuckles tattooed on his skin.

Their two friends are leaning back from behind the dumpster, one prick with his pants halfway down.

Fury burns through me at the sight of these bastards. Pathetic things. I charge, ripping them off the girl pinned in the corner, looking petrified. Her black hair is wild from the fight she's been in.

Her frightened gaze clashes with mine.

"Hold on," I tell her.

Unrelenting anger pounds in my veins, and I lose myself to the attack, tearing into the gang, blood spattering, and by the time I'm done, the alley is painted in red, bodies twisted and strewn in the gutter where they belong.

The realization that they weren't much of a challenge, and that they're now dead, is a downer. I had just been warming up.

Still, I walk over to the girl who has blood splashed on her cheek, and I offer her my hand. "Hey, you're safe now."

She pries open her teary eyes. The girl is maybe eighteen or nineteen and by the looks of it, the assholes didn't hurt her too much, aside from the purple bruise beneath her eye and her waitress uniform torn across her shoulder.

"Take my hand and I'll help you back inside."

Glancing around at the remains of her attackers, she bursts into tears, and I pinch my lips, knowing she needs time. Humans are such fragile creatures, so I crouch down and take her into my arms, then carry her into Chuck's.

"Let me give you a word of advice," I say. "Don't take your lunch break in the alley."

With her safely back inside and after giving her boss, who recognizes me instantly, a summary of the incident, I head outside. I leave the dead bodies in the alley for him to clean up.

Then I continue my brisk walk back home, like it's just another blissful day in Andover City.

Hopefully Drac won't be too pissed I took down some of the Spades' scrubs. We are supposed to be laying low until the merger pulls through.

Eh, should be fine.

Once inside the Tower, I jump into the elevator. When the doors ding open, I step directly into the foyer of our penthouse. The polished hardwood floors and floor-to-ceiling windows always invoke a strange nostalgia, like inhaling a scent from easier times.

From the moment I found this place and entered the top floor, I knew that we Kings had to live here. So I bought the whole damn building. Complete with picturesque views of the sprawling city stretching outward like an ocean and mountains sitting in the distance reminding me that beyond this concrete jungle lies a wilderness I can escape into.

I've done my fair share of wrong, and nature helps balance my tainted soul. Though most days, I doubt that I even have a soul.

"Cassius," Dracon's deep voice calls from his trophy room, stopping me mid stride on my way to the wet bar.

Running a hand through my blonde hair, I lick my lips and head down the hallway instead.

"You've got blood on you," Dracon says the moment I enter the room. He's reclined on a leather couch, his cell phone beside him, along with a manila folder with the corners of papers sticking out. Despite looking polished, his fiery amber eyes always look primal and furious, just like the beast inside him.

"Franco's roaches tried to kill me." That makes me look innocent enough.

"And…" he asks, his attention falling to his phone as if expecting a call.

"And I showed them that was a big mistake."

His gaze snaps up to my bloody clothes again, his lips pressing into a hard line.

"Listen, Drac, I know we're trying not to make waves, but they were runners. Insignificant–"

He holds up a hand to stop me.

Ah shit. Here it comes.

I brace for impact.

"Any survivors?" he asks instead, which shocks the shit out of me.

I blink, unsure if I've even heard him right. "Uh, no. Of course not."

His eyes drop back to his phone. "Good."

Okay then. Not what I was expecting at all but I'll take it.

When he lifts his head again, his hardened eyes turn a

darker golden color. "I'll double the enforcers in the area to see if it's a problem or a one-off incident. Where did this happen?"

"Chuck's Diner," I reply.

He nods once.

When Dracon loses his shit, his beast is terrifying, but when he's like this—silent, calculating, a monster trapped in a cardboard box—it scares me even more.

A beast I can see coming. I can predict the danger, dodge and fight. Dracon the man always rides a thin edge of restraint. You never know when he's going to blow.

Unlike him, I'm chaos all the time. I love a good fight, to feel warm blood running through my fingers, to hear my prey begging for help as I stomp the lives out of them.

I'm a sadistic son of a bitch.

"Have you seen Knox? We need to talk," Dracon states, his voice tight and breaking me out of my thoughts.

I shrug. "Ninety-nine percent of the time, he's in his morgue, you know that. Why?" I stride across the room before propping my ass on the arm of the couch across from him. I look down and sigh at the blood spots on my shirt, unsure if the stains will come out. Another shirt destroyed. If I keep going this way, I'll have to buy shares in Armani.

"We had two containers of guns stolen down at the docks from the delivery last night."

I jerk my head up. "What the fuck?" I jump to my feet, annoyance vibrating through me. "I was there and counted the stock personally with the crew."

Dracon raises to his feet, equal in height to my six-foot-five frame but twice as broad at the shoulders. We're not men anyone should cross, and right now, I'm fucking fuming with the news of theft on my watch. "All the stock was accounted for."

"I'm not insinuating that you were in any way at fault," he says firmly. "But someone must have been watching our team receive the shipment. Our storage was broken into. There were signs of forced entry, and our cameras were tampered with."

A beat of silence passes between us.

I stiffen, my brow furrowing. "Mother fuckers." How could someone steal right from under our noses? "I'll deal with it."

I start making my way to the door, ready to tear someone's head off.

"Not now, Cassius. We have the dinner coming up with Cobra Strike and then the Lords' auction night, and I need you and Knox to be my eyes and ears. The place will be filled with every gang leader from across the coast," Dracon demands. "Call Knox. He needs to know what's happened at the docks."

It takes a while, but I'm able to reel back my fury. These auspicious nights are the most dangerous, everyone is armed to the hilt. So, I agree with Dracon about being alert.

Ever since we lost Saxon, our world has been turned upside down. Our power is wavering, our reputation shaken, and that's something we can't have. We've worked way too hard to get where we are now. Dracon more than all of us combined. Saxon was his closest friend, but even he hasn't had a second to mourn his death. Part of me thinks he doesn't want to.

As for me, I'll be all over the missing guns tomorrow.

I head for the door, but before I leave, I glance over my

shoulder again. Dracon's staring down at his phone's screen again, as if he's trying to will the thing to ring.

"Let me guess," I begin, pausing in the doorway. "Another treasure?"

He doesn't answer, and in his silence, I hear the truth. I learned a long time ago that Dracon is the kind of man who can't silence his mind, so he's always on the go, got his fingers in a hundred fucking pies. He's a collector of sorts, constantly finding new things to hang on his walls. There's barely any space left in this room, but he somehow always finds a spot. Most of the relics are from his glory years, centuries ago.

To each their own kink.

His hobby keeps us on our toes, and he pretty much hunts down a new piece every damn week. But as weird as it is, he's family, just like Knox, so I've always got their backs. Though some days, I wonder if unaliving them for pissing me off would be easier. Of course, I wouldn't... But that's family, right? Pushing all your fucking buttons.

"Please don't let it be like the last one from that mummified priestess. Fuck, nearly lost all my fingers with that thing."

"It's King Arthur's sword," he responds plainly.

I arch a brow. "No shit. That's real?"

A dip of his chin for a nod. "So, are you going to get Knox?"

"Yeah, yeah," I answer, pulling out my cell phone from my back pocket and jab the screen with my thumbs, texting Knox to get his Hot Topic-looking ass up here.

When I don't get an immediate response, I hit the call button. It goes straight to voicemail.

I curse. Why the fuck did I buy him a cell phone if he's not going to keep it charged or turned on?

Dracon's phone buzzes next, and when he answers, he pushes to his feet and begins pacing across the room. By the sounds of it, the conversation has nothing to do with Knox and everything to do with the sword.

I turn on my heels, march out of there to catch the elevator down to the basement. The building is twenty-six stories tall. Well, soon to be thirty with our new penthouse being built. Knox and I named it the Tower as a little poke at Dracon's love of dragons and all those prissy fairy tales he hates so much.

And now, I'm going to shove Knox's phone down his throat for making me have to fetch him.

I was born in a world of carnage, and it took me a long time to learn that strangling someone for merely looking at me the wrong way wouldn't cut it here on earth unless I intended to become everyone's enemy. For a while, I considered it, but seeing as this was now my permanent home, Dracon showed me a few tricks to deal with my wild temper.

The Black Spades pricks in the alley come to mind. They were no challenge for me, but they served their purpose. Now my mind is wired up on punishing whoever stole our cargo during my watch, rather than waiting until tomorrow.

Once the elevator doors open, I'm confronted by the intense darkness that swallows the basement. I stroll forward, my sights set on the stream of light coming from under the door at the end of the open planned area. Being Death, Knox is naturally drawn to anything…well, dead. He's like our resident crazy goth. He's also the best person to inflict torture to get the information we need or exact revenge. Those unfortunate souls get brought here–to Knox's morgue–to play a part in his deranged fantasies.

I'll give it to the guy, though. He's good at death.

A female voice makes a half-moan, half-cry from the room, and I grin to myself. No way… He's got a girl in there? A *living* girl?

Is that why Knox didn't pick up the phone?

Lucky fuck! Good for him, getting laid. About damn time. I was starting to think he was a eunuch.

That has me walking faster and pushing open the door, eager to catch the entertainment.

But then, that's not exactly what I find in the room.

A gorgeous little thing is on her back, strapped down to his autopsy table. Unruly platinum blonde hair hangs around her face and dangles off the table. She's gagged, wrists tied down in leather straps by her sides, ankles bound in the same manner. And around her, a white magic circle has been drawn on the concrete floor, the kind I've only seen Knox use when he's dealing with someone brutally dangerous and not from this dimension.

He's on top of the girl, straddling her hips, grasping a long blade, blood dripping from the tip. And that's when I see the cuts on the girl's arms and a few on her body. Not deep, but definitely made to hurt. He's mumbling something I can't decipher, but then again, we're talking about Knox here, who uses death magic. I'm convinced he gets off on it.

He's a psycho like that.

But I'm curious. What did this blonde do to invoke his wrath?

Here I thought he was banging her, but in fact, he's going all Texas Chainsaw Massacre instead. By her painful groans and whimpers for escape, I am going to go out on a limb here and say, she's not who he thinks she is.

"Typical Tuesday night?" I ask loud enough to break

through his murmurs as I lean a shoulder into the door frame.

Knox surprises me by turning around slowly and grinning.

The girl's head turns my way and her glistening green eyes widen in desperation. With a rag stuffed into her mouth, she tries to scream around it.

I'm usually numb to hearing the pleas of Knox's victims, but for some reason this one makes me hesitate. Maybe it's everything that happened with the Spades and the waitress from Chuck's Diner, but I have a feeling Knox may have gone off the deep end here.

"Weren't you supposed to be tracking down Franco? Who's the chick?" I ask, crossing my arms.

His smile turns sickly sweet.

I follow his gaze to the workbench at the side of the room, covered in a myriad of his torture tools glinting beneath the fluorescent lights.

"She held my Mortem Blade, Cassius," he says. "She's been possessed by Aris."

"Wait, you found the thing?" I ask, shocked. He's been obsessed with tracking it down for months. I was starting to think the damn blade never existed and it was just another one of the dude's psychosis. But searching for it had kept him busy most days, so Dracon and I never bothered with it.

Knox waves the blade to prove his point. "It's finally back home."

I swivel my jaw, unconvinced Knox's arch-enemy is inside this girl. For one, Knox has always been paranoid as fuck. And for two, if the big dick himself were here, the world would be shuddering from his mere presence.

"Why do I think you got your wires crossed?" I push

away from the doorway to creep closer but pause at the edge of the magic circle. She may be a complete mess, but even beneath the tears and blood, she's stunning.

She thrashes on the table, seeming to be swearing behind the gag.

Oh, she's feisty.

The longer I let my gaze linger over her big sultry eyes and beautiful face–even if panicked–the more I'm intrigued. Her delicious tits are on full display, barely covered by a black bra. They rise and fall with each rushed breath, while I'm drawn to her curvy hips and the supple little tummy peeking out over her pants. My fingers itch to explore every inch of her.

Fucking tempting.

If I let myself stare any longer, I'll be hard as stone.

So I change my focus to my skin, itching from the heavy magic Knox used to enclose the girl, causing the hairs on my arms to stand on end. With all that energy, she'd be frothing at the mouth if anything resided inside her.

"She seems normal to me," I suggest.

"Didn't you hear me? She held my blade. No mortal or supe on earth can do that," he growls.

There Knox goes again with his super inflated ego–obviously someone other than him can touch his fucking blade because this girl did.

My phone dings with a text and I grit my teeth as I read Dracon's message.

Are you and Knox returning anytime today?

Rolling my eyes, I stuff the phone back into my pocket. "Looks like you're going to have to put your torture project on hold. We've got an shit to do tonight and Drac's waiting."

"I'm not leaving," he snarls, lifting his blade.

Her shoulders rear back against the table, her cries muffled by the gag in her mouth. While I would normally pull up a chair and grab a bag of popcorn to enjoy the show, I also don't want to deal with Dracon's bitching. And something about this scene feels… wrong, so very wrong… and I shouldn't give a shit.

But it's the whole image. The despair on her face, the way she trembles. It screams: someone who's in the wrong place.

Seems like I'm suffering from a personality complex today when it comes to saving damsels in distress.

"You know if you don't come back with me, Drac will be an insufferable prick, and I really can't deal with his attitude anymore today. I'm at my limit."

Knox pauses and glances down at the girl one last time, debating. The three of us have been together long enough to know Dracon can be one scary bastard. Silent, emotionless, but fucking deadly if triggered. Like a landmine. Just one tap and…*boom*. He'll take out everyone in a fifty-mile radius with his rage.

Narrowed eyes never leaving the blonde, he carefully climbs off the table, sheaths his blade in his belt. Then, he glances at the wall of cold lockers where he's stored many bodies before–dead or alive–until he was ready to play with them again.

"Put her upstairs somewhere. We'll deal with her and the blade thing after we see Dracon," I say and head for the door. Glancing over my shoulder one last time, I sigh loudly and shake my head. "Whatever you do, just hurry the fuck up."

CHAPTER SEVEN

EVE

I'm thrown into a bright room.

I hit the cement floor with my knees and lift my head to see the psycho who'd kidnapped me and sliced me up, glaring at me with glowing eyes as he closes the door. Panic surges. He's going to lock me in here!

I try to scramble to my feet to get to him, but with my body still riddled with pain from the fight with Franco and the fresh cuts, I'm too slow. The door slams shut, the lock clicking in place. I grip the handle, twist, and yank as hard as I can, but it doesn't budge.

"You crazy fuck! Let me out of here!" I bang my fists on the door over and over.

His heavy footsteps fade away as he heads down the hall, leaving me alone.

I whirl around, facing the unfinished room. A wall of floor-to-ceiling windows stare back at me, and beyond it, the city of Andover stretches out. I don't know how many stories up I am, but it's high enough to see every road, building, and park. I can even see downtown and the red glow of Kat's Kradle's sign, as well as the harbor and shipyards.

Holy shit. Where am I? This must be the tallest building in the entire fucking city. And who were those two guys? More Black Spades? Had to be.

How had I gotten myself in this mess?

My gaze scans the large room, which seems to be freshly built with concrete floors, exposed drywall, and naked wires. Rolls of plastic and various other building materials are scattered around the space. It's a construction zone in here.

That means I may be able to find something useful to help me escape.

I rush to the middle of the room. When I spot a rusty toolbox, I praise my luck and pop the thing open. There's got to be something in here, a hammer or a paperclip, anything I can use to pick the lock or smash my way through the door. Sure, it'd make a lot of noise, but the tattooed guy–Cassius, the maniac who'd cut me up had called him–had said they had to go meet someone named Dracon. Maybe I'd get lucky and wherever he is, it's far, *far* away from here. Either way, I have to move fast.

Shifting through the box's contents, I find it's full of wrenches, different size attachments, loose screws, and a cut up dirty t-shirt that looked like it had seen better days.

I glance down at my blouse. The buttons cut off and split up the middle, putting all my goods on display. There's blood, I'm cut in multiple places…

Yeah, the ratty t-shirt is looking better and better, especially if I have to go to the cops after this. Can't show up at the station looking like a busted up prostitute. They'd never take me seriously.

Quickly, I shimmy out of my shirt and pull on the raggy

one. It's big on me and smells like sweat and grease, but I don't care, it'll do.

One problem solved, but a bunch of wrenches and screws aren't going to help me get out of here.

I could use my power–that could get me out of here *easily*, but it could just as easily bring down the entire building on top of me.

There's a reason I never tap into the magical part of me. My power is destructive, wild, and uncontrollable. It's telekinesis but on steroids. And supercharged with a shot of electricity. Times ten. Trying to move something an inch causes the walls to start shaking and things start flying around–it's terrifying. I've always thought I might be some kind of witch, but I've never come across anyone like me, and I've met *a lot* of people in my profession.

Asking my mother has always been out of the question, since everything escalated after I'd left. The stress of being homeless and fending for myself didn't help any, but I refused to go home. Even for answers. So, I toughed it out and solved the problem by never tapping into that part of myself again. It was safer that way.

There are times when the power sneaks through–like when I was being sliced up on the table like a steak dinner. Things started to shake and swing, especially when the pain of the cuts increased, but the psycho barely noticed. Though, if he did, all he could think about was getting to *Aris*, whoever the fuck that is. I sure as hell don't know. As attractive as he might be with his shoulder-length black hair, tan skin, and hazel eyes, the man has too many screws loose.

By the extreme hard-on he got while cutting me, he was thoroughly enjoying himself by making me scream and bleed.

The sick fuck.

All the more reason to get the fuck out of here. And fast.

Shoving over a stack of two-by-fours and some pink insulation, I spot something useful and my heart leaps with excitement. A screwdriver. I won't have to worry about the door being locked if I can just take the doorknob off, right?

Perfect.

I hurry back over to the door and press my ear against the wood. Silence echoes on the other side.

Maybe I should wait a bit, just to make sure those monsters are far enough away, but even the thought of being in this place with that part creepy torture chamber, part morgue, has my nerves crawling under my skin.

Hands trembling, I jam the flat end between the metal plate and the door and wiggle fiercely. It pops off, revealing four tiny screws. I unscrew them one by one. It doesn't take too long for me to get them all out and rip the knob off the door. I pull out all the pieces, including the latch bolt, and chuck them all to the side.

I stick my fingers in the hole where the doorknob just was and yank as hard as I can. The thing swings open with ease.

Ha! That was a cakewalk. Finally, something's going right for me.

Cautiously, I step into the hallway, but keep the screwdriver in case I bump into any of Franco's men and need to defend myself.

Like the room I'd come out of, the rest of the floor is being worked on too, although the hall seems to be farther along with fresh paint on the walls at least. There are no decorations, carpets, or lighting fixtures yet, but it's in progress. Cold air rushes past me from somewhere unknown, making me shiver all over.

Glancing left and then right, I see nothing but more closed doors on either side. I spin and head right. The hall opens up suddenly to a wide foyer-type space with a spiral staircase covered in plastic, an elevator, and another hallway disappearing down the opposite side.

Excitement bubbles up at the sight of the elevator–my ticket to freedom.

I rush over, but my stomach sinks when I see the card access point above the buttons.

Maybe it hasn't been programmed yet?

I push the down button and say a silent prayer while I wait for the doors to open. The panel lights up instead.

Dammit!

Okay, forget the elevator. There has to be a set of stairs for emergencies, right? Fire escape access?

Remembering how the emergency exits at Kat's Kradle were always exposed to the elements outside and therefore cold during these months, I head back down the way I came, where the frigid air feels the strongest. It has to be over here. Somewhere.

I start opening doors and peering inside. Each one leads to another partly done room with either a wall of windows or high, curved ceilings. My god, this place is enormous. It must cost a fortune to live in one of these apartments.

The hallway turns suddenly, and when I follow it, I come face to face with a wall of hanging plastic. It's freezing here, and I quickly realize why. Beyond the plastic are only cement walls and a temporary wooden staircase leading both up and down. There are openings for windows to one day go in, but right now, the space is completely open to the winter elements and the temperatures.

I don't care. As long as it goes down to the first floor, it works for me.

Clutching the screwdriver, I rip the plastic aside and fly down the steps. Even though my body aches terribly, my adrenaline keeps me going. I almost trip as I sprint down the stairs.

One…two…three…four…

Shit, how many floors are in this construction?

Nothing's labeled, so I lose count after a while, but I have to be near the first floor by now. As I make the next turn, I'm halted by a door instead of more stairs, and fear twists my gut. I must've gone too far. I sure as hell don't want to end up back in the basement.

I'm about to turn and hurry back up a flight, but the sound of classical music halts me in my tracks. I glance over my shoulder to see another one of their card access panels, but the door is open a crack. So no card needed.

Slowly, I tiptoe over, pull it open a smidge more, and pass through.

This floor is finished, unlike the others, and painted in coal gray with white accents and furniture. Clean, sharp lines, minimalist decor, and dark wood floors that all screams *single rich male*. There's not a feminine touch to be seen.

I creep down the hallway, happy for once not to have my heels on. Even with the music playing, they'd be too loud on this floor and give me away.

Like the stories above, at the end, the corridor opens up to a grand room with a large circular staircase and high ceilings. Unlike the ones above, though, an elaborate antler chandelier hangs in the middle, reminding me of a hunting lodge somewhere up north.

A ding sounds behind me, and I whip around to see the digital display above the elevator showing an arrow pointing up.

Panic rocketing through me, I run back toward the emergency staircase, but when I hear the gears churning and the metal doors sliding open, I know I'm not going to make it without being seen. I turn the nearest door handle, shove it open, and throw myself inside an unknown room. I'm just able to get it closed again when I hear thundering voices on the other side.

Fuck. Fuck. Fuck. Fuck. Did they see me?

I cross the room. The same ski resort aesthetic with the chandelier continues in here. Only more so. There's a huge stone fireplace, a circular leather couch, tons of dark wood paneling, and various bookshelves and treasures mounted on the walls.

Who lives here?

"I wait for no one." A deep voice booms outside, and I freeze on the spot, gripping the screwdriver like my life depends on it. And it just might. "And that includes you and Knox."

Knox?

"Listen, Drac, you're preaching to the choir here," a familiar voice replies. It belongs to the tattooed guy who'd found me and the gothic Fabio in the basement. Cassius.

Uh oh. That means this Drac he's talking to is the Dracon he was warning the other one about. The one they both seemed to obey.

"But Knox was busy with a girl–"

"A girl?" he sounds surprised.

"Not like that. But I was hoping."

"Then how?"

"Oh, you know him. He can't get off unless someone is tied up,begging for mercy, bleeding."

So, Knox is the crazy one.

I shift on my feet, and the floor creaks under my weight. Every muscle tenses and I hold my breath.

"What?" Cassius barks suddenly. "What is it? Did you hear something?"

"Where did you say the girl is now?" Dracon begins carefully. I can hear his footsteps as they slowly come down the hall, toward my hiding place.

"Upstairs. Twenty-seventh floor. Knox threw her in one of the rooms up there–"

Dracon's sharp shush cuts him off.

I clamp my mouth shut. How can he still hear me? I haven't moved, but my heart is pounding against my rib cage.

"Not anymore," Dracon says, and his words made my legs weak. If this guy is as big and bad as the other two say he is, a rinky-dinky screwdriver won't help me.

I glance around the room for another weapon. And spot an ornate looking axe mounted above the fireplace mantel. It looks old, almost medieval, and has engravings along the wooden handle and a large chunk missing from its sharp edge. But if I was facing another monster like Franco, I needed something deadly, and broken or not, it would do.

Chucking the screwdriver, I hurry over and pull the battle axe off the stone. It's heavier than I expected, but that won't stop me from using it. I move further into the room, searching for another way out of here. There's a door that leads to a bedroom and bathroom, and lots of windows that show off the city and the scaffolding outside from all the construction, but that's it as far as I can see.

As I glance out the windows, I notice they aren't all fixed panes, like the other room had been. These actually open.

Maybe I could climb my way onto the scaffolding and make my way down the building.

No fucking way. Too dangerous.

Turning, I see shadows dance under the crack of the door. They're going to come in here.

I glance back at the window. I'll take my chances being a monkey because there's no way on this planet I'm going back on that autopsy table with Knox.

The doorknob turns, and I'm already unlocking the window and pulling it open. I don't know who in their right mind would have windows that open wide like this so many floors up, but right now, I'm thankful for the design flaw.

The moment I step outside, I'm slammed from all angles by biting frigid air. It whips up my hair and whooshes past my ears, cutting out any other sounds. I stagger back and grip onto the side rails, somehow unable to get enough oxygen into my lungs. When my gaze drops to the streets below, my stomach instantly turns and my head spins.

Why did I think this was a good idea again?

Inside the room, the door slams open. And my body leaps toward the ladder automatically.

Oh yeah, that's why. I have Black Spades trying to kill me.

"Are you crazy?"

Chest heaving, I peer back to see Cassius half hanging out the window; the wind whipping through his hair, too.

"You're going to get yourself killed!"

"Fuck you!" I shout. The scaffolding rocks and I stumble sideways. My side hits one of the bars, and a scream claws up my throat.

"Holy shit–Dracon!" He spins. "Drac? Where the fuck did you go?"

Wait, Dracon's not there? Where did he go?

The boards and pipes groan and whine all around me from the power of the wind.

Cassius is waving for me to come back. "Get over here and I'll pull you back in!"

I chance another peek down, see the deadly height, and my head spins again. Heat crawls up my neck and my vision wavers. I'm going to faint.

"Aw, fuck." Cassius reaches for the scaffolding, about to step on it with me. "Why am I always cleaning up Knox's messes?"

The mention of Knox has me dropping to my knees and crawling frantically over to the ladder. There's no way I'm letting anyone drag me back. I'd rather leap off the scaffolding right now.

Fate seems to want to grant my wish because the wind becomes violent, pulling the braces off the wall. The scaffolding sways and rocks so hard, I end up rolling off the edge and falling.

I'm still holding the stupid axe, and it feels like it's only pulling me down faster. I wave it desperately, trying to lodge it into something to stop me, but I can't reach anything.

Above me, I see Cassius's face watching in horror. His mouth opens as he screams something, but I can't hear it over the roar of the air and my own blood-curdling screams.

For a few terrifying seconds, I'm convinced I'm going to die, but then something snatches me around the middle, and I'm halted abruptly.

It all happens too fast for me to register. One second I'm plummeting to my death and the next I'm suspended in mid-air–being pulled back toward the wall. The wind isn't helping. Swinging wildly, I smack into the side of the building hard, and pain explodes through my skull as my head hits. Then my knees.

A fierce growl rumbles above me, and when I look up, I see I've been saved by a dark angel.

He's breathtaking. With short, dark hair, animalistic amber eyes, and ruggedly handsome face, he makes my brain fog. Or maybe that's just the concussion setting in. Hard to tell.

"Don't you dare drop it," he says through clenched teeth.

I stare at him in confusion.

"The axe!"

What the fuck? He cares more about the stupid axe than me?

Okay, not an angel.

He's half hanging out of the window, and even with the drop and my weight, he's able to hoist me back inside easily. Too easily. I know I'm no size two, but the guy tosses me around like I weigh nothing.

I'm thrown into the middle of the room, his precious axe flying out of my hands and sailing across the room. When my body meets the soft carpet, I want to weep. I'm so cold, but the realization of what happened is what has me trembling. *I almost died! And I would've been nothing but a stain on the pavement!*

Cassius appears in the doorway, out of breath like he

had just run down flights of stairs. "Sonofabitch, Dracon! You caught her!"

Arms shaking and breathing hard, I peer up at the mountain of a man standing in front of me with his lip curled in a furious snarl.

This is him?

Dracon.

The Dracon.

Now I'm not sure being saved was such a good thing.

CHAPTER EIGHT

DRACON

"Fuck!" I holler, staring at my broken axe on the floor, snapped in half.

I squeeze my hands into fists, my attention zeroing in on the blonde I'd just dragged in from falling off the scaffolding. "What the hell have you done?"

This tiny beauty who's literally crashed into my home tilts her head to the side, blinking at me like she's having trouble understanding my words or the significance of my axe. She's curvy, her body sinful, and those tits…fuck I want to lick them.

Something sharp twists in my gut at the sight of her. This is new.

Long golden hair cascades to her tiny waist in messy waves. Her soft, shapely legs are in tight jeans, and she's wearing an oversized white tee that is so thin… I easily follow the curves of her bra. She has fresh cuts on her arms, no doubt from Knox. Her lip is swollen, her feet are bare, and she looks like she's on the verge of hypothermia.

She's much shorter than me, and she's trembling, yet she holds herself bravely. Even with Cassius grasping onto her arm, she attempts to pull away from him. I can't look away from her. She's the most beautiful woman I've ever seen, which surprises me. I'm caught so off guard by her looks that it does something to my brain and my beast rises within me, growling, *Mine*.

It begs the question… who exactly is this creature Knox brought into our home?

As if summoned, Knox walks into my trophy room and stops short at the sight of the three of us. He doesn't say a fucking word.

The girl arches a thin eyebrow, her anger simmering behind those gorgeous green eyes. "Are we talking about me escaping after that crazy dick," she tears her gaze from me and turns to Knox, her voice escalating, "kidnapped, imprisoned, and tortured me, and then he," she lifts her chin toward Cassius at her side, "did nothing to help me when he found me tied to a damn autopsy table? I did what I had to do to get the fuck out of this hellhole. What the hell is wrong with you people?"

"To be fair, he's done worse. You were fine by his standards," Cassius adds, to which she shoots him a glare.

Her narrowing gaze lifts to me. "Who the heck are you three, anyway? Franco's shitheads?"

A growl rolls through my chest, while Cassius chokes on his next breath, sputtering and coughing like her words punched him in the throat.

It takes him a while, but when he finally regains his composure, he says, "The oversized cantaloupe wishes we were on his payroll."

I cut a glance to Knox, who shrugs a shoulder nonchalantly. "I tracked down my blade to the Spades' warehouse. They had kidnapped her, and somehow she used the Mortem Balde to escape."

"Wait, what?" the girl asks. She appears genuinely confused by the whole thing. "The Mortem...*what?*"

Knox continues, ignoring her. "You know no mortal can wield my magic without dying. She has to be Aris. *Has to be.*"

"So you brought her to your morgue to torture." Cassius puts the pieces together. "Because you're convinced she's your long lost brother come back to kill you."

Knox blinks. "Well...yes."

She barks a loud laugh. "You are all fucking crazy."

I sigh. Knox's obsession with Aris has gotten us in shit before. And now, it looks like it's tangled us up in the Black Spades. Right when we're supposed to be keeping low and building more to our arsenal from behind the curtain.

Fury whirls inside me. This is exactly what he was warned not to do. Don't draw attention to us until the merger with Cobra Strike goes through. It's not that fucking hard, but it's like he can't control himself.

If he wasn't a horseman and deadly as fuck, I probably would've taken him out myself by now. He's a liability, but it's better–smarter–to have him on our side than against us.

No one can beat Death.

The girl he's dragged in seems to like pushing his buttons though. She continues to glare at him with a mask of anger, not fear. "There is no Aris! I'm Eve! Eve! I don't know what the fuck you're talking about."

So...her name is Eve.

"I told you, Knox. You fucked up again," Cassius grunts.

Walking over, Knox reaches out a hand to touch Eve's cheek, almost affectionately, but she slaps his hand away. Grinning, he addresses me and Cassius again instead of her. "She must be influenced by Aris in some way. She's as fragile as a little dove. There's no way she'd be able to wield my blade without him."

Her face scrunches up with anger. "Fuck you, asshole."

"Do you have anything to contribute to make sense of this, Cassius?" I bark, getting angrier by the second. "At this rate, I'm about ready to throw all three of you back out that window and start this group from scratch."

Eve's gaze whips over her shoulder to the open glass where she had almost plummeted to her death mere moments ago.

Sighing, Cassius pushes his fingers through his hair. "I don't think she's Aris. I'm not even sure that's really the blade Knox has been griping about for months–"

"It is!" he snaps automatically but Cassius keeps going.

"I don't fucking know. Maybe the magic's changed since you last handled the thing, Knox. Maybe it's weaker and other people can touch it now. It may be wiser for you to focus on that then stuffing a gag in her mouth and dicing her up like yesterday's leftovers."

"Go suck a dick," Knox blurts, not willing to hear any alternatives.

"Well, while you three enjoy your little loony party," Eve begins as she glances between the lot of us. "I'll let myself out."

She rips her arm from Cassius's hold and runs right past me for the hall.

Clearly, she has no idea who she's dealing with.

Before she can even make it out the door, I snatch her arm and yank her close. "You're not going anywhere," I murmur in her ear before pushing her back into the room. She stumbles, almost tripping over my broken axe where she dropped it.

Her tits bounce, and I'm instantly picturing them bare and in my hands. Hmm…Maybe I can fuck the attitude out of her…

Except, this temptress broke my relic, and no one goes unpunished after taking something of mine. The piece was priceless. Nothing can replace it. And fuck! No one's talking straight or telling me what the fuck's going on. Or how Franco got involved.

Knox and Cassius are still bickering about the damned blade. While I stand here, my heart sprinting in my chest like a wild beast.

Eve, on the other hand, eyes the broken axe as if she's deciding whether or not to pick it up and use it against me.

Interesting… Even after everything she's been through, she's still willing to fight?

She's a fighter. Like me.

"I wouldn't do that if I were you," I say, eyeing her.

Her fierce gaze clashes with mine. How can someone so gorgeous be so irritating?

"I hope you know that I don't plan on staying," she replies.

"And I hope *you* know I'll be the one that decides whether you walk out of here alive or not." My skin itches from my beast, pushing to be freed. Every inch of me pulses with a thumping beat to unleash and allow him to serve his own brand of punishment for what we lost by someone who doesn't seem to give a shit.

The tomahawk axe is a trophy, a prize I took from one of the last tribes I fought and defeated way back in the days before civilizations spawned. From each battle, I claimed a reward. However, this axe is unique. It holds power–for anyone who can actually activate it. It's why I kept it on the wall in my room with my other invaluable objects: Masks and blades, blessed with ancient power.

Eve studies my axe, her brow knotted, still debating what to do.

I move to her with purpose, and in that split second, she makes her choice, snatches the weapon with both hands, and raises it with an intention to strike.

Cassius and Knox try to step forward to intervene, but I'm faster. I grab the broken handle in her grasp. That's when the hairs on my arms suddenly lift.

Power skates down my spine, and energy jolts through me so hard that I convulse.

Everything turns to darkness in seconds.

And just as fast as the surprise crawls through me, I am no longer standing in my apartment.

My vision blurs, my head dizzy, and I'm in an ordinary person's living room. Sunlight peeks in from the closed blinds.

There's a woman, maybe in her late thirties, with blonde hair lying on the couch, her arm tucked under her chin. She looks like she's sleeping. She's wearing a pale blue dress that has wormed its way up to her thighs.

The door suddenly opens and a young, perky girl, maybe thirteen or fourteen years old, with blonde a ponytail, drags herself into the house. One look and I instantly recognize those green eyes. It's Eve, and I'm watching a piece of her past.

"Mom," she calls out only to pause when she finds her mom groaning from the couch. "You're asleep?" Eve asks with sarcasm in her voice. "Are we still going shopping to get a sleeping bag for tomorrow's school camping trip?"

Her mom's head lifts and her eyes snap open. "What time is it?"

"Almost four."

Her mom groans and pushes herself to her feet. "Oh, I lost an entire hour. Why are you home late from school?"

"I had track practice, told you already."

Eve's mom pats down her messy blonde hair, then tugs down her dress. "Look at the time. We have to be at the fundraiser in twenty minutes."

"Mom," Eve raises her voice. "We have to go shopping first. I can't go if I don't have a sleeping bag. You promised me."

Her mom's face hardens. "We don't have time, Evelyn. That's what happens when you're home late. Now get ready."

Eve clenches her fists, and she kicks a cushion on the floor. "No," she insists. "I am going camping tomorrow. I told everyone I'm going this time. I've been telling you about it for weeks. Please, Mom."

The woman pinches her lips and walks over to collect a set of heels from the hallway, murmuring something under her breath I don't catch, but Eve must have because she's shaking.

"No. No. No. You promised. Why couldn't you for once put me first? Just this once, I needed you. I want to go with my friends and be normal."

Her mom's face twists like she's about to spit fire. In her straight dress and heels, she looks every part the pristine woman, always in her best clothes, always fake smiling, always sprouting how much they do for everyone else. Except for their own family.

She marches toward Eve and snatches her arm, nails digging into her flesh.

"You're hurting me," Eve cries out.

"If someone had helped me clean up the house and finished baking the muffins for today's fundraiser, then I would have more time to go shopping with you. I'm tired of you not doing enough around the house. Your room is a mess. Maybe you should focus on studying instead of going camping. Getting a B

in trigonometry is not good enough, Eve. I am so embarrassed when I have to speak with your teachers."

Eve's face is red with anger, and she looks ready to explode.

The walls start shaking around us, and I peer up, thinking it's an earthquake. The paintings on the wall shudder, and one falls, the glass smashing.

"Eve, you will end up in hell if you don't listen and stop this." Her mom stiffens, shoulders square, and irritation contorts her expression to one of pure anger. "And don't look at me like that, or I get the belt, and you'll be sorry. Instead of camping with your wild friends, you will stay home. Go get cleaned up and put on that yellow dress I bought you. God have mercy on you, but I will make a half-decent, respectable girl out of you."

She grimaces with disgust as her mom collects lipstick from her purse and goes to stand in front of a mirror on the wall to smear it on her lips.

Eve screams in frustration and runs out of the house. The walls are still once more.

My vision immediately blurs and fades as fast as it came.

I now find myself standing on a sidewalk with the sun setting, throwing the decrepit neighborhood into darkness. I'm nowhere near my indulgent apartment in the city, but somewhere run down and poor. A violent wind thrashes through the street, tossing trash down the sidewalk.

Across the road, green eyes catch my attention.

It's Eve, she's older now. Maybe sixteen or seventeen. She's huddled with her back against a building, sitting on a piece of cardboard and hugging her knees. The blanket around her shoulders doesn't seem to be doing much. Her face is red with cold. She looks at everyone passing by to get their attention, but not one person gives her the time of day. Resting her chin on her knees, she closes her eyes just as the cap in front of her, to collect money, is snatched away on the breeze, blowing down the street without her even noticing.

A man with silvery hair and in a suit crouches down by her side. He's talking to her, then offers her what looks like a small stack of cash.

She lifts her gaze, then shakes her head.

He persists and tries to push the money at her once more, but she shoves his hand back into his face. The guy falls on his ass from the shove, clearly not expecting her to fight back.

The jackass gets to his feet, dusting his jacket, and kicks her before leaving.

I step forward, something in me rearing up to teach the fucking dick a lesson. A growl scratches in my throat as I realize how much I want to smash his head into the concrete sidewalk.

But my vision blurs in and out once more, a reminder that I can't do shit in a past that's already happened.

I'm now in an alley with dumpsters. I know the place. Kat's Kradle. Eve's at the back door, holding onto a black garbage bag in one hand, her clothes hanging off her thin frame, blonde hair messily pulled into a ponytail. She's talking to an older woman in the doorway. Kat, the witch who owns the club. I'd recognize the ginger curls anywhere. The woman has sway in this city.

She offers Eve a hand and then takes her inside.

My mind flashes with images that make no sense now, and my head spins.

Ripped from the visions, I stumble back, my breath lodged in my lungs. The snippets of Eve's life leave me looking at her differently. She's fought for just survival, something I can relate to.

My axe drops from our hands to the floor.

"What was that?" she whimpers, her face pale, her eyes glistening like she's about to burst into tears.

I stay perfectly still, not trusting myself to move yet, as I realize that not only had I just been privy to her tragic past, but that she's seen mine. A horrific past that leaves me fighting the urge to find a way to steal back those memories from her, from her ever seeing them.

That's how the magic of the axe works, after all. It shows you the past of the person who holds it… something I haven't been able to activate since it broke all those years ago in battle.

Eve's hugging herself, blinking at me with huge eyes. And I pity her for having to lay witness to anything in my head.

A horrible, decrepit past I loathe.

"Are you alright?" I ask cautiously. But she doesn't respond. Her eyes glazed, lost in the terror.

The thing about us three Kings is we all have pasts, stories to tell, dark reasons we don't share. Things that have left us bent and twisted beyond repair. And mine is one I keep under lock and key from everyone but these two. Until now. This girl caught a glimpse of the darkness I was born from. Possibly even the monster within. And by the tears flooding her eyes, the pain on her face, she's not coping well with what she's seen.

My body goes cold, and while I have no idea which parts of my past she experienced, it's not something I intend to talk about now or ever.

"I think you broke her," Knox says.

Straightening, I snap my stone-cold facade in place and stare her down. "It seems our little blonde figured out how to activate the power of my axe," I say.

That's all he and Cassius need to know. They're aware of the power the axe once held and what that means.

"Did you see anything good?" Knox asks a bit too cheerily. "What's Dracon been hiding for us?"

The bastard loves seeing people suffer and struggle.

Eve's trembling in place, and for a long moment, she can't even seem to form words. After a while, she turns to me and manages in a low voice, "He... You..."

Ah, shit. Whatever she's seen, it wasn't good.

"Horrible," she blurts out next. "Absolutely horrible."

Cassius and Knox glance my way, wanting more explanation, but this isn't the time. I'm not sure there will ever be a moment to reveal such things. Even to them.

"Carnage," is all I say. "Death."

"Sounds like our kind of thing," Cassius jokes, but when I throw him a hard look, he clamps his mouth shut.

"Not like this," I assure them. "*Nothing* like this."

Then, I turn back to Eve, who's now rubbing her arms and muttering nonsense in an effort to console herself. "It'll be smarter for you to forget what you saw. If you want to keep your sanity."

They'll always be haunting memories to me, ones that refuse to leave.

Eve licks her lips, and the three of us watch her intently. She takes several moments to compose herself, to blink away the tears that collected in her eyes.

There's an unfamiliar urge to take her into my arms and soothe her, and just the idea startles me. She's a stranger. A nobody.

And I'm...*me.*

But my hand swings out anyway, despite my reservations.

She pulls away. "Don't."

Which part did she see?

Me shackled and chained to a tree like a dog, fed scraps when they remembered to feed me? When they called me a demon for not understanding that I could shift into more than one animal. Beating me to keep my animal side at bay, to make me so weak, I couldn't fight back.

I was just a fucking child. Eight years old. My parents treated me like a plight in their lives. Something they had to hide. It still guts me each time I recall them.

Or had Eve seen the fights I'd been thrown into for sport, enslaved and then forced to battle for the sole purpose of being other people's amusement, while beaten close to death?

Cut. Bled. Broken.

Over and over.

Or had she seen me kill…

My body trembles at the memories I've driven to the deepest crevices of my mind. Along with the hatred of a world that left me so scared that some days I want to burn it all down. Every. Last. Piece.

Heaving for each breath, Cassius is at my side, his hand on my back. He gives no words because none are needed. He knows what happens when I lose myself, but even he doesn't know my past. None of them do–not really. The only person who I'd confided in was Saxon and look where he is now. Ashes in the wind.

Shaking off the memories from a long time ago, I remind myself that this is a different time and place. I'm stronger now. Powerful. My abilities are celebrated. Envied. Feared. And I embrace it.

"I'm fine," I murmur under my breath, shrugging off his hand.

"So what now?" Knox asks, annoyance tinging his tone. His fingers dance along his blade's handle, clearly itching to use it again. "We're all twisted here. We all have demons."

Cassius snorts.

"I'm sure this little dove has had her fair share herself," Knox says, tilting his head Eve's way. "But I think we should focus on the real issue here. Like how the fuck she was able hold my blade?"

"And activate the axe's power," Cassius adds.

"When you say it that way, it sounds pretty bad, but I swear to you, I have no idea what any of this means. None of it," Eve says and clears her throat. "You should just let me go."

"Right back into Franco's waiting arms?" Cassius replies.

Eve grows rigid, rethinking her request to leave.

I, on the other hand, have no idea what to do with her. Part of me is intrigued about what she is and what kind of powers she possesses. It could be useful to add to our arsenal, especially since Saxon's death has left us weaker.

But at the same time, do I really want someone as tempting as her around here? Can we afford the distraction right now?

I don't think so.

I grit my teeth. Letting her go would be the same as hand delivering her to Franco. She's a dead woman walking.

And why do I care?

Good question, one I'm not sure I can answer right now.

"What are you?" The question whips from my lips.

Taken off guard, her eyes widen. "Wh-What?"

"What kind of supernatural are you?" I repeat more firmly. I try to keep her gaze but she drops it to her feet.

"I'm...human."

"Someone's lying," Knox sing-songs.

I hold up a hand to stop him. Thinking back to the

vision Eve and I had shared with her bitch of a mother, her living on the streets, and then finding solace at Kat's Kradle. It all seemed *human* enough, but there has to be more to her… Has to. I can feel it.

Eve shifts uneasily under my stare.

"A human wouldn't be able to tap into the magic of the axe," I say.

"Or even *think* of touching my blade," Knox interjects.

"So, I suggest you cut the shit and tell us straight out what you are or Knox will take you back down to the morgue and get the truth out of you that way."

She pales instantly.

"What do you say, little dove? You wanna play some more?" Knox asks with a serial killer smile spreading across his face.

"I-I–" In that second, she makes a run for the elevators behind me, again.

Getting tired of this game, I snap my arm out once more and hook her around her waist, pulling her into me.

Didn't she learn the first time?

"Let me go," she cries out, her fingernails biting into my arm as her other hand lashes out. Sharp points dig into my cheek, and I groan, grabbing her wrist.

"She's a fighter, this one!" Knox is practically salivating with each word.

Big emerald eyes burn into me. She's scared and knows she stands no chance, but she isn't backing down.

Oh, I like that about her. I like it a lot.

She'll fight tooth and nail. I respect that, but she also needs to know who's in charge here.

Me.

"Get off me, you bastard," she hisses. She's small, curvy, and shaking as I spin her around, so she's facing away from me. Just as fast, I walk her forward until she's caged between the wall and my body, with her cheek flush against it and my groin pressed into her gorgeous ass.

With one hand tangled in her hair, I wrench her head back until she yelps in pain. "Let's try this again, shall we?"

CHAPTER NINE

DRACON

*I*f looks could kill, I'd be dead.

"Go fuck yourself!" she snarls.

I make a tsking sound, pressing in closer to her. All I can focus on is her scent. I breathe it deep into my lungs. She smells like clementines and something floral. But beneath that, something raw and purely her. Whatever it is…it's taking all my strength not to fuck her against this wall.

Noticing movement out of the corner of my eye, I turn to see Cassius and Knox coming up to my side, waiting for my next orders. Except right now, I have none to give. None except *watch and learn.*

I tug her hair again for good measure, loving the soft whimper that escapes her lips. "Let's start with the basics. Who are you?"

"You go first," she fires back just as sharply. "You have a very colorful past."

I stiffen at her words, remembering that she's seen what haunts my mind. Then I reiterate in a low, guttural voice. "You are in my house, my domain, so speak." I pull her head back, and she sucks in a sharp breath.

"Okay, okay! Fine!" she gasps. "My name's Eve Dalton. I work at Kat's Kradle and unfortunately caught the attention of Xavier Franco. The guy doesn't take no for an answer, which seems to be a common theme in this line of work…"

Cassius laughs. "Ain't that the truth."

"Yeah, well, I stabbed him in the eye with my stiletto, and now he wants me dead. That's when this psycho showed up and brought me here. The end." She nods toward Knox.

Franco. Just hearing his name uttered from her has heat rising across my neck. Knowing the moose tried to rape her–it boils my blood.

We've never been friendly with the Black Spades. Never. And Franco's always irked me to another level, but with everything going on, we can't afford to pick fights with anyone right now. Then there's this annoying, gorgeous girl who really means nothing to me, yet my beast stirs inside my chest, wanting blood for simply putting his grubby hands on her. It doesn't make any sense.

"Now back to the original question," I press. "What are you?"

"Human," she repeats.

"One that happens to know about supernaturals and magic?"

She pauses. Clearly, she didn't expect me to trap her so easily. "I…was introduced to it at a young age," she settles with.

Cassius shakes his head, not buying any of it. He's not the only one. "Riiiight. And I'm the tooth fairy."

Knox's brows knit together. "No you're not."

Cassius rolls his eyes, but doesn't even try to explain what sarcasm is to the immortal. Again.

"Believe it or not, it's true." Eve tries to shove off the wall, but I shove her forward roughly. Her cheek slams against it, and she grunts out a curse.

"Wrong answer." I lean down further, my lips brushing against her ear. "If you keep wanting to play this game, you're not going to like how I win." Her seductive scent grows heavier, and the need to taste her, to make her moan, plays on my mind again. But not yet... at least not the way I want her.

Her body tenses against mine, but her face flushes a pinkish color.

"You don't scare me," she says, but her body is betraying her.

"That's because you haven't seen me angry," I answer.

She freezes suddenly, and a whimper escapes.

Or maybe she has...

Oh fuck, what did she see in the vision? She probably thinks I'll hurt her, and if she were anyone else, I definitely would. And without hesitation. But there are other ways to make a person submit than mere force. The cuts on her body tell me that Knox had tried that tactic with her and failed.

"You need to learn who's in charge," I begin as I trail my nose down her neck. "You will stay here until I'm satisfied with everything you have to tell me."

"And we learn how she was able to wield my blade," Knox calls from my side.

Eve attempts to escape from under my grip, her body wriggling, her elbow slamming into my ribs. I groan, the pain fueling me, and I press my foot between her feet and knock them apart. Then wedge my knee between her thighs.

There's dread on her face when she twists around to glare at me. The beast stirs within me, just below the surface of my skin.

"Do you still think you can get away?" I purr in her ear, my fingers sliding across her collarbone and her throat. "No one crosses me, Eve. No one."

Her breath hitches, and her sweet scent mingles with fear and arousal. She's so vulnerable right now. I could so easily tear her jugular out and be done with this.

Silence sweeps between us.

"Ready to talk?" I whisper in her ear.

"Have you thought of asking nicely?" she gasps between raspy breaths. "Because fear mongering does nothing for me."

Liar.

"This is me asking nicely. Otherwise you'd be dead." My fingers twitch around her neck, tightening just a fraction to feel her flinch.

"I'd hate to see how you treat your girlfriend."

A husky laugh escapes me. "Monsters aren't capable of love, little one."

"Well, you're wasting your time with me," she says softly, almost convincingly. "I already told you everything I know."

"You'd be surprised what I can get people to confess," I growl, frustration flaring over my chest. There's something deliciously alluring about her, something that is making me want to push boundaries even more.

In one swift move, I spin her around to face me. Sliding my knee between her legs silences anything she's thinking of saying, and instead, she groans softly.

Fuck me, but she's exquisite.

I quickly slip my hand to the back of her head, fist her hair, and bring her to me. Our lips crash, and I devour her mouth.

Mmmm, she tastes like sweet berries. Does the rest of her taste just as sweet?

She claws at my shoulders. Trying and failing to shove me away from her. Chest to chest, I feel her tits pressing against me, her heart beating ferociously. Everything she's doing–all her fighting–only has my cock hardening. For me, it heightens the urgency, the feel of the hunt, and finally the claim of the prize. Especially when her breaths become more rapid, as gasps, and her thrashing grows more desperate.

I hiss when her fingernails tear across my neck, drawing blood, then seize her wrists in one hand and pin them over her head.

Completely helpless to me, I kiss her harder. Finally, she gives in and her tongue clashes with mine, battling, and giving me what I seek.

With my free hand, I traced a path to her gorgeous breast, perfectly filling my palm. Pinching her nipple, I hear her moan, and her back arches, pushing her further into my touch.

The sound of heavy breathing pulls my attention, and I notice Eve's gaze on Cassius and Knox enjoying the show.

Those bastards are getting off on this, especially Cassius. The fucking voyeur. He fucks a new girl every second day, but Knox...surprises me. Most of the time, he walks away when we have women in the Tower. Yet, he's still here.

With my distraction, Eve suddenly bites down on my lower lip.

"Fuck," I shout. The sharp pain sent a shot of arousal straight to my dick. I snarl, shaking from the delicious high.

She has no idea what she's unleashing.

I pull back and suck on my bleeding lip, the copper taste of blood on my tongue.

Her grin grows wicked, and her eyes sparkle.

I growl, pushing my hard cock into her lower stomach. I'm barely holding back from ripping her clothes off and fucking her right here.

The only thing stopping me is my inner beast telling me that the first time I fuck her can't be like this... No, it wants it to be a moment she'll remember for the rest of her life. Today's lesson has to be something different. A message of what I am—of what *we* are—and if she wants to see another day, she must obey.

I rip open the zipper of her jeans, holding her stare, and watch as her smile quickly vanishes.

Flicking my tongue out, I lick the blood from my lip, and her eyes track the movement. It almost looks like she wants me to kiss her again. Holding her gaze, I slip my hand under the band of her underwear, finding the warmth between her thighs. Fear paints her face and her eyes widen, but she never says stop.

"I hate you," she pants.

"That's good."

Despite her words, her cunt is soaking wet, proving how much her body craves my touch. I draw the scent of her sweet arousal, savoring how she smells.

I guide my fingers between her folds, stroking back and forth. The pad of my finger pauses on her clit, then I lazily make circles, wanting her to fall deeper. To beg me for more. Her breathing speeds up, and when I push two fingers into her, I expect a protest. Instead, she moans louder.

Her cheeks redden just as quickly as she balances on the edge of losing herself. I smile and pull out of her, then I trace my finger over her clit again, this time in slow and sensual swirls.

Her eyes flutter.

She's burning up as I bring her closer to her climax.

Her eyes remain on me, the battle in them wild. She wants to push me away but can't bring herself to do it. She loves what I'm doing too much.

"Asshole," she breathes heavily, quivering beneath me, and I know she's close.

It takes every ounce of my strength not to fuck her, not to flood her cunt with my seed. She smells divine. And the tiny moaning sounds she's making are everything.

Her hips surge forward, her body bracing for the escalating release. My heart stops at the sight.

Beautiful. Just beautiful.

I stop rubbing her, and she's moving of her own accord, sliding her sweet cunt on my fingers, taking what she wants from me. She's absolutely hypnotic, and the thought of having her come on my hand undoes me.

What would it be like to have this girl in my room to fuck her brains out?

Her eyes close, and she tilts her head back, her body shaking.

The sight of her on the verge of an orgasm is mesmerizing. An image I know I'll think about later tonight.

A deep growl rumbles in my chest with the need to find out how sweet she tastes, to fall to my knees before her and suck on her pussy.

"Please," she begs softly. "Almost…there…"

My gaze never leaves her. She's trembling furiously as she hangs on the edge of her climax. The whimpering sound she makes has me tempted to take her now.

Too bad.

Instead, I withdraw my hand from between her legs, and her eyes fly open. I suck the two fingers I fucked her with into my mouth, savoring her honeyed taste, craving her to sit on my face and suffocate me.

"You taste delicious," I whisper. Her expression is frozen in utter shock. "But that's enough for now."

And just like that, her green eyes flash and burn into me. Her anger flaring. "Are you kidding me? You fucking asshole."

"You belong to me. I own you and will do as I please with you."

I give her a few seconds for the words to sink in, and her eyes glisten. That's when I know she understands. What she doesn't need to know is exactly how much I want to sink my cock into her, to give her the release she craves.

Not yet.

Not now.

"Good girl." I release her hands from above her head and zip up her jeans. "Now come with me." I take her wrist and pull her from the wall. Her huge, expressive eyes pass over Knox and Cassius again, who are still watching in silence.

"Fuck you. All of you." Eve's tone is vicious, but her voice cracks, revealing her vulnerability.

"If you wish," Cassius muses.

"I'll slit all your throats while you sleep."

"Is that a promise?" Knox asks. Of course, he'd say that. Nothing is ever enough for him.

As I pull her across the hallway and toward the elevator, I'm drowning in the scent of her. It surrounds me, filling my senses, the taste of her still on my tongue, and suddenly I'm wondering if I've made a grave mistake.

"Where are you taking me?" she shouts, trying her damndest to rip my grip off her. I'm so in my head at the moment, fighting an internal battle I never expected, that I almost miss her question completely. The punishment was meant for her, and yet here I am, contemplating finishing what I've started. My cock throbs, and my hands twitch at my sides. I ball one into fist, trying to calm my chaotic thoughts.

I punch in the access code to the panel, and the moment the elevator's metal doors roll open, I toss her inside.

Stepping in right after her, she glares at me.

"Hello! Now you're suddenly deaf? You can't just...just do *that* to me, you know. And then throw me around. I have rights."

My heart thunders, and my adrenaline races. Letting her go now would be the easier thing and killing her would be the easiest, but the look of pure ecstasy on her face and her moans for more will be burned in my brain for fucking ever.

My whole life, I fought for everything–against the darkness, forcing myself to learn how to control my needs... my wants.

But Eve is a weakness I never expected, and as much as I know I shouldn't, I want to keep her.

Fuck! I'm stronger than this. She's just another woman. I'm a damn King! I have more restraint and discipline than most–so then why am I bringing her down two floors to lock her in one of the guest bedrooms?

"Hello!"

A growl tears from my throat, sounding animalistic, and it's enough to make her freeze on the spot.

"You have no idea who you're dealing with, do you?" I say, voice low and threatening. When she doesn't answer, I go on, making sure to emphasize each word. "We're the Kings of the city. You are now ours, our property, and that means there's no way you're getting out unscathed."

She inhales loudly as the realization of the danger sinks in.

That's all I have to say–Kings–and she knows who we are.

Good. Then our name and our reputation still mean something around here.

The Kings.

I've been taken by the Kings of Eden.

Fuck, fuck, fuck!

This is so not good.

I thought being wanted by the Black Spades was bad, but they're like innocent fluffy kittens next to these three maniacs. They've got all the same power, money, and influence as Franco but are supes, which makes them more deadly.

I don't even know what kind of supernaturals they are, but just from the little time I've spent with them, I know they're more than your average spellcaster or shifter. Their magic buzzes across my skin, even now that I'm alone. It's…unsettling.

Knox is full of darkness. His power is ancient. I've never sensed anything like it before. Cassius is like a firecracker—fast, fiery, and unpredictable. It's like being drugged, and the high is exhilarating and terrifying at the same time.

And Dracon…he's a different kind of beast entirely.

What I saw... I don't even... Can't... Ever since we both touched that stupid axe, I've tried to shake the images from my head, but my thoughts keep wanting to replay them over and over. An area lined in stone and lit with torches with a younger Dracon and another man staring each other down, both practically naked, while a group of onlookers watch at a safe distance. Blood streaks across their skin and sticks in their hair, but that's nothing next to the body parts strewn about. Arms, feet, fingers, and god knows what else...

Bile hits the back at my throat as I fight the images to leave me. What I saw next was the most brutal and horrifying fighting I've ever seen, and it was all without weapons. Only nails, teeth, fists, strength, and sheer will.

It took me a bit to realize one of the men I was watching tear into the other was Dracon—a young Dracon—but he was just as vicious. Cruel. Unforgiving.

The way he played me like a fiddle and didn't even bat an eye, even when I took a chunk out of his lip... I'm convinced the man isn't a man at all.

Then, to be even more sinister, he had the balls to bring me so close to orgasm, only to leave me hanging like that. My clit is still pulsing from it.

I glance around the bedroom I've been tossed into this time. Not the construction site of the first one, and not the hunting lodge aesthetic of the other. This one is rather... normal, with sage green painted walls and pine furniture. No big windows—or scaffolding—thank god, but an incredible view of the city. There is a queen-size bed with clean bedding, but it doesn't look like it's ever been touched. This must be one of the guest rooms. One of the dozen. This place is huge, and not only do the Kings of Eden own the entire thing, but they're adding more to it. In this city, that's insanity. It screams to just how much power and wealth they have.

As I continue to inspect the room, a tiny red light shining in the far upper corner catches my eye. I creep closer to it and squint to get a better look. When I see the glass dome thing hanging from the ceiling, fury lashes inside me.

A camera? They're watching me?

Sick bastards.

I flip my middle finger to the camera, hoping they're watching me at this very second and can see it. When no one comes thundering in here, I sigh. It may be stupid, but it makes me feel a little better, but just a little.

I don't understand why I am even still here. Am I their prisoner or something? I didn't do anything wrong, and clearly, Knox made a mistake in thinking I'm some guy named Aris. They should let me go.

Or the Kings might just kill me instead. It'd be easier.

My throat tightens.

I need to find a way out of here, but just thinking about it has exhaustion pressing its heavy hand on me. With the adrenaline dissipating, every cut and bruise I've gotten in the last forty-eight hours decides now is a great time to rear up and let themselves be known.

Everything hurts. Every inch of me. Even my eyelashes hurt, and I don't even know how that's possible, but it's true.

Sighing, I make my way over to the bed and flop down face first into the feathery pillows. When I lift my head, I see a small red smear painting the fabric and grimace. I touch my forehead and wince as a sharp pain slices through me. When I look at my fingers, they are bloody.

Perfect.

Must've happened when I slammed into the side of the building.

I'm surprised I don't have a concussion. Or maybe I do.

Great. Just great.

This entire situation is fucked up to the nth degree.

I roll over and sink into the soft mattress underneath me. I'm so tired, my eyes close automatically, and the moment they do, I'm assaulted with images of Dracon's past, and then in stark contrast, his body pressing against me. The way his heated gaze seared into mine and his fingers dove past my underwear to make me melt.

I shouldn't be feeling a fucking *thing* for these Kings—these monsters—except fury. But just thinking about Dracon fingering my pussy sends heat prickling across my skin and my imagination speeding into overdrive.

Then I think about Knox leaning over me, holding that curved blade covered in my blood, with his hard cock straining against his pants and his breathing coming out ragged. And Cassius watching with that wicked grin twisted on his lips, ready to dive on me the moment he sees an opening.

God, I'm fucked up.

I hate that I want them, despite everything they've done to me.

Stupid emotions. They're always getting in the way.

Forcing my eyes open, I stare at the ceiling. My mother used to tell me I was going to get into some sort of trouble like this one day. That if I kept on the path I was going down, I would end up raped and left for dead. Or worse... *burning in Hell for all eternity.*

I snort. Living in that house with her was Hell.

But I don't want to think about my mother and my

fucked up past. I just want to go to sleep peacefully for once. Why is that so hard?

Sighing, I readjust myself against the pillows and close my eyes again. Instantly, my thoughts go right back to being pressed against that wall, and anger mixes with the desire. I should've done something more to stop him from touching me; I definitely shouldn't have enjoyed it as much as I did. The fact that I had no control over my own damn body pisses me off.

Fuck hormones. And my lust-drunk vagina.

Fuck Dracon for making me feel anything at all. And for not finishing what he started. I'm still squirming from not reaching that delicious peak.

What an asshole.

You know what? While I'm at it, fuck them all. Cassius and Knox in that mix too because they're all fucking guilty.

I wish I could get them back for doing this shit to me. If I was in control of my powers… oh, they'd be toast. Maybe I wouldn't kill them, though. Not right away. Maybe I'd just play with them a little. Paralyze them, strip them naked, cut them up like Knox did to me, make them bleed, and then fuck them.

Yes, perfect.

The untamed power inside me buzzes through my veins just at the thought.

Ugh, no. I can't.

I push the swell of magic back down, knowing from experience that it's too wild. I can't use it like that–although I wish I could. It'd let me get my sweet revenge.

Still, my hand glides between my legs, under my panties, to the place where I burn the most. I groan when I find myself already incredibly wet.

Dammit. Dracon did this to me.

Wait. What if they found out how much I desire them? How much my body reacts whenever they're around?

Would they take my body like they took me? Better yet, would I let them?

Running my finger up my slick seam, I circle my clit and imagine it's a stranger's hands on me. No, not a stranger—one of the three Kings. Teasing me, exploring, making me gasp as the delicious pleasure builds.

Yes, fuck.

My pulse races as I think of all their strength, aggression, and power directed at me.

I lift my knees and rock my hips faster, needing more. I find my nipple with my other hand and pinch it through the fabric. Hard. A loud gasp escapes at the pain, followed by a moan of pleasure. These men are brutal. Everything about them hurts. The way they fuck wouldn't be any different.

Vision foggy with lust, my gaze slides to the ceiling again, where the camera light blinks.

Oh, shit. I freeze for a second. I completely forgot I'm being spied on.

Tingles of excitement spread over my body, my embarrassment quickly switches to confidence. Let them watch. I hope they enjoy the show because I'm getting out of this place and away from them ASAP.

Yeah, consider this my parting gift.

My mind goes back to Dracon and those fiery amber eyes, the way they burn me up when they narrow on me. So much fury inside me, caged in like a wild animal. His wide shoulders and muscular arms tensing as he holds me in place, wanting to dominate me completely.

My fingers, slick with my cream, rub my clit, circling, teasing, all while I imagine Dracon holding me still, glaring at me with burning desire. Maybe he's keeping me in place for someone else to explore me–Cassius. He's the one touching me and peering up at me with that twisted smirk on his devilish face.

Chasing the building orgasm, I squeeze my breast and let my nails dig in. The cuts there sting, and the pain makes me think of Knox. He likes pain more than the others, so he'd be using his knife on me again, leaving little knicks and slices on my skin, but this time, he's using his mouth as well. His tongue swirls over me, sucking and biting. Slow. Torturous.

I moan and push a finger into my pussy. In and out. The muscles clench around me, wishing my finger was one of their cocks pumping into me instead.

Fuck…

They would be relentless. Their hands would bruise and mark me as their own.

And I'd want it all.

Fucking them would be a violent torrent of hatred, anger, and raw power, of all of us wanting to resist but needing it too much to stop.

My orgasm tears me apart. It zaps through me with such force that I cry out, my back arching off of the mattress. My entire body shakes as waves of pleasure course through me, and I fuck myself, extending the pleasure, knowing damn well the Kings wouldn't stop with just one orgasm. No. They'd continue to push for more. To control my body and tell me when I'd had enough.

When I can't stand it anymore, I collapse onto the bed, panting for breath and waiting for my frantic heartbeat to slow back down to normal.

The imagination can do wonderful things, can't it?

Like, take a pretty fucked up situation run by three clearly psychotic assholes and turn it into pure pleasure.

I glance back up at the camera again, hoping one of them is on the other side, enjoying the show.

The Kings of Eden have captured me, and I've just used thoughts of them to get myself off.

Maybe they aren't the only psychotic ones here…

It's starting to look like I'm just as crazy as they are.

DRACON

*M*y eyes are glued to the screen. I can't tear my gaze away from the stunning beauty gripping her breasts and riding her fingers to the point of ecstasy. The way she keeps fingering that tight little pussy the same way I had. Fuck, but I want to be the one exploring those folds again. Tasting her wetness and watching her eyes glaze over in pleasure because I'm the one forcing the orgasm. Not her.

Growling, I watch her climax and see those perfect tits lift into the air when she arches her back.

Yes. She knows exactly what she's doing. And although I know she's putting on a show, like she must've done at that dump of a strip club, I'm enthralled. I can't look away, even if someone came in here and forcibly ripped my eyes from my head. I'd still watch Eve.

There's something about her that has nothing to do with the way she handled Knox's blade, or the way she activated my axe's power. Although those things are just as impressive.

I shake my head and turn from the screen to look at another before I lose myself in watching her. This one's a hell of a lot less interesting–staring at the empty emergency staircase, and it's not long before my gaze drifts back to the one I really want to see.

There's clearly more to her than meets the eye–or more than I read on paper. Naturally, after getting her full name, I called on Taliah to pull her background from our best informants. It cost a pretty penny to get the information on our unexpected guest this fast, but I need to know who it is we're dealing with. I don't have the time or patience for games. And if Knox is right this time, and Aris is involved with her in some way... well, then death will be coming for her, no matter how gorgeous she may be.

Evelyn Dalton is her birth name, but most people know her by Eve. She works as a stripper at Kat's Kradle downtown and has quite the reputation and following there. She has a mother, still alive, and although I'd been privy to her in my vision, her father is deceased. He'd died tragically when she was still young.

Even more surprising is that Eve left her parental home at sixteen and was able to graduate high school and then college on her own.

But that is all the boring stuff. What interests me the most is what kind of supernatural she is.

According to the research, she's human. As is the rest of her family tree.

Sterile of any magic at all.

How is that possible? There's no way.

I don't understand.

The door behind me creaks open, and I turn to see Cassius strolling into the surveillance room. His gaze instantly finds the screen with Eve's room that I've been watching, and he closes the distance in two quick steps.

"Well, well, well... What do we have here?" he asks,

licking his lips. On the monitor, Eve still has her hand buried in her panties, while the other teases her nipple through the grimy, oversized shirt. He reaches over and flicks the volume button to make her sweet moans and pants louder, and the delicious sounds send electricity shooting straight to my cock.

When her eyes shoot open again, and she stares straight at the camera, Cassius jerks upright. "Holy shit. She's a sexy devil now, isn't she?"

Interesting choice of words coming from a demon. Or part demon… Or whatever the fuck Cassius actually is.

"She's trouble," is all I say back.

He glances at me, and that stupid side smile is back on his face. "Is that why you were watching her fuck herself? Like a peeping Tom?"

A growl rumbles in my throat, and I clench my jaw. "She did it to get a rise out of me." Which is true. It's clear she's trying to get some kind of revenge for what I did to her before.

His gaze drops to my lap and back up. "Looks like she got what she wanted."

I take a swing at him, but the slippery fucker dances back, holding his hands up in surrender, and laughs. "Hey now! No judgment here. I mean, how can you *not* watch? It's like porn, but better because it's happening in real-time, right next door. You can jump in anytime." He pauses, scratching his chin as if considering that very thing. "You know what? Maybe I will."

The shifter part of me rages at that, not liking the idea of another person encroaching on what's his. And that's what it sees Eve as. *His.*

I'm out of my seat in an instant. "Cassius."

He halts in the doorway and dramatically spins on his heel. "Mhmmm?"

Even after all these years of knowing and working together, there are still some things that Cassius does that drive me up a fucking wall. The first being walking away when I'm not done talking to him, and the second being him always thinking he can do whatever the fuck he wants, whenever he wants.

And right now, he's doing both those things.

"Don't you fucking *dare* go into that room, do you hear me?"

He blinks innocently. "And why not?"

"Because if Knox is right–"

He holds up a hand to cut me off. "I'm gonna stop you right there. Do you hear yourself? You and I both know Knox is far from rational on a good day, but when Aris is involved, he's a full on sociopath. He doesn't know his left from his right, or up from down. The dude's brain is like scrambled eggs. He's not all there. This is going to end up being just some big mistake that we're going to have to clean up after, like always."

He's probably right. Knox's obsession with his archrival has made him completely irrational at times, but he seemed adamant that she wielded his blade. And I not only witnessed but experienced the axe's power triggered by her touch as well, after centuries of being dormant. That may be easy for Cassius to overlook, but not me.

"We will bring her to Ladir to be sure," I say. Ladir is a witch doctor equipped, better than any, to tell me what the fuck is going on with her. And I need to know, not just for my own sanity, but for the future of us. The Kings of Eden. If she's got enough power to do the things she did, then she's dangerous. And she's too stubborn to be an ally, which means I need to be prepared for the possibility of having to crush her as an enemy.

"I don't get it. You and Knox got to play with her. Why is it a problem when I want to do it?" he whines.

I went too far with her–I know it. But I wanted answers, and I had to touch her. She's a temptation I gave into too easily. One I want to give into again, especially after watching her on that screen.

But I harden my voice so Cassius knows I've made the final decision on the matter. "We bring her to Ladir, and then, if she's clean, you can play with her all you want."

He grins at that. "Okay... Until Knox kills her, you mean."

I nod, knowing all too well that Knox will want his piece of her too. If she's smart, Eve will cooperate because how long we keep her alive will depend entirely on her.

CHAPTER ELEVEN

CASSIUS

Screaming rips me out of my sleep, chilling me to the bone and spurring me into action before I'm even aware of what's happening. I'm on my feet in an instant, trying to shake off the last bit of grogginess. It always feels like I'm chasing sleep lately, and tonight is no exception.

As I open my bedroom door and step into the hallway, I realize all the commotion is coming from the guest room where Drac threw Eve.

She's not only screaming, but there are other sounds… violent sounds, like fists and feet colliding with something else. Slapping, kicking… Fuck. Are we under attack? It sounds like she's brawling in there.

It better not be Knox torturing the girl again. I swear to fuck…

I slam my shoulder against her door, ready to kick ass. The sound of the lock popping open marries Eve's terrified screeches as I push my way inside. Heart pounding, my gaze sweeps the room, searching for someone to kill, but there's only Eve thrashing against the mattress with her sheets tangled around her arms and legs.

I stop short. *What the hell?*

Eyes closed, she's screaming her head off and fighting with an invisible attacker, one I can't see or help her fight off because it's in her own imagination.

She's having a nightmare. And a pretty bad one at that, by the looks of it. Sweat plasters her blonde hair to her forehead and neck, and she continues to buck wildly on the bed.

Sympathy tugs at my chest. Between Knox and Dracon, she really has been through a great deal in the little time she's been with us. And fuck knows what happened when Franco had her. From what she told us about his wandering hands, I don't blame her for puncturing his eye with her shoe. The dickhole deserves worse.

Slowly, I approach her and watch as she swings her fists. The girl's got some moves, but that comes from living a hard life. Or afterlife, in my case. It's something I can relate to, except my nightmares are real, blood-thirsty, Hell creatures.

Despite Dracon's warnings to stay away from Eve and every damn instinct I own, I stride to her side.

Shit, this is a bad idea. A really fucking bad idea, but those are usually my favorite kind.

Against all better judgment, I sit on the edge of the bed and gather Eve in my arms. She lashes out at first, thinking I'm one of her inner demons, but pain's never stopped me before—even when one of her fists lands a pretty decent shot to my jaw. I hold her tighter, pressing myself into her curves, hoping that somehow it'll be enough to calm her down.

She keeps shouting angry, incoherent nonsense, and

when she throws her head back and nails me in the nose, stars dance before my eyes.

Goddammit, she got me good. But at least I don't taste any blood, so it's not broken.

This isn't working like I hoped, but I'm not sure what else to do. I settle for stoking her hair with one hand, while holding her in place with the other. My fingers comb through her soft curls, and after a few moments, her frantic screams turn to sobs. Eventually, her body sinks against me, and she calms enough for me to just hold her without risking bodily harm.

"Shhh… I've got you," I whisper into her ear as my hand glides from her hair, to her shoulders, and down her arms. Still wrapped in sleep, her muscles ease under my fingertips, so I keep going.

Night terrors aren't something that form out of nowhere. Someone hurt her, and I don't mean today. She's come from a lot of pain. Darkness. A sordid past.

Like us.

She may not want to hear it, but she's more like the three of us than she realizes.

I've faced down *real* boogeymen, the worst of the worst, both in Hell and the living world. As much as they like to think they're not, humans aren't any different than demons. And I know, being a demon myself. The only difference I've found is that demons are proud of the chaos and destruction they create. Humans do the same thing but cloak everything in secret. They want to plot your demise but pretend to be your friend to have a front row seat as your burn.

Once Eve quiets and her breathing becomes even, I gently lay her down onto the pillows and get off the bed. Trying not to make any loud noise, I creep across the room but find myself pausing in the doorway. When I glance back at her, she appears peaceful with her gold hair fanned out around her face, her pink lips parted, and her cheeks glistening from crying.

It's my cue to leave, I know. I shouldn't even have come in here in the first place, and if Drac finds out, I'm guaranteed to get an earful.

Sure, Eve's a pretty little thing, but this city is full of fine pieces of ass just like her. She's just another pussy. That's all. Yet I'm still finding it difficult to walk out of her room and I don't know why.

We're meeting with Ladir in a few hours to get more of a read on Eve, and I need my beauty sleep too. So, begrudgingly, I force my feet to step further into the hall and lock Eve's door behind me before making my way back to my own bedroom.

The next morning, I find Drac and Knox in the living room. Knox is admiring his blade like it's some long-lost lover, sharpening it while testing how easy it slices through his skin when he runs his finger across the edge.

What a freak. The dude seriously needs to get laid.

Drac's no better. He is mindlessly staring out the room's windows, listening to his boring-as-sin music that he likes so much. Classical shit, like the stuff pretentious douches listen to.

Even though I've found them ignoring each other like this before, there's something different about this time. There's a tension lingering in the air between them, and it's obvious the cause is Eve. She's the only thing that's changed in our lives recently.

And, let's not forget, we all want to fuck her.

Even Knox, though the crazy bastard doesn't want to admit it.

What could possibly go wrong?

I sprawl across the couch, shooting them both a shit-eating grin. "You guys really do talk too much."

Knox glances at me before continuing with his blade. Drac doesn't even look up.

"Soooo…. When are we off?" I try again.

Knox mutters under his breath. "I still say she's Aris in disguise."

"Hey, she might be a crazy bitch, but I seriously doubt she's some crazy war horseman." If the guy even exists… With Knox's instability, it's hard to tell.

"Would you stake your life on it?" Knox asks, examining his reflection in the blade's face.

Did horsemen have night terrors like Eve did last night? Doubt it. "I do actually."

"I'll take that bet."

I roll my eyes. "Look, if she was actually Aria–"

"*Aris*," Knox snaps the correction. Pronouncing it like *heiress*.

I bark a laugh. "Whatever. If she was *Aris*, then she would've killed us by now. Right? If that bastard is as psychotic and powerful as you say, we'd be dead. You especially. You'd be dust."

He blinks rapidly as if my common sense had completely blindsided him.

Scrambling for an explanation, he says, "Maybe he's been weakened somehow…"

"Uh huh, right."

Knox glances at Drac for backup, but when his eyes

drift to him and then back to the window, dismissively. He grunts.

"You're only staying quiet because you finger fucked her," Knox tosses back.

Dracon's yellow eyes slide his way and his lips curl curl back exposing his fangs. A growl rumbles in his chest as a warning.

Okay, great. I see how this day is going to go, and it's going to be spent keeping these guys from each other's throats.

With three powerful supernaturals living in close proximity to each other–let alone three alpha *men*–things tend to get tense around here. Hell, I'm no angel. I have days when I can't stand looking at Drac or Knox's ugly mugs. But there's always been more animosity between Drac and Knox. Even more so since Saxon died. The bastard seemed to be the glue that was holding us all together, and we had no idea.

Now it's just me with an ancient deity and one of the horsemen of the apocalypse. We're like the start of a bad sitcom or something.

These are the fucking clowns I have to live with.

Drac is what they call a True Alpha or an Apex. Meaning, he is a shifter with unlimited shifting abilities. He can turn into any predator he wants, mostly the big and bad kind.

I've been around the block, if you know what I mean, and I've never met anyone else like him. Apparently, he's a rare breed. But forget asking him about his past. I can't get anything out of him besides our gang business. He's not only a closed book, he is a closed book sealed with super-glue, trapped in cement, and then locked in a titanium box.

The fucker's a mystery. We don't even know his real name. Dracon, or Drac, is what we began calling him because of his favorite animal to shift into: a dragon. With his massive size, quick temper, animalistic instincts, and hot-headed nature, I'd say it fits.

The only reason he's taken the lead role in our little group is because Knox relents most of the time. He's too mentally shifty to deal with the business end of what we do, so whenever the two go toe-to-toe, he's always the one to step back. Which is exactly what Drac wants.

Me? I deal with my aggression by killing assholes. Otherwise, I stay the fuck away from all that testosterone bullshit. I got enough of it in Hell—men fighting to dominate, to be the head honcho. But I don't give a shit about being in charge. I run to the beat of my own drum, and I always get mine in the end. Naturally, it drives Drac crazy, which I only see as a perk. Pushing his buttons is just too much fun.

But then there are times, like now, when I have to be the voice of reason and make sure we stay focused on our objectives. And at the moment, that's taking down the Black Spades, finding out what the hell Eve is, and if, by some chance, the two are connected.

"I'll go make some coffee," I offer. Pushing myself off the couch, I head into the kitchen.

***

A couple of hours later, we're on our way with Eve sandwiched in the back between me and Knox in the nondescript black sedan looking like she's ready to spit acid.

For me, this is better than any sort of daytime drama on television. Real-life is always much more interesting.

And our little blonde dancer is all kinds of interesting.

"Tell me again why we're not meeting Ladir at his compound?" Knox asks. His fingers drumming an inaudible tune on his thighs like he can't sit still.

"Who the fuck knows anymore," Dracon says with a grimace. "First, he's adamant he can't leave his place, and suddenly he's saying over the phone that it's not secure anymore. Manic fucker."

I lift a brow at that. "And he thinks a warehouse in the harbor district is going to be better? He's out of his fucking gourd."

Knox shrugs, his fingers still tapping out a beat. "Who gives a shit? If anything happens, we do what we always do. It's the way things have always been." The corners of his mouth slowly rise. He looks like the fucking Grinch about to steal Christmas.

I spare a sharp glance over at Eve, wondering how things are supposed to be the way they've always been if we have her to worry about now.

This morning we had some…difficulties with her. So, her hands and feet are bound together with magical ropes to keep her from hurting herself or us. It was the only way to get her out of the building. Otherwise, her knee would be right up there between my legs. It's either her comfort or my balls.

And I'm pretty fond of my jewels so…

Dracon expressed mild concern that she'd potentially ruin another one of the precious treasures he hoards, but oh well. The bewitched ropes are doing their job by keeping her still while the spell seems to be keeping her calm. Like giving her a Xanax. But to be even safer, we've gagged her with a rag too.

We finally pull into a small alleyway between two abandoned warehouses, and the hair on the back of my neck stands to attention. Narrowing my eyes, I peer out the dark tinted window, but see nothing. None of the freaks are out, but that doesn't lessen the creep factor or risk. And I don't put anything past either the Black Spades or the Lords of Night.

Ladir's been on our payroll for a decade. He's trustworthy, but a paranoid motherfucker, rivaling Knox. After almost being taken out by the Lords, he rarely ever leaves the safety of his bunker, so I'm shocked when he asks us to meet him in the business district in the middle of the day.

Nothing sketchy about that at all.

The car pulls to a stop, and Drac and I are the first to climb out. After tugging Eve outside too, Drac's head whips to Knox, who's lagging behind

"Knox, fetch," he says, which is his cue to go ghost and search the area for any hidden threats.

He grins like the sadistic bastard he is, and the moment his eyes roll back into his head, his body collapses onto the seat, seemingly dead. Seconds later, a small touch of air whispers by me, telling me Knox has left the limo in spirit form. The only reason I can sense it is because my soul isn't fully alive either, being a demon and all.

Drac's itching to move, so he grabs Eve's tied wrists and tugs her along. With me taking up the rear, we stroll through the open door of the abandoned textile factory. All the windows in the place have been busted out, letting sunlight and the freezing temperatures stream inside.

Eve's gaze shoots up to the ceiling and follows the perimeter as if seeing something we can't. Is it Knox? Can she see him or something else? Eyes widening, she starts to mumble something around the gag, and seeing her distress, Drac rips it away from her mouth.

"What is it?" he rumbles in annoyance.

She juts her chin to the ceiling's corner. "Look! There!"

We both glance in that direction to see a pair of tiny blinking red lights staring back at us.

Eyes?

No. Cameras. Infrared cameras.

How perceptive of her.

Gaze sweeping around the rest of the space, I find several more watching us.

"Ladir, you coward," Drac grumbles. Facing down screens or camera lenses is never uncommon when meeting with Ladir. He goes through great lengths to make sure he's not being double crossed in some way, which, in our line of work, isn't a crazy notion. So it looks like for whatever reason, Ladir's moved his order of operations here. At least for the time being.

"Is this the girl?" his high pitched voice booms from all around us. He must have speakers hidden in the shadows too.

Drac growls, showing fang. He's never been fond of Ladir's use of technology. He much rather do business in person—you know, so he can strangle you easier.

"Yeah, this is her," I shout to the rafters, feeling like an idiot. "What the fuck are you doing here now? Outgrew your old place?"

"Rat infestation," his voice echoes back, and I'm not sure if that's meant to be a joke or not, considering his bunker was in the sewers of the city.

"Can you come out here?" Drac asks through gritted teeth. "I'm sure you're going to want to examine her."

"And do your magic voodoo shit," I add.

His harrump sends static crackling through the sound system. "Are you sure you weren't followed?"

Drac gives the ceiling a deadpan glare, his head swiveling from not knowing where to direct it. "Get the fuck over here."

There's a long moment of silence from the other end.

"Where's Knox?" Ladir asks finally.

"Doing his job scoping out the place," I reply. "Making sure your precautions are working."

Aggravation growing, Drac pulls Eve more to the center of the floor. The magical rope allows her to walk a few steps on her own—shuffle, more like—but Drac's got a firm hand on her to prevent her from toppling over. "Let's go, Ladir. We don't have all fucking day here."

The sound of gears churning cuts sharply through the quiet, followed by the piercing wail of metal grinding on metal. Eve's eyes snap up and I follow to see a cherry-picker basket descending from above.

And who else is riding it down to ground level but the witch doctor himself–Ladir.

Not looking like the kind of voodoo man one might see in the movies, Ladir wears headphones, a video game comedic T-shirt, cargo shorts, and square-framed glasses. He reminds me of more of a M.I.T. drop out than a powerful witch doctor.

Once the platform hits the ground in front of us, he steps down, holding a thick controller in his hand with a dozen buttons and wires sticking out of it. Like always, he's too twitchy, constantly glancing over his shoulder, waiting for someone to jump out of the shadows at any minute. What a tortuous way to live, always being on high alert.

Drac shoves Eve closer to him. "This is her. Evelyn Dalton."

"It's Eve, you asshole," she spits back with venom, and it's enough for Drac to put the gag back in place. She glares at him with enough fire to burn the place down to the studs.

My kind of lady.

"Eve then," Drac says with a cocky smile.

Unease flutters over my skin, and I can't shake the feeling that something's off. But Knox hasn't gotten back yet, so he must be still scouting the place. If he'd found anything suspicious, we'd know.

Ladir's nerves are contagious, I guess.

Pulling the totem necklace from under his shirt, he grasps it tightly in his hand and begins to circle Eve, muttering incantations in gibberish to awaken the magic. The totem glows purple, the light emitting through his fingers, and when Eve sees it, she squirms against Drac's hold.

"Stay still–"

The screech of tires skidding over pavement floods the night. That's when Drac and I realize Eve's not fighting him because of the building magic. Behind Ladir, car headlights blaze through the broken windows, growing brighter by the second.

My stomach plummets. It's coming right for us!

The car–no, the *limo*–crashes through the wall, engine smoking and wheels peeling out.

"Shit!" I manage to snatch Ladir and throw us both to the right just in time. Drac does the same with Eve, the limo narrowly missing all of us. Her muffled screams fill my ears as Ladir and I roll and tumble across the pavement.

The limo comes to a halt in the middle of the room, causing dust and debris to rain down all around us.

"What the fuck?" Drac's voice booms on the other side. I drag Ladir to his feet. He's shaking like he's having a seizure and the remote in his hand has been smashed during the fall.

"We're under attack!" he shouts. "I don't understand–my alarms!"

As if answering him, the blare of sirens erupt throughout the place.

Drac roars, unleashing his fury.

"What the fuck is going on?" I shout at Ladir, who can barely hear me over the piercing whistles and horns. Frantically, he bangs his remote to try to stop the alarms.

The limo's driver door is thrown open, and to my complete shock, Knox stumbles out. Less surprising–he's covered in blood. Drenched in it. And he's breathing heavily.

Drac and Eve round the limo to meet us. Furious, he grabs the remote out of Ladir's hand and crushes it in one hand. It does the job, the sirens stop, and we're engulfed in silence once more. "Someone better tell me what the fuck is going on or a swear to fuck–"

"Vampires!" Knox and Eve answer in unison. Her gag must've fallen out during the scuffle.

A swarm of the bloodsuckers leap from the broken windows and ambush us from all directions. Thinking quickly, I fist Ladir's shirt and throw him into the limo's front seat. Drac follows my idea and does the same with Eve.

"Stay inside and lock the doors!" he shouts. They don't have to be told twice. After locking down everything, they scramble into the back seats.

Drac turns back to me and Knox and gives us a subtle nod, his blessing to do what we do best and take them all down. A familiar bloodlust settles over me as I jump into the action.

Heart thundering, I tear into the nearest vampire with my bare hands. Usually vamps are confined to the dark, but when they're all hopped up from a recent feeding, they can spend a brief amount of time in the sun. So since these fuckers aren't bursting into ash right now, they must have fresh blood running through their veins.

That means all their abilities will be heightened, which makes for a more exciting fight. Which I realize instantly, when the vamp I'm wrestling with is able to twist out of my grasp and land a kick to my stomach. I stumble back.

Beside me, Knox is slicing through vamps like it's nothing. The second his blade makes contact, blue sparks dance along the edge, stealing their souls, and they drop like a sack of potatoes.

Well, shit. That's one powerful weapon.

My vamp is a lanky thing with spiked hair and sharp cheekbones. Rolling his shoulders, he hisses at me, thinking I'll be an easy target next to Knox.

Boy, is he wrong.

Drawing on my anger, the fuel of my power, I let it roll over me and awaken the demon I normally fight to suppress. Like the fires of Hell, the monster consumes me, bringing with it immense power and strength. My brow extends, my vision sharpens, and curved horns push from my forehead.

I smile. Sometimes I do miss it.

When the vampire sees me now, he hesitates.

I don't give him a chance to change his mind though. I rush at him and punch him so hard in the chest, his ribs collapse, crushing his heart. Blood spurts from every orifice.

No need for a fancy knife here.

As he falls, dead, I catch a brief glance at my clothes, which are now covered in blood splatter.

Great. Another fucking shirt ruined.

Glancing around the factory, I spot Dracon tearing into two vampires at the same time with arms half-shifted into bear claws. They slash through muscle and bone with ease.

Are these vamps from the Lords of Night? We're supposed to have a truce with those fanged assholes. This would mean war.

Eve's panicked scream snaps my attention right, and that's where I find two vampires on the roof of the limo, beating on the doors to try and get inside. One rips off the handle and uses it to try and break through the bulletproof glass windows.

My demon rages. He doesn't like the idea of anyone else touching his busty blonde with thick thighs.

The glass gives way, and the vamp quickly rips the rest away to crawl inside.

I'm flying across the room in the next second, seizing the vamp by the back of the pants and hauling him out of the limo. Tossing him through the air, he slams into the metal wall and lands on his head.

A scream rips through the air, and I whirl around to see that the other vamp had managed to break the opposite window and was dragging Eve out of it by her hair.

Over my dead fucking body!

With the ropes still binding her, she's defenseless. Ladir attempts to help by leaping onto her legs, but the fucker pulling her out is stronger than him.

I'm about to climb onto the roof and tear into the

bloodsucker when the ground trembles under my feet, taking me off guard. Looking at the limo, I find it's shaking too. Earthquake? Or another car about to speed through here again?

It only lasts for a split second, and when things settle, I wonder if I've imagined it. But I don't have time to worry about it because the vampire on the other side of the limo has Eve halfway out the window, his fangs inches from her neck.

I leap onto the roof just as the fanger does the unthinkable. Instead of biting her, he lifts a shiny tube-like thing into the air and shoves it into the side of her neck. A syringe.

"Fuck!" Poison? Drugs?

Eve's yells cut off abruptly, her eyes widening with panic.

My brain struggles to catch up with the rest of my body, but my demon is doing most of the work anyway, and he's beyond furious. Somehow, I'm now behind the vamp that stabbed Eve, his head in my hands. One sharp twist and his spine snaps. Not dead but paralyzed for now. We'll need at least one of these fuckers to question later.

During the commotion, Eve landed on the cement, face down near the back wheel. I drop beside her and find she's shivering madly. The empty vial lays next to her head, and my blood runs cold.

What the fuck did he shoot her with? Better yet, why?

By some miracle, my demon recedes on its own. Usually it takes hours—sometimes days—to free myself of it, but seeing Eve hurt seems to chase it back into its box inside me. Once the horns sink back into my forehead, I gently flip her to her back and bring her head into my lap.

Her face is badly scraped up and the injection site is red, swollen, and angry.

"Hey, it's okay. I'm here now," I whisper to her.

Her eyes flutter open as if she's struggling to stay awake. "Where were you…a second ago?"

I should have been faster. I shouldn't have gotten distracted.

Ladir pops out of the window, staring down at us with horror on his face. "Is—Is she okay?"

"I've been through worse," she wheezes, and for some reason, her words pain me.

Not caring if I'll get shit for it, I tug off the magical ropes still binding her wrists and ankles and toss them away.

"Can you stand?" I ask her.

To answer my question, she tries to push herself up but wobbles once on her knees. I hook my arms under hers and help her the rest of the way.

"Thanks," she says flippantly. She may hate me, but she doesn't push away this time. She lets me hold her up.

Staring down into her eyes, I watch as her pupils dilate and worry spreads through me. I know enough about drugs and their effects to know whatever that vamp spiked her with, it's working fast.

Across the way, I see Knox slamming his boot down on the other vamp's head, the one I'd thrown, extinguishing the last bit of life in the creature's eyes.

Dracon rounds the limo and takes in the scene. When he spots the vamp and the needle nearby, his amber eyes narrow on me.

"He jabbed her," I explain, guilt spiraling through me. "I wasn't fast enough to stop him."

Not saying a word, Dracon moves to take my place and lifts Eve into his arms. She curls herself into his chest.

"She's drugged, Drac," I say. "What do we do?"

"We get her home," he says through clenched teeth, and I don't know if he's just mad at me or the situation. Maybe both.

"What about me? What do I do now?" Ladir asks, fear clinging to him. "The vamps, they'll come back!"

"You may want to go back to the rats," I suggest. "It's still safer."

Ladir nods frantically, already making up his mind.

"Knox!" Dracon calls from over his shoulder. "We're leaving. Now."

Knox pulls his bloody blade out of one of the vampire's chests and sheaths it, coming silently to our sides.

"The limo...do you think it still runs after that grand entrance?" I ask the pair.

"Only one way to find out." Drac kicks open the back door and gingerly lays Eve across the back seat before climbing in himself. Ladir scrambles to the other side of the cabin without a word.

"Bring that one back with us," Drac commands, pointing to the vamp on the ground still breathing. Without hesitation, Knox picks him up and chucks him inside too.

With the back of the limo now full, Knox and I take our places up in the front with me as the driver.

The leather is slick with blood, and red handprints are all over the dash and windshield. There was a massacre in here.

"Shit, Knox. What the fuck happened?" I ask as I throw the limousine in reverse. To my relief, the thing obeys and backs out of the factory but trembles violently. More smoke swirls from under the hood, and cross my fingers we'll be able to make it to Ladir's place and the Tower before it spontaneously combusts.

Knox studies the blood coating his sword, grinning like a fool. "I saw the Lords circling the place, but when I went to rejoin my body, the limo was gone," he starts.

"With your body."

He nods. "They stole it and our driver was dead, so I had to track the limo down before coming back to warn you."

"So you decided to drive it into the factory," I say, glancing at him from the corner of my eye as we pull onto the street on shaky wheels. I watch as Knox licks the blood off the blade like a goddamn psycho. But when he catches me staring, he only shrugs.

"It was the quickest way to get to you," he says simply.

To his logic, it makes perfect sense, right? And from all the blood staining the interior of the limo, it looks like he had quite some fun in the process.

I slam my foot onto the gas, speeding the rest of the way through Andover.

CHAPTER TWELVE

EVE

"Open wide for me," Dracon's growly voice snaps.

I pull my knees to my chest on the couch, squeezing tighter and drawing my dress over them. My gaze sweeps from him and to the other two guys behind him. "You can't just order me around," I protest.

The Kings are standing there, watching me like wolves studying their prey before they attack.

Three incredibly handsome—almost too handsome to be real—men. Rugged appearances, chiseled faces, and angled muscles.

It's a strange thing to feel torn between making a run for it and giving them what they want...me.

Of course, the answer is obvious, and yet here I sit, unable to tear my gaze away.

At first sight, they're the kind of men you do a double-take on as you pass them in the street, then wish you were brave enough to ask them for their number.

And if you're anything like me, you are also wondering how big their dicks really are based on their size.

You see, I'm clearly broken in the head. But these three men. I suspect it will do more than impress me. They'll blow my mind.

I glance at Dracon, who is inflated with so much arrogance, I'm surprised he hasn't choked on his own ego yet. I despise him, yet I'm captivated by him. Lips that promise me every fantasy I've dreamed of leave my face blushing the longer I watch them. Short dark hair, styled so perfectly, I just want to run my fingers through it to mess it up.

His golden gaze skates over my body, leaving me trembling. He's clean-shaven and immaculately dressed in dress pants and shirt that I know cost more than my whole wardrobe. He's the biggest of the three and devastatingly handsome. The kind of man who takes what he wants without question. The kind of man that has everyone trembling in his presence. My dark angel.

I glance past him to the other two.

Wild, black hair frames Knox's strong face, while his piercing black-rimmed hazel eyes stare into my soul. And the shadow of growth on his square jawline has my hands itching to run my fingers over it. He's twirling a switchblade in his hand. I don't think he goes anywhere without a knife.

Next to him, Cassius slouches on one leg, his head tilted to the side, eyeing me up and down. Knox might be crazy, but something about Cassius makes him unpredictably dangerous. Sandy hair buzzed along the sides, and golden skin. Notches have been etched out of his eyebrows, bringing your focus to mesmer-izing blue eyes. They remind me of a stormy sea, changing in hues. The longer I look into them, the more they rouse a deep, throbbing desire in the pit of my stomach. And the tattoos...

These men are enormous and beautiful. They're terrifying as hell and watch me with sinful stares.

Dracon bends forward at the waist, his shadow falling over me, and I flinch back into the couch. He studies me like he might be trying to see into my soul.

"I asked you to do something," he says. "In my home, I am your master. And you belong to me."

Arousal bursts through me at the primal hunger in his eyes, at the way Cassius and Knox step closer. The emotions in my body are all wrong.

You're supposed to fight monsters, not secretly wish they'd fuck you.

Dracon places soft hands on my knees, his touch feeling right, like it's always meant to be on me.

I stiffen, and my reaction has him smiling.

"Now be a good girl." He pulls open my legs, and I don't fight him. I know I should, but with this man, every fantasy and all my pent-up desires rush through me, demanding release.

I blush wildly at how easily I allow them to make me feel vulnerable.

He grins as his gaze lowers, his fingers following a slow path down the inside of my thighs.

Heat pulses between my legs and dirty thoughts swarm my mind, involving Dracon and me playing out scenes from a Pornhub video. Any will do, as long as it involves him making me scream.

"You will always belong to us."

I should protest, except my heart beats louder at the notion of them having their way with me, and I'm panting instead of getting out of here.

He holds my legs open, and I feel my thong clinging to me with how soaked I am.

Cassius snarls. It's a sound I'd expect Dracon to make.

Filthy sensations curl through me, growing hotter by being surrounded by these men who are barely holding themselves back.

Dracon's hand slides lower and runs the tips of his fingers across the edge of my underwear, along my bikini line. I shiver and a small groan grazes my throat.

"You know what happens to bad girls who don't listen,"

Dracon growls. "They get punished."

His words steal my breath, and every nerve in my body twists in on itself.

Dracon slides my underwear to the side and runs a finger up and down my slippery, aching pussy.

I moan out loud, my body shuddering, coming alive. My legs easily fall apart wider while he's got me pinned to the couch.

He snarls as he takes in all of me, his jaw clenched tightly.

"I want in," Cassius murmurs, his hand squeezing his thick, swollen cock over his pants.

"Me too." Knox steps closer, grinning so wickedly that I whimper my approval.

"P-Please..." I can barely speak.

Dracon pushes a long finger into me, and I come undone, my legs quivering. Desperate hunger builds within me, mounting faster and faster, pulsing through me, pushing me towards something more powerful.

He calls his friends with a nod of his head.

"Does this feel good?" he asks me.

I can't respond. I'm rocketing into an escalating orgasm.

I won't last, not when I crave this like oxygen. I'm so close... so fucking close to bursting that I'm about to scream the whole fucking building down if they don't hurry up.

But instead of unbridled desire rocking my world, Dracon draws back, sliding his finger out of me.

I start to groan, aching for his touch again. "No. No. Don't stop."

"That's enough for now," he says, almost maliciously.

"No!" I shoot up from the bed, eyes snapping open. I'm drenched in sweat. Fire throbs between my thighs with such ferocity that I'm going to explode.

"Goddammit," I growl hoarsely, coming back down to

earth, remembering I'm still in the Kings' penthouse. With it comes the memory of Dracon bringing me so close to an orgasm, then stopping. Not just in the dream, but in real life.

Fucking asshole.

Since that first day when he pushed me up against the wall, I haven't been able to get him out of my mind.

Pushing my legs out of bed, I grab the bottle of water I left on the floor and gulp down several mouthfuls. The tepid water does nothing to cool me down.

I've been living in the penthouse, having sex-induced fever dreams, and waking up too tired to do much else beyond lying in bed or on the couch.

Something is wrong with me. And I'm not just talking about my mental state. About craving my kidnappers, or acknowledging that I'm suffering from a severe case of Stockholm syndrome.

No. It's more than that.

I'm constantly burning up and I have no energy. I think whatever the vamps jabbed into me during the attack is the reason.

I drag myself into the walk-in closet to find something to wear. Yesterday, the guys surprised me by having some clothes delivered, only the most expensive designer brands, still with the price tags. A pair of jeans alone cost more than I'd earn in a week, and that's saying something since I take home thousands a night at Kat's. But if they have money to burn, I'm not going to complain.

I pick out a simple blue dress with spaghetti straps in a light cotton fabric. Next, underwear. A round hat box grabs my attention, and inside, a small selection of panties. I have no clue who chose my clothes, but everything is in my size.

Though, I do notice, no bras were delivered.

With a white thong and the dress in my hands, I walk into the bathroom.

With the strange fogginess still clinging to me, I get dressed. The funny feeling makes it hard to plan my escape, but I bide my time and watch everything.

I'm always listening for movement outside my door. When the Kings of Eden come and go. When food is delivered. Anything that will give me a window of opportunity.

Once I'm done, I contemplate crawling back into bed. My whole body feels heavy and my brain isn't firing normally. Instead, I decide to test out the doorknob's lock for the hundredth time today.

To my astonishment, the handle gives way and the door opens.

Excitement skates through me. This can be it. My chance to get out of this place.

My heart thunders even more when I scan the hallway and find it empty.

Can I really be...*free?*

On tiptoes, I hurry right to the grand foyer and elevator only to be confronted by the access panel again. Fuck, that's right. I need a keycard or pin code to use the damn thing.

Wait! The stairs!

I rush in the opposite direction, down the hallway away, to the other end. When I find the emergency staircase door, I wrench the handle.

But it's locked.

Shit! No, no, no! Please!

I pull at the thing over and over but it doesn't open. No matter how much I curse it off.

With one final kick at it, I spin around and press my

back against the metal. Exhaustion slams into me, and I blink rapidly just to keep myself awake. I did something so simple yet I feel like I've run a marathon.

Something's definitely not right with me.

Without the codes to the elevator and the emergency exit inaccessible, I'm still trapped here.

No wonder why they hadn't bothered to lock my bedroom door. They knew I couldn't get far. I'm sure as shit not going to try braving the scaffolding again.

Feeling defeated, I stroll to the living room, hoping to drown in some daytime soap opera. Since I'm still stuck here, I might as well enjoy the free cable. Maybe even raid the fridge.

Scratch the food. Just thinking about eating right now makes my stomach sour. Yeah... laying on the couch and vegging out to some mindless TV is sounding better and better.

I fall onto the C-shaped leather couch and rest my head on the pillow, feeling feverish and sweaty.

Their whole penthouse is extravagant, so it surprises me that they are building an extension. But I guess they want something with more opulence. Kat once said that the difference between the mega-rich and us common folk is simply how we use our time. And I guess when you are rolling in cash, you build empires and the largest towers in the city. Must be a "who has the biggest dick showoff" thing.

I twist my head to look up behind me to the railing and hallway on the next floor. No one's there, watching me for a change. Good.

Time to go exploring. I need to move around a bit before I fall asleep again from the exhaustion I feel right down to my bones.

Slowly, I climb the stairs that come complete with ornate railings, shining as though they're made from black opals, and enter another long stretch of hallway. I check every door I pass, finding a few more bedrooms, a fully functioning gym with every piece of equipment you could imagine, and a conference room. It's a bit hard to imagine the Kings conducting actual business, like something a CEO of a fortune 500 company would do, especially with how rough around the edges they are, but I guess it's possible.

Dracon's room is up here too, which I don't dare enter, since the last time I was there I almost died. Best to skip that one.

Some doors are empty, but I find one with a leather couch facing the wall of windows showcasing the city and snow-capped mountains in the distance. Bookcases cover the rest of the walls in the room, each one full of thick hardback books.

A library. Interesting.

Behind the next open door, I find an enormous bedroom with a king-sized bed draped in rumpled black sheets. Clothes are strewn all over the floor, and a pair of handcuffs hang off the edge of the bedside table.

Well, someone's into kink. I just can't figure out whose room this is.

The walk-in closet door sits open to reveal more clothes on the floor. Others remain on the hangers untouched, as though someone struggled to decide what to wear.

I've been there. Some days, everything I put on has me swearing I look like a sack of garbage

Figuring I've snooped enough for now, so I head back downstairs and go in search of the kitchen for a glass of water. I'm overheating again, my stomach somersaulting, and might go crash in my room after this.

The moment I reach the main floor, a soft moan comes from my left. I glance that way to find the kitchen I was looking for and a dining area. But both are empty.

What was that?

Another groan sounds, seeming more male than female, and in more pain rather than pleasure. And here I thought I was the only one home today.

Cautiously, I follow the sounds until I come to another ridiculously large room. This one's painted from floor to ceiling in black and darkness is so jarring that it takes my eyes a while to adjust. A simple bed with dark linens that look like they've never been touched and random furniture, but everything's neat and tidy.

Well, that is, until I stick my head further into the room and see Knox standing with his back to me in front of a man who is hanging from the ceiling by his wrists. A plastic tarp is spread out beneath him, catching the blood dripping from the array of cuts littering his body.

I blink, my heart racing in my chest, trying to decipher what I'm seeing. Especially when my mind isn't exactly sharp right now.

Knox shifts out of my line of sight just enough for me to see his victim. And I instantly recognize the man... or more like the son of a bitch bloodsucker who had attacked me at the factory, the one who had jabbed a needle into me after ripping me through a window.

And now, seeing him bloody, slashed, his clothes barely hanging on him, I smile at his agony. At him bleeding, wincing.

I should be appalled. Disgusted. Freaked-the-fuck out. But I'm not.

Quite the opposite actually. I'm happy Knox has him, is torturing him. I hope he makes it slow and as painful as possible. The fucker deserves it for what he did to me.

Mesmerized, I continue to watch in silence. The vampire's chin remains tucked into his chest, and as he spins in place, I see that there's a bloody hole where his ear should be.

My breath catches.

Holy shit!

Knox is so lost in what he's doing, that he doesn't notice that he has an audience. The guy loves torturing people, doesn't he? He's very much in his element. At first, I called him a psychopath, and the more I get to see him, the more I believe I nailed my first impression.

Speaking of first impressions, I'm actually pretty surprised he doesn't have this vamp on his autopsy table in the morgue downstairs, if that's where he likes to do this dirty work. Why is this low life getting special treatment?

"What shall we remove next?" Knox asks him, turning to him, with a blade in his hand. Not his Mortem Blade, I notice, but any weapon is a deadly one in Knox's hand. He could probably kill someone with a pencil eraser if he really wanted to.

When the vampire doesn't respond, Knox shrugs. "Fine. My pick."

He bends over and grabs the vamps bare feet, which are bound together, then slices off two toes. They fall to the floor, splashing in the blood.

My mouth falls open.

The vampire unleashes an inhuman screech, his head snapping up. Both his eyes have been removed, the sockets bleeding profusely.

I should be horrified, but instead, I'm on fire. My dress

clings to me from the heat overwhelming me.

Knox tsks and places the flat side of the knife to the vamp's mouth, dribbling with blood. "Told you before. You keep being a screamer and I'll cut your tongue out next." He's talking loudly, and that's when I see the earbuds in his ears. He's listening to music or something as he works.

The vamp fights against his restraints, kicking and bucking wildly. I want to feel sympathy for him—I really do—but I can't seem to muster up even an ounce for him and I don't know why.

Maybe it's whatever he'd shot me with, or maybe I'm fucked up in the head, but either way, I can't tear myself away from the sight of him mangled up and on the verge of death. My heart's drumming against my ribs, the excitement of what's coming next taking hold, and I wonder if Knox is doing this for information or…for me.

Silence fills the room. Well, aside from the humming sound coming from Knox's headphones.

He grabs a rag from the bookshelf near him and wipes down his arms, then he drops the blade and picks up a pair of pliers.

My pulse kicks up another notch. He's beyond psycho.

"We could have had so much more fun down in my morgue, but I'm supposed to be babysitting my little dove, you see. So we have to make do up here," he says.

His little dove…

That's what he called me before.

He cracks his neck. "You hurt her. You *violated* her, and so you're going to tell me what was in that syringe or I'll be removing your fangs from your skull next."

Heat floods me again, but this time, it pools at my core. He *is* dicing up this guy because of me—because of what he did to me.

I tremble, a mix of dread and curiosity. Whatever is wrong with me, whatever I am feeling right now, it has to do with whatever that asshole injected me with. And I want him to scream in agony. To suffer even more.

I remain pressed against the door frame, my mind scattered. My feelings are torn. Knox's torture should repulse me, and yet strangely, I can't look away. And the more I watch the way he mutilates the vamp, with the way I'm burning up, an awful amount of lust flows through me.

I swallow hard. I don't know what's going on with me, and all I can do is picture Knox's large hands on me, a delicious shiver moving down my spine. My mind remembers last night's dream, the way Dracon's fingers slid into me, how I woke up aching for more and dripping wet.

I always thought that the type of man I wanted as my forever guy would be strong but tender. The opposite of all the hardship I'd faced in life. Yet, look at me now. I'm craving the roughness, brutality, and pain.

The weight of what I've been through bears down on me. At the same time, the reality of how much trouble I'm in buzzes in every fiber of my being. And now a frantic sensation climbs through me that I'm sick, and I don't know if there's a cure.

It becomes too much, and I stumble from the room and into the hallway. Head swimming, I stagger, trying to remember how to get back to my room. Combine the fever burning me alive, to the raging lust licking at my insides, and I'm a complete mess.

A sharp pain slices through me, and I groan, clutching a hand to my chest. God, am I having a heart attack? It sure feels like it.

What's happening to me?

CHAPTER THIRTEEN

EVE

I teeter down the hallway towards my bedroom. The pain…it's agonizing and I feel like my veins are on fire. Whatever is going on inside me, it's getting worse.

I don't even hear the elevator announce its arrival, or see anyone step out until Cassius is standing right in front of me, blocking my way. I almost collide with him in my stumbling, but he's quick to grasp my arm and help me stay upright.

Heat rises to my cheeks and my heart flutters. "I-I didn't see you." My voice sounds muffled to my own ears. Like I'm talking underwater.

"What are you doing out of your room?" he asks, confusion wrinkling his brow. He glances behind me. "And where's Knox?"

"Vampire…room…" is all I manage to get out between shallow breaths. But Cassius seems to understand. He rolls his eyes.

"Of fucking course," he mutters. "I leave him alone with you for five minutes—"

I sway on my feet, feeling like the penthouse is spinning around me.

"Eve, are you okay? You're pale as a ghost."

"I think… I'm sick," I sputter.

Cassius's gaze darkens, and the next thing I know, I'm cradled in his arms. "I've got you," he says, sweeping me against his chest.

I find myself leaning closer into him, finding solace in his arms. I take a deep inhale of his masculine scent–spicy cologne, perspiration, and something woodsy. It's intoxicating.

"You smell so good," I murmur.

He places his lips on my forehead, and my nipples pebble at the innocent touch.

"You're burning up." His voice is almost panicky, and then suddenly he's walking quickly down the hall. I think he's going to bring me back to my room, but when we pass it and walk into another, I realize he's taking me to his.

I shiver in his arms. When he lays me down on his bed, I cry out in pain as my body constricts. Sharpness stabs me in my chest worse than before.

"I might be dying." I whimper, arching against the pain.

"I'm here. Just relax, okay," he pleads softly. "I'm going to figure this out."

My stomach tingles to hear him speak to me in such a caring way.

"Have you been vomiting blood?" he asks, sounding concerned.

I shake my head. "It feels like someone's built a bonfire inside me. And everything is turning me on. I'm so aroused, I might explode." The truth falls from my lips. Apparently, my filter has been disengaged, but I don't care when another wave of agony cuts through my body. I grasp the sheets, biting down on my tongue to ride through the episode.

"Well, that's new," he mumbles, but there's no humor in his voice. An expression of worry knits his brows instead. "It's going to be alright."

"Touch me, please," I beg, reaching my hand out to him. "I don't know how or why, but being next to you makes it bearable."

Something flashes over his gaze, as though my words triggered a memory.

I shut my eyes, scrunching up my face. I don't understand what's going on with me.

The mattress dips from where he sits next to me, and he brushes the hair out of my face. "I know exactly what you need."

"Aha." I open my eyes and press my palm against his forearm, his skin smooth and cool beneath my touch. It gives me a moment of reprieve from the ache.

"This is going to hurt a bit though initially," he warns me. "Then it will be bliss."

"Okay," is all I manage. Whatever it is, it can't be worse than what I'm experiencing now. It's like barbed wire is being dragged through my insides.

He leans in closer. "Just take a deep breath."

But all I can do is stare into his blue eyes and think about how lush his lips look. Maybe I'm losing my mind, but I reach up, cupping the side of his face, and I kiss him.

Unexpectedly, he returns it with his own searing hot kiss that eases the pain and leaves me hopeless. His touch is my salvation—soft, responsive, and demanding. Lips, hands, our bodies entwined. Tasting, searching, licking.

His kisses are like fire, his hands pressing against my

back, drawing me closer. Chest to chest, I can't hide how much I need this. How much I need *him*.

Except kissing him might have been a huge mistake, one that'll come to haunt me because I'm now completely lost. He's left me breathless, the echo of my need flowing through me so suddenly that desire claws at my insides.

When he breaks us apart, I want to cry, needing those perfect lips pressed against mine again.

Agony radiates through me once more, carving a path to my soul with how deeply it hurts.

"Please." I hate begging, but right now I'd do anything.

His gaze is one of fear as he looks at me.

"What's wrong with me?"

"I think you've been poisoned, but I'll know soon enough."

Swallowing the reality of his words, I remain silent, stunned to find that not only did Franco want me dead, but now the vampires? What have I ever done to them?

"Do you trust me?" Cassius says, drawing my attention to him as he pulls off his shirt.

I'm shaking my head because hell no, I don't trust him, yet the words are lodged in my throat as I take in his godly appearance. Bare chested, he has me drooling. Muscles everywhere, and a defined eight-pack. Angles and dips of muscles, all begging to be explored. A myriad of tattoos runs across his chest, while light blonde hair travels down his muscular abdomen.

He slides his hands under my thighs, and in one swift move, he's got me to the end of the bed, my dress driven all the way to my waist. I'm flashing him my white thong.

Frantically, I'm pushing down the skirt, but he swats my hand away while my ass remains perched on the edge of the mattress.

"Lay back and let me do my thing," he instructs.

When he falls to his knees before me, a slight panic grips me. All my thoughts go to an unholy place, and I don't understand how feasting on me can help if I've really been poisoned.

It may help a few other things though...

I wrench myself up to a sitting position, and the room starts spinning. I'm having a major déjà vu moment from my dreams right now, with me spread out in front of one of the Kings. Shaking away those thoughts, I push my hand against his forehead as he leans in closer.

"What do you think you're doing?" I ask with a croaky voice.

He arches an eyebrow. "Did you know there's a major vein that runs down the inside of your upper thigh? It's called the saphenous vein, and it'll serve my purpose well. I need to bite into it and then mix your blood with mine."

"You're going to bite me?" I blink at him, confused, I hate how fuzzy my head is, how hard it is to think straight. I just want this painful nightmare to end.

My breathing speeds up, and despite pushing him away moments ago, I reach for him. "Why does touching you help so much?" I whimper, not understanding anything that's happening to me.

He cups the side of my face, and I lean into it. "I'm not exactly human," he says.

"That's obvious," I respond and whimper, barely holding on. "I know enough about the Kings of Eden to know that."

"Well, while you might know I'm a demon, you wouldn't know that my blood carries healing properties that could help you. My family bloodline isn't exactly *pure*, you could say."

Keeping my gaze focused on him seems to grow harder. I take in his words, though they confuse me. I'm just too tired to make sense of them.

"Now, lie down for me, gorgeous, and let's get you feeling better." He runs his tongue along his bottom lip as he watches me lean back onto my elbows.

I don't have any other options. "Help me."

There's no pause. Cassius lowers his gaze and runs a strong palm along the inside of my left leg, pausing just inches from my bikini line.

Shyness isn't something I usually feel. I'm a stripper, a pole dancer for fuck's sake, yet around these men... they bring out all my insecurities, like now. I'm not exactly a thin girl, and maybe that's something they're used to. So, I mean, to have a huge hunk who is not only a demon but one of the dangerous Kings between my legs is unnerving.

He's gently massaging my inner leg, and I flop back onto the bed, needing this to just happen already. It helps that his touch aids in dulling the pain cutting through me. His warm breath dances across my thigh, and I hear him inhaling deeply.

I shut my eyes. "Can we just hurry up," I urge him.

"You smell divine," he purrs.

I bite on my lower lip, lust slipping down through my body.

He releases a low chuckle, and I feel his hair dancing delicately across my skin.

Soft warm lips caress my skin, and it's close to impossible to ignore his touch when everything about this man screams sex.

Fingers slip higher along my leg, pausing just inches from my underwear. So close that my mind swims and my heart thumps with the uncertainty of what he's going to do next.

Goddamn demon is just teasing me, isn't he? He's taking his time, getting an eyeful.

What's taking him so long?

I crane my head up, and he meets my gaze again, but this time, his blue eyes have darkened. They're almost black, and he's grinning at me.

I say, "Look, if you're getting cold feet, then–"

His mouth slips open, his canines sharp, stealing my words. Then he bites down into my inner thigh with a growl.

Sharpness pierces my flesh, and I cry out, dropping onto my back. I wrench my head to the side; the bite throbbing up my leg, spreading like lightning. My spine arches and I tense up as panic has me second guessing my decision to allow him to do this to me.

The initial burst of pain is short-lived though. And I shudder as a fiery desire carves right through me. Pain and pleasure entwined deep within me.

The demon's slurping sound pulls my attention. I think he's rather enjoying himself.

"Cassius–" My voice cracks, coming out husky.

He unlatches himself from my leg and lifts his head, blood coating his lower lip, which he greedily licks.

"I don't feel any different."

"Be patient," he growls at me like I should know better. "I need to give you my blood to heal you."

"Then why the hell were you biting me for so long?" I hiss.

The corner of his mouth curls up while he collects a switchblade from the top drawer of his bedside table. "I first needed a small taste to confirm you still had poison in your system."

"A *small* taste?" I eye him, unconvincingly.

He quickly slices the meaty part of his palm with the blade, and blood instantly bubbles to the surface. Then he lays the cut against where he bit me, pressing them together.

I clench my teeth from the sting.

"You should feel the change fast, sweetheart."

He removes his hand, then places his mouth over my bite. His tongue laps at the cut, and I won't lie, it's sexy as fuck.

He offers me his cut hand, a drop of blood rolling down the inside of his arm. "Drink," he demands, while he's tending to my wound. Hunger flares in his eyes.

There's no hesitation as I lean forward, accepting his blood in distressed panic, and press his cut to my mouth. A metallic, coppery taste floods my mouth, and I don't even think about the fact I'm ingesting a demon's blood.

Cassius comes up from my leg and kneels before me, watching me as I greedily suck his blood.

It's only when he drags his arm away from me that I realize I've been digging my nails into his skin to hold on. The earlier pain isn't there anymore, but the haziness is even stronger than before. But it feels almost...euphoric now.

"How are you feeling?" Cassius asks, running a thumb over his bite mark on my thigh. A simple gesture, but my skin is hypersensitive, so it feels like so much more.

I'm having a hard time finding my voice as the magic of his blood sweeps through me.

Cassius is suddenly in my face, bending over me. He

cups my face and his thumbs stroke my cheeks. "Perfect. It's starting to take effect," he says.

My gaze falls to his mouth. "Thank you for taking care of me. I just hope I don't regret it tomorrow."

"You may feel drunk for a while, and there might be a slight hangover." We're so close now, him hovering only inches from laying on top of me. "But this is nothing compared to what else I could do for you."

"T-To heal me?" I murmur, sounding like I'm drunk and slurring.

He's shaking his head, studying me, leaving me imagining all the things I'd let him do to me, and that single thought arouses my earlier desire. Being this close to him makes me so horny, and I have no idea how to stop myself from falling.

When he pulls away, I shuffle back up the bed, pushing down my dress. I've never felt this drawn to another man before, but maybe it's his blood coursing through my veins.

That's the lie I'm going to keep telling myself anyway.

Large hands suddenly roll me onto my side.

"Hey, what are you doing?"

"Hush," he says. "You're just too beautiful." Then he's bunching up the fabric of my dress and pushing it to my waist, exposing my hip and backside. But it's nothing he hasn't already seen, right? I giggle to myself at the thought, then I completely forget why I found it funny.

I'm losing my mind. And with each passing moment, that perfect drunken sensation overwhelms me further. Numbing me. Making me exist in my body but relinquish all control.

"All the men I dance for would pay a fortune to manhandle me like you're doing now." I'm humming a rock ballad stuck in my head, and I love how free I feel. When

Cassius doesn't respond, I continue because I'm suddenly in a chatty mood.

"It's almost as if you care about me," I murmur, arching my back so that my ass pushes against him. His body stiffens suddenly, and I laugh again. "Saving me from the vampire… Holding me… Giving me your blood…"

"Maybe I did all those things for myself," he teases me.

"Hmmm…" I nod. "Maybe."

"Do you want to know the benefit of my demon blood coursing through your veins?"

"Yes…well, no. You said it heals me and I feel like I'm floating. Is that strange?" I'm rambling, I know. I can hear my voice, but I can't feel my lips moving to form the words.

"My blood is like morphine, so you'll feel almost no pain, but it'll also give you one hell of a high, so enjoy the ride."

I try to turn back around to face him, but he presses a hand against my shoulder, so I remain on my side. "Nope, stay right there for me, gorgeous. I haven't finished with you."

But when I sense him leaning away from me, I twist my head around and the room spins. For that split second, I focus enough to see him fiddling with his switchblade again.

"What's that for?" I muse, reaching for the blade in my attempt to roll me onto my back. But his knee is there, stopping me, and he pushes my hand away. Truthfully, having him lightly slap my hand has me laughing. "Hey, do it again, but on my ass."

"Oh, Eve," he purrs, the sound is delicious. "You have no idea what you're saying right now. And you're driving me insane."

He runs his large hand over my hip, his fingers digging into my skin. His touch slips down to my ass and squeezes. "Perfection."

I moan and stick my ass out more. "Your touch is heaven. Keep going, please, Cassius."

His growl turns me on even more.

When the soft cushion of his lips presses where his fingers were seconds earlier, a velvety sensation races up my spine, and a shiver strokes my slick core.

"I'm not sure I deserve a beauty like you," he breathes near my ear, "but I'll make you mine."

My eyes half close while my body hums. Is it a good thing to be his? A demon's? He did just save me and took away my pain. And if a simple kiss made me moan, what else could he do?

Something digs into the side of my hip.

"Ouch," I cry out and lift my head, thinking he's just pinched me. "What are you doing?"

"Shh," he coos, running his fingers up and down my hip. His touch feels icy cold all of a sudden. "You're safe now. Let me take care of you."

"Fuck, there you are, little dove!" Knox's explosive voice booms through the room. "I thought you were still in your room."

I crane my neck to look at the doorway. Knox is gripping the top of the door frame with his fingers, practically hanging there. He offers me a tight smile while every muscle in his arms and shoulders stretch as he leans into the pose he's pulling, and just looking at him leaves me breathless.

His shirt rides up his stomach, revealing the sharp angles and ridges of his muscular stomach and the drool-worthy V just over his hip bones. I clench my thighs together at the sight. He studies me with a wildness in his gaze.

How can these men all be so ridiculously handsome?

I try to sit up more, but Cassius's strong hand holds me down. "Not yet, sweetheart. Almost done."

Done? Done with what?

Knox's gaze sweeps over me, leaving a trail of goosebumps in its wake. There's blood in his hair and smeared across his neck, but instead of freaking me out, it makes more desire awaken inside me. Especially when I remember that he was cutting up that vampire for me.

I hope he's dead.

"You know, Knox, you were supposed to be watching her," Cassius says from behind me in a scolding tone. "I came home and found her wandering the halls in so much pain, she could barely stand up straight."

His brow wrinkles in confusion. "Pain?"

"The poison," I blurt out, unable to control the volume of my voice. "I was dying."

Knox glances at Cassius. "What did you do? Did you drug her?"

"Pretty much," Cassius laughs. "I gave her my blood."

I don't hear the rest of their conversation when I lower my gaze to Knox's sweatpants, at how low they sit on his hips. The thin fabric of his pants conceals nothing. I can see every curve of his cock, every line, and just how big it dangles.

"Sweet Jesus..." I gasp. "Is that a dragon in your pants?"

"Dracon's not going to be happy about this..." Knox gives him a deadpan expression as Cassius tries to roll me onto my stomach.

"What he doesn't know won't hurt him," he replies. "Why don't you stop griping and help me."

Knox jumps down and walks over. When he climbs onto the bed and puts his hands on me, a groan rolls through my chest. The way he's kneeling next to me has my face so close to his dick. I lick my lips in anticipation.

"I think she likes you," Cassius chuckles, which wins him a sharp glare from Knox. "Fine, just hold her still."

Knox turns me gently so that I'm practically on my stomach between them with my ass exposed.

"Would you rather do it from behind?" I burst out laughing from my terrible joke. I don't know where this bravery is coming from, but right now, I feel invincible.

But at least Cassius thinks I'm funny too and howls with laughter. "Don't you love how spontaneous she is?"

"She's not herself right now," Knox states dryly.

An argument erupts between them, but I tune them in and out.

A pinching ache flares from my hip again, and I whine. Then, I lower my gaze to where Cassius is running the tip of his blade across my hip. It should hurt more, but I can only feel it vaguely.

Releasing a long exhale, I let myself sink against the mattress.

"I think she's passing out." I hear Knox say, but his voice sounds far away as heaviness tugs at my eyelids.

"Ah, good. She's going to need her rest to heal up. She'll feel better when she wakes."

"Wait until she sees what you did," Knox says. "She's going to kill you."

"She can try."

Unable to fight the exhaustion anymore, I let it envelope me and close my eyes. Within seconds, I'm tugged deep into dreamland.

CHAPTER FOURTEEN

KNOX

I slap my hand down on the other side of the dining room table where Cassius and Dracon sit. Both their gazes snap up to me, and a smile escapes. I can't help it. I love what I do, and they're going to *love* to hear what I discovered even more.

"Guess what I found out?" I say, wiping my bloody hand down the front of my shirt to clean it. After Cassius and I brought Eve back to her room to sleep off her stupor, I went back to the vamp in my bedroom. It took a few more hours since he was a stubborn one, but I finally got him to tell me some useful information.

Cassius watches me, intrigued, from over his mug of coffee—the demon drinks enough to make a human go into cardiac arrest—while Dracon eyes me unimpressed, like always.

"You got the vamp to talk?" Cassius replies excitedly, which causes my smile to grow. At least someone appreciates my skills in this place.

"Did you ever doubt me?"

"When it comes to death, not even for a second," Cassius says.

Now he's just flattering me.

"Of course, I got him to talk," I tell him. "Didn't take too long. Actually, I wish he put up a bit more of a fight."

"You're one crazy bastard, you know that, right?"

I only tilt my head to the side. Is he still complimenting me? I'm not sure.

Impatient, Cassius waves for me to go on. "Out with it. You can't leave us hanging here. I want to know."

I stretch my neck first to the left and then the right, working out the kinks. I don't need any of the fancy gadgets and whatnot that humans use to extract information. I like to do it the old-fashioned way, and I'm not afraid to get my hands dirty.

Boy, it was nice to just splay that vamp open and feel his blood color my skin, especially after what he'd done to Eve.

"Knox," Cassius snaps, reminding me they're still waiting.

"Ladir changing the location wasn't because of rats," I tell the others, leaning over the table as my excitement bubbles up. The rush of killing someone is a high like no other for me. As if I just took whatever drugs Cassius is taking nowadays, I'm still jittery from it. Hopped up on the memory of watching his soul leave his body. The terror in his eyes the moment he realized he wasn't leaving my room alive.

Oh, it was exquisite.

"And?" Dracon's deep voice finally injects into the conversation. His brow is cocked, his patience wearing thin too.

Better skip to the end.

"The Lords of Night got to him," I say.

Cassius shakes his head before saying, "But he's terrified of the Lords."

"Exactly, and so getting him to cooperate was easy." I curled my fingers into a fist at my side with enough force to have my knuckles cracking. "Ladir was a plot to draw us and Eve to them."

"Eve? What does she have to do with this?" Dracon asks.

"They wanted to bring out her power and figure out what the hell she really is."

"So we're not the only ones who know there's something about her." Dracon snarls. His fury makes his irises flash–the beast lurking just beneath the surface, ready to come out and play. I'm surprised there isn't smoke curling out of his nostrils.

If he shifts right here in this room, he'll flatten us all.

"Apparently not," I reply.

"But we have a truce with them. Why would they break it over something as miniscule as a girl?" Cassius asks. "They'll have a full on war on their hands."

"This would be the time to try and push us out. With Saxon gone," Dracon answers.

Cassius takes another long sip of his coffee. "The vamp could've been lying. Ever think of that?"

Gaze zoned out on the ceiling, Dracon considers that option for a while. "He could be..." But his tone reveals that he's not convinced.

"So Franco *and* Marius want her?" Cassius says. "We're about to have a gang war over some pussy?"

The dim thought in the back of my head tells me it's my fault that Eve's here. I'm the one who found her in Franco's warehouse and tried to figure her out. If I'd left her there, if I'd left her for the Spades to ruin, then things might be different for her.

I wouldn't fucking care about her. None of us would, and we wouldn't have to worry about going up against the Black Spades or the Lords of Night. Unlike now.

"I wonder if the Spades found out about her first, and that's why Franco went and paid her a visit. That motherfucker," Dracon grounds out, his control slipping.

"Franco's human. He doesn't know about supes," Cassius adds in.

"We don't know that for sure. He might have figured it out by now. And maybe Eve is how he plans on leveling the playing field."

Interesting thought…

"It's time to show them all that they can't fuck with us," Dracon says, clenching his fist on the table.

"This definitely changes things." Cassius taps his chin with barely veiled curiosity. Leaning forward, his tongue darting out to wet his lips.

"What are we thinking?" I ask the group.

"Something is clearly going on with her. Eve. Who is she really?" Dracon pushes away from the table with such force, he accidentally sends the thing skidding away from him. "It's time to do some of the ground work. Check into her friends, her workplace, how she lived and see what we can find out."

"Didn't you already have her files pulled? Her lineage traced?" I ask. It's not like Dracon to do anything half assed. He's the most fucking anal out of all of us. Cassius and I can't be bothered with that kind of shit.

"We need more than what's written on paper. There has to be something else we're missing."

"I can go talk to the girls at the club where she used to

work." Cassius's lips peel back in a cold smile at the proposition. He'll jump at anything to get him out of the house. He hates monotony and routine. An hour without excitement is too long for him.

For me, I can sit alone, lost in my thoughts, forever. That's one thing Dracon and I have in common, I guess. We don't mind the silence. But that's as far as my similarities with the Apex go. Unlike Dracon, I've been by myself for most of my existence, and I embrace my monster. I don't fight it. Living with two other creatures, let alone interacting with the living in general, is new to me. I'm still getting used to it, even after all these years.

And now...this woman. Eve. She's really spun things on its head for me. I tell myself I'm not interested in her beyond mere curiosity. Not one bit. But even when I thought she might be Aris coming back to dispose of me, I couldn't deny the strange pull she had on me.

Hell, even my cock betrayed me. When she was on my table, at my mercy, I wanted to fuck her so fucking bad...

And that's just *not me.*

I curl my nails into my palms, stabbing myself with their sharp pointed ends, like the pain will somehow help ground me. To remind me of who I am.

She's the only person I know who can handle my blade, which makes her either the most fucking spectacular creature on this plane of existence or something I need to kill. I'm not opposed to either option.

I could make her death spectacular too. But I'm the only one who can do it. If anyone else lays a hand on her...

A fist knocks into my shoulder, and I whirl around with a hiss. Cassius is staring at me with a smirk, like he knows the struggle going on in my head and is getting a good laugh because of it.

Annoyance pricks at me, and I glare at him. "What?"

"Just keep your torture to the vampires, okay?" he says with a chuckle. "We can't do anything to Eve until we figure out what she is."

"Don't you think I know that?" I snap back.

Dracon's gaze roams over me. "He's making sure you remember."

"And I don't need you on my back either."

Dracon shifts slightly. The movement would seem unimportant to an outsider, but I know the animal of a man in front of me. He's waiting to see if I make a move first and challenge him. I've seen it enough over the countless years we've spent together, so he can try to rain hell down on me. He's waiting for a reason to take me out.

But Dracon doesn't scare me. No one does.

I stand straighter and meet his glare head on. He may be bigger than me, in size, and I know I need his and Cassius's help while I'm cast out on this plane, but I'll kill him if I have to.

He wants Eve too. It's obvious. I watched him fuck her with his fingers the other day and knew it had been more than a simple power play on his part. He'd gotten to her first; I can't help but think that's strategic too.

"Stand down, Knox," I hear Cassius say by my ear like a pestering gnat, and anger rises within me. I don't understand why he always has to interfere, why he's always telling me to step back. He knows just as well as I do that sometimes Dracon needs to have his ego deflated.

Cassius reaches to touch my shoulder, and in one swift move, I jerk away from him, rip the Mortem Blade out, and twist it to press against Cassius's throat. Fear flicks in his gaze, but it's fleeting, soon replaced with mirth.

"Knox, are you going to kill me?" Cassius laughs, eyes wild.

"Knox," Dracon's warning rumbles. He takes a step around the table but pauses, nostrils flaring. "We need to work together."

Cassius seems unbothered. He only continues to laugh like it's the funniest thing in the world that I could eradicate him in a second. The fucker's as nuts as me.

Because I wish it was Dracon on the other side of my blade and not Cassius, I lower it. Cassius rubs his neck, still grinning wickedly. "Boy, that was a rush. Thanks."

"Anytime," I grumble.

Dracon shakes his head, and somehow, the action forces the rigidness out of his muscles. "Enough of this bullshit. We need to figure this shit out before a fucking woman brings our empire crumbling down around us."

"Drac's right. We need to work together," Cassius pipes in.

I hate how they're both staring at me. Like I'm the fucking problem in this trio.

Spinning around, I trudge across the kitchen.

"Knox! Come on, man," Cassius shouts.

I stop.

Turning, I narrow my eyes on both of them. "It's not me you have to worry about."

With that, I stride down the hallway, leaving them with my words. I know Dracon is stewing behind me, hating that I took control of the conversation, but that only makes a smile tease my lips.

Fuck that fire-breathing prick.

The game we play, the calculating steps we take toward and around each other, is welcomed right now. I'll accept any distraction that keeps me away from Eve and whatever it is that's happening between us.

I'd take on a thousand Dracons rather than developing feelings for this woman.

EVE

It feels like I've been asleep for days.

When I wake, I glance around my bedroom finding that it's unchanged despite all the time that's passed by me.

After a moment of taking stock of my body, I can honestly say that I'm feeling much better. Whatever mysterious sickness that plagued me seems to be gone. So that's a win right there.

But when I try to think back on my time with Cassius, I can't seem to remember what happened after he gave me his blood. Things are blurry from there on.

Did I just fall asleep on his bed and then he brought me back here? Or, shit…did he do something to me *after* I fell asleep?

Wait…wasn't Knox there too? Why do I have a twinge of memory of him holding me on my stomach?

Then I think about how I'd come to find him torturing the vampire in the black room, but that definitely hadn't been my imagination. That part had been very, very real.

Finally, I rouse myself enough to shift up on my elbows, pushing the sheets aside. My dress is bunched up at my waist from sleep, but when my gaze falls onto my hip, I gasp.

There's a mark on my skin. Wait, not just a mark. Letters. Deep and red and raised from healing.

I squint and lean in further for a better look.

C-A-S-S-I-U-S.

MOTHER FUCKER!

That demon carved his name into my skin! Branded me!

Fragments of memory float to the surface. Him holding the switchblade... The pinching feeling on my hip as he soothed me with his words and caresses... How he had asked Knox to help him hold me still...

What a deranged, possessive asshole!

I probe the area to find it still tender and raw, and pure fury lashes through me. It looks like some poorly done prison-made tattoo. I'll probably have it forever.

He's going to get a kick in the dick the second I find him.

I rub a finger over the mark, hissing at the pain, and then jump out of bed.

That's it. This is another level of fucked up. I'm done. I'm getting out of here *immediately*.

These Kings messed with the wrong woman. They have no idea who I am or where I've been in my life. They also have no fucking clue the lengths I'm willing to go to survive. I've scraped and clawed and fought to provide myself with a good life. And they are not going to take that away from me.

I need to figure out a way to get out of here. With the cameras on me, it's going to be a challenge. I'm their private peep show, after all. But surely the Kings have much better things to do than watch me all day, right?

I'm going to have to take that risk.

Grabbing the door handle, I test it to be sure. Unlike last time, it's locked. Of course I couldn't get lucky twice.

Guess I'm breaking the damn thing down then.

Not thinking twice, I throw all my weight against it like it will somehow budge.

Nope, not moving. So, how am I going to do this?

I peek up at the blinking red light and listen for any sounds of footsteps in the hall. When I don't hear anyone coming for me, I try again. All it wins me is a sore shoulder, one that makes tears well in my eyes.

Hissing, I rub the area and stare at the wood. Shit, I stabbed Xavier Franco in the eye with my heel. I can do this.

Right?

Right.

Kicking the door doesn't help. Punching it doesn't either, it only leaves bruises on my knuckles.

Frustration bubbles through me, my anger picking up on it. How the fuck am I going to get out of here?

Grabbing the door handle again, I yank it hard, grunting out my aggravation. At the same time, lightning snaps through me as my power seizes its opportunity to rear up through my emotions. It whirls out of me like a tornado, throwing up my hair and pushing forward so fast, I can't even register what's happening until I'm thrown backward across the room. My back hits the bed, my body bouncing off the mattress and sending me slamming into my stomach. All the wind is knocked out of me, but it's not as bad as the booming explosion that echoes throughout the penthouse.

Oh, shit! The Kings are bound to know something's up now. It's going to be impossible to explain away this one.

Scrambling to my feet, I realize the door has been ripped off the hinges. It stands crooked on the frame, holding on by a thread practically.

Pulse racing, I gape. I did that? And without even trying?

Oops.

I'm losing control over my power. First in the warehouse with Franco, with Knox in the morgue, and then the other night with the vamps… It's been slipping through my barriers a lot easier ever since I was kidnapped.

Not good. Not good at all.

Footsteps thunder from somewhere in the penthouse. They are coming toward my room.

My heart skips with panic. I really can't stand here and freak over this now. I have to use these precious seconds to get the heck out of here. The Kings already think I'm hiding something, and after this, they are going to *know* I am. If I stick around, who knows what they'll do to get it out of me.

Just the thought has me rushing into the hallway. Behind me, the door completely detaches from the wall and crashes to the floor.

"Jesus fuck, what was that?" Cassius's shouts have me practically leaping out of my skin. His blond head appears at the end of the corridor near the elevator, where he's met with Knox, who's gripping his curved knife and breathing hard.

Their heads whip my way, and my breath freezes in my chest.

Heart thundering, I sprint in the opposite direction. And of course, they chase after me. They're closing the distance fast. I don't even know where to go or if there's another way out of this maze, but I'm running for my life now. At least, it sure feels like it.

"Eeeevveee!" Cassius sing-songs, and a shiver darts up my spine. "Why are you running, sweetheart?"

I glance over my shoulder to see the two men sprinting for me with the same predatory looks in their eyes. A scream climbs up my throat.

Cassius and Knox are terrifying in their own right, but I'd take both of them over—

I slam into a wall—no, not a real one. A wall of muscle. As I stumble back a step, disoriented, strong hands seize my arms to steady me on my feet, and when I look up and see those familiar gold eyes and ruggedly handsome face, my heart stops.

His stare bores into me. "Think you're going somewhere?"

Shit.

Almost as if he's reading my mind, he chuckles low under his breath before saying, "It was a nice try."

I've never wanted to punch someone and kiss them at the same time in all my life. Talk about confusing.

I settle for trying to step back instead, but Dracon's fingers dig into my flesh, holding me in place.

"You're hurting me," I gasp and attempt to pry him off me, but he's unmovable. I settle for punching him in the arm instead.

As if I'm not more than an annoyance, Dracon cocks a brow. "And how did you get out of your room?" he asks. "Did you use your powers, I assume?"

My spine stiffens at the mention of my powers.

What do I do? What do I say? He's not going to believe me if I say I Hulk-smashed my way through the door. I mean, look at me.

But revealing myself can only end in something much more deadly.

"Maybe," I say in a mocking tone. "Maybe not."

Using his grip on my arm, he spins me into him and

grunts when the curve of my ass presses against his thighs. Now I'm staring at Cassius and Knox, who have both stopped short in front of us and are watching with narrowed eyes. Unlike the first time they'd witnessed Dracon manhandle me, I see jealousy flashing in their gazes.

Dracon doesn't seem to notice though. And if he does, he doesn't care. He brings me in close and leans forward, pushing his mouth right up against my ear, so I can feel every hard plane of his body, and my heartbeat picks up speed. His hot breath caresses the side of my face when he speaks again.

"All you have to do is tell me what you are, Eve," he mutters against my ear, sending tingles dancing across my skin. "And I can make this as painless as possible for you."

"But what's the fun in that?" I retort. The slightest wiggle of my hips and his cock twitches against me.

I'm not going to lie, it feels *good.* And I love how much I'm affecting him even more.

"You like pain?" he breathes, his voice dropping. "You like when it hurts?"

"It's all I know."

The memory of me fucking myself to the thought of the Kings being rough with me rushes forward from the dark recesses of my mind, and for a moment, I wonder if Dracon had seen me play with myself after all.

That's when I realize he's just trying to get a rise out of me again, but I'm not going to let him. I know better.

How amazing would it be to be *his* undoing?

An idea is stirring–a batshit crazy one, but remembering how he caged me against the wall and finger-fucked me to the edge only to leave me hanging has the taste of revenge on my tongue.

"Powers or not, it seems to me that you aren't too worried," I murmur.

Wouldn't it be absolutely *delicious* to have him squirming under *my* touch? Get him so close to the point that his head is spinning and he doesn't know which way is up?

"About you escaping?" His nostrils flare. "Absolutely not."

"No. About your friends seeing you in a compromising position."

He tilts his head to the side as he stares at me, but loosens his grip enough for me to wiggle again. His cock stiffens even more against my back. "What are you talking about?"

Here goes nothing.

I twist suddenly, taking him off guard, and drop to my knees in front of him. With quick hands, I drag down the zipper of his jeans.

"What the fu—"

His cock springs out from his jeans right into the palm of my hand.

For a second, I'm stunned at the size of him. He's massive and thick–I've never seen a dick so big in my life. And in my line of work, you see quite a few.

My tongue sweeps across my lips, and my brain fogs. For a second, I forget what I'm supposed to be doing.

Oh, yeah. Revenge.

It's time for a little payback.

I flick my tongue along the underside of his erection, making sure to peer up at him the entire time. Hmm... He's salty and sweet in the best kind of way. And so damn hot on my tongue. It's as if he has a lit furnace under all that height and muscle.

Dracon tries to swallow his groan of surprise, still trying to appear uninterested, but I'm no fool. I can see that arrogant facade cracking in front of my eyes.

When his body stiffens, I know this is actually how I'm going to beat him at his own game.

"What's the matter, Dracon?" I tease before sucking him deep and releasing him with a pop a second later.

His hands fist at his sides, his fingers clenching and unclenching. He's itching to touch me in some way, but whether that's to hold my head to encourage me to go on or snap my neck… I don't know. I'm not even sure he's blinked since running into me.

"Are you having a *little* problem?" The flirtatious tone I use does the trick, but it's not the reaction I'm hoping for. Instead, his brows pinch together.

"*Little?*" He growls out the word.

I blink up at him. "Oh, I'm sorry?" I suck his cock into my mouth a second time and listen with pleasure to his sharp inhale. "Did I insinuate something about your big, massive…"

Trailing off, I start to work his shaft in time with my mouth.

He can't control himself for long. A few seconds in and his hands fist in my hair, tugging with a sharp bite of pain that has desire swirling in my core. It is a nice cock; I have to admit it. One I wouldn't mind taking for a spin…

If I don't die in the next few minutes, that is.

Focus, Eve. Focus.

"Leave!"

The command fires through the air like a gunshot, but when I realize his fingers are still tangled in my hair, I know he's not talking to me.

He's talking to Knox and Cassius.

Wow, I'd completely forgotten they were there. Watching us. Not saying a word.

I can't move from my spot–Dracon has me pinned in place where he wants me the most–but when another "I said leave!" rumbles past his lips, it's clear his two friends weren't clearing out fast enough for his liking.

Cassius and Knox's footsteps fade away, followed by the slamming of doors, and once Dracon's sure we're alone, he peers down at me again.

"I like you this way," he purrs, a grin splitting his lips. He thrusts his hips forward, pushing his dick deeper into my mouth. "Quiet. Obedient."

What a jerk.

The urge to bite down and chomp his dick right off is tempting. That would definitely get me revenge, but it would also most certainly end in my death.

His hips jerk forward in time with my sucking, with his hands keeping my head in place. Of course, he needs to stay in control. It's his thing, dominance. Even when it comes to pleasure.

But I'd be lying if I said I wasn't enjoying this too. Against all common sense, heat is pooling at my core, and the desire to take this a step further is rooting itself in me. It'd be so much easier to hate his guts—hate all of them, if I'm still being honest—if they weren't hotter than sin.

I'm going to Hell for this.

Oh, well.

Soon enough, he takes over the movement and I have to grip his thighs and brace myself to take all of him while he fucks my face. Dracon's cock hits the back of my throat with such force that tears burn the corners of my eyes, but I take him all, never breaking eye contact with him.

"Hmmm, yes. That's it. Fuck." His eyelids flutter close as

his head falls back, lost in the moment. "You like it when I fuck your face, Eve?"

I don't reply–how can I? But I do. He quickens his pace to give himself the answer he wants. "Good girl. Yes, take it all. Just like that."

His dirty words and all the praise, lights a fire in me. My throat is burning from his roughness, but I don't care.

"Look at me," he growls suddenly.

I must be too lost in the moment, and so I stare up at him through my lashes to find his eyes glowing as if they emit light on their own. They're hypnotizing.

"Yes…" he growls. Finally, his hands fall away from me, and he slows a beat. "You're going to swallow all of me down, aren't you, Eve? Every last drop."

A squeak escapes me. A mother fucking squeak, like a goddamn mouse.

His hips jerk, his muscles tensing, and I know what's coming. He's about to blow.

Come on, Eve. Now this is your time to get him back. Remember how you got on your knees in the first place?

Shit, my subconscious is right.

Oh, and payback is going to be the best feeling in the world.

Grabbing his thighs, I push myself backward enough to slide his cock out of my mouth. Automatically, he reaches for me, trying to get me back in place, but I jump to my feet and slip out of his reach.

Then, wiping the corners of my mouth, I say, "Oh, I think that's enough for now."

The look on his face is priceless.

Pure shock and confusion. He's locked in place from it, eyes wide and mouth hanging open. I'll remember this image of him for eternity. It's pure gold.

Doesn't feel so good to be on the receiving end, does it, big boy?

It doesn't last long, though. The moment he recognizes the similarity to my words, fury blazes across his face. In a blink of an eye, his hands are on my hips, and he's slamming me against the closest wall. The back of my head collides with the plaster and colors explode before my eyes.

I cry out. My feet are dangling off the floor; he's only holding me up with one hand plastered against my rib cage, and it hurts. Everything hurts.

Then, with his free hand, he rips my pants off me like they're made of nothing more than wet paper. He drops them like the trash they now are, and my stomach flips with a scary mixture of fear and anticipation.

This...beast... He could destroy me with just a simple snap of his fingers, and for some fucked up reason, that turns me on to no end.

Dracon steps closer and positions himself between my splayed legs. His stone-hard cock now presses against my panties, the thin fabric the only thing blocking him from entering me. I try to clench my legs, to deny him access, but it's no use.

"My house," he reminds me, his voice rough and his syllables grinding together. "You're in my house. You follow *my* rules. You do as *I* say."

My panties are off me in a flash, the shreds of fabric fluttering to the floor before I even know what's happened. He's done playing around.

I swallow hard. The head of his cock is pressing against my pussy, demanding entry.

"Get off me," I bite out, but my voice comes out too

shaky to be taken seriously. Not only that, but he's sure to feel how wet I am now.

His nostrils flare, and his pupils dilate with hunger.

Oh, no… Can he smell my arousal too?

When his lips split into a grin, I see fangs. He's about to devour me.

I shouldn't want him to fuck me with all that cock, especially when I need to escape, but he's soooo close. So close to giving me what I crave, what I've been imagining would happen since the moment I came to the Tower and met the Kings. I'm arching my back, pushing my ass against the wall and wrapping my legs around his waist. Ready for him to take what he wants, push himself inside, and—

"Dracon!"

Cassius's voice bursts through my subconscious. Both me and Dracon whip our attention back down the hall. Cassius is striding towards us, glowering, with something in his hands.

"What the fuck do you want?" The statement is loud enough, forceful enough, to shake the wall at my back.

Cassius doesn't even look at me. With a frown twisting his lips, his stare stays trained on Dracon.

Dracon grunts. "I told you to leave!"

"We have a bit of a problem," Cassius cuts him off abruptly. "We got a gift."

"A what?" he snaps back.

Finally, Cassius glances my way, but only briefly. Then he holds up a dark wooden box to show Dracon. "We got a *gift.*"

That must be a code word for something important because Dracon suddenly pulls away and lets me go. so I can slide down the wall to my feet. Quickly, he stuffs his cock back into his pants, while I struggle to pull down my shirt to cover my exposed goods. Though, it's not like Cassius didn't know what Dracon and I had been doing. He did see me drop to my knees, after all.

"From who?" Dracon booms.

"Don't know. It's addressed to Eve."

My eyes widen in fear. "M-Me?" I don't understand. Worry tumbles inside me. "I don't know anything about a gift."

"Of course you don't," Cassius replies. There's uneasiness in his expression that makes me anxious. Cassius is always so carefree, the opposite of Dracon's seriousness. It's disturbing to see him this way. "I doubt it's really meant for you. It's a message for us."

Stepping up to Dracon's side, I watch as he tentatively takes the box from Cassius and lifts the lid. What I see has my breath seizing in my lungs.

It's a finger... A *person's* finger.

My stomach heaves, and I back away.

The severed finger has been cut from the bottom knuckle, the pointed nail painted a fire engine red. The same color my boss, Kat, always wore to match her fiery personality.

Wait... Cassius had said this *gift* was addressed to me.

That's when I see the faded infinity tattoo just above the knuckle, and my heart slams against my ribs.

No...it can't be.

Dread rolls through me.

"Oh, my god!" My voice trembles, and I have to slap a hand over my mouth as bile hits the back of my throat. It's hers—it's Kat's. I just know it.

Someone killed her.

Cassius and Dracon exchange looks.

"You know who this belongs to?" Cassius asks carefully, referring to the finger.

All I can do is nod. Because if I open my mouth again, I'll vomit.

"There was a note, too," Cassius adds. He closes the box, for which I'm grateful, and then pulls out a folded piece of paper from his jeans pocket. "It says we need to meet them down at the docks on Friday night. And to bring Eve. Or next time…" He pauses.

I stiffen. Friday… That's in a few days.

My pulse is thunder in my ears.

Dracon is growing more impatient by the second. "Next time…?"

As much as I wish he wouldn't finish the sentence, Cassius sighs before going on. "Next time, the woman's head will be in the box."

Kat's head. She's still alive, but this was a warning. They'll kill her in a heartbeat if we don't follow his instructions.

Friday. At the docks.

I can't let anything happen to her.

I can't—

Darkness swirls around the edges of my vision. I lean against the wall for support, convinced that if I don't throw up first, I may just pass out.

"Who do you think it's from?" Cassius asks Dracon, too lost in business to notice my distress. "The vamps again?"

My mind is a jumbled mess, but I know it can't be the Lords of Night. Whoever did this has to be someone who knows me, where I worked, who Kat is to me…

"Franco," I gasp as the realization slams into me. I'm shaking all over, panic clawing over my skin. "It has to be him."

They both look at me. There's a flicker of sympathy in Cassius's gaze, but Dracon's glare is ice cold, his expression tense like the rest of him.

How long until they decide I'm more trouble than I'm worth and kill me?

"The Black Spades are challenging us," Dracon snarls. His fury is all-consuming; it makes his body shudder where he stands. "Franco's grown too cocky."

"How do you want to handle this, Drac?" Cassius asks him.

Dracon grunts, his irises turning a molten gold. "We do what we always do in situations like this," he says before turning to look at me. "We fight for what's ours."

CHAPTER FIFTEEN

EVE

I barely slept last night. When I woke up, it had been with Kat's name spilling from my lips. And now, I'm pacing. Her severed finger hasn't left my thoughts; I keep imagining how much she screamed and cried when it was cut off.

Because of me.

I curl my hands into fists. I want to punch something. I want it to hurt, to wash away the guilt that's destroying me.

Friday, the note had said, which means she'll hopefully be okay until then, right? Kat is a strong witch who's endured hardship in her life. She grew up in a family where her stepfather beat her, and she eventually moved in with her druggie boyfriend. But she got out. And ever since, she's been a fighter. She doesn't deserve this.

The muscles in my abdomen bunch up, and the weight of her being tortured eats away at my soul.

Outside the window, a storm is brewing. The night devours the land and dense gray clouds block out any light from the moon and stars. Normally, I find snow calming and peaceful. The way it turns an ugly world into a magical wonderland has always given me hope. Today, it reminds me of an ominous warning hanging over me.

I mean, how much worse can things get?

I inhale deeply, my breath shuddering in my lungs when a knock comes at my newly installed, passcode protected, metal door, wrenching me out of my thoughts. "Who is it?"

Lucky for me, Dracon's been too busy with whatever is going on in gang-land to force me to explain how I was able to blow the other door off the hinges. But that didn't stop him from having a crew in here a half an hour later to install this new monster in its place. It reminds me of something a bank would use to keep all the money safe.

"It's me, little dove," the voice on the other side answers.

Knox.

"Come in," I say, nervously. As much as I want to turn him away, he'll end up coming in no matter what, and I honestly don't have the energy to fight right now.

I hear the chimes of the mystery five digit code being punched into the panel outside and then the zip of locks moving and unlatching. A robotic woman's voice says, *"Enter"* in greeting and he does, taking long strides into the center of the room.

His gaze swallows me whole, and anxiety crawls over me. Is he here to take me to the morgue? To get me to admit that I'm harboring some crazy, untamable power?

At this rate, I may just tell him. It's not like they'll let me go otherwise–that's clear.

As his eyes look up and down my body, my pulse gallops. Everything about him is dark and sinful. From the black pants to his matching Henley shirt that hugs the muscles across his chest and biceps. He's wearing his hair in a ponytail at the nape of his neck, giving him an older, more distinguished flare that I'm loving. It's the complete opposite of his manic personality.

"I have a gift for you," he breathes the words, his voice calm.

Oh no.

The last time I heard those words and got *a gift*, it was Kat's finger in a box.

"Uh…Oh."

He waits, not moving, and I realize it's probably not the reaction he'd been expecting from me. I try again, "I'm sorry, it's just that I've had my share of gifts lately. You know what I mean?"

Blinking, he regards me silently as if he's trying to work out what I mean. Or maybe why I am so upset about it. But instead of asking those things, he says instead, "This gift is different. No body parts."

"You promise?" I force a laugh, my nerves getting the better of me.

He takes several steps forward but then hesitates when I flinch.

"I'm sorry," I apologize in a rush. "It's just–I mean, I didn't–"

"It's okay," he whispers as if he completely understands. "I just wanted to show you that I don't think you're Aris anymore. And…" he trails off, shaking his head as he rethinks his next words.

Well that's a relief. If only he realized it a little sooner.

"You're on edge still," he says suddenly, taking me off guard. "Maybe I'll just come back another time." He heads for the door.

His vulnerability has me stumbling and so damn

confused. I hurry to stop him. "No, no. Look, I'm sorry. Don't go."

He pauses and glances up at me.

"I didn't mean to be rude… I just didn't expect to get anything from you, being what you are."

Wow, that sounds bad too. I'm batting a thousand here.

"Death, you mean," he says.

What kind of supernaturals the Kings of Eden actually are have been a mystery. Demons, shifters, bigfoots…the rumors are vast and sometimes funny. Knowing they are dangerous has always been okay with me–I never needed more of an explanation than that–but spending time with them has made me curious. Cassius is a demon, he's revealed that to me already, but why he's on earth and not in Hell…I don't know. Dracon's some kind of shifter, I think. From his massive size and need to control everything, he screams Alpha. Like with Cassius, the details I don't exactly know, but when it comes to Knox…he's crazy and he has a magic blade. That's all I got from him. So is calling himself Death an ego thing?

I'm not sure.

"When you say Death…" I begin, unsure how to approach the subject.

"That's what I mean," he says and reaches into his pocket. He pulls out a small black box that's delicately wrapped with a blood-red ribbon. "I'm Death."

I stare down at the box, too afraid to move. The man standing before me is something else. His very presence lashes out with dread, leaving me trembling to my bones. Even the air around him chills, like it knows he's not a creature of this world. Traumatizing energy vibrates off of him, and all sense of feeling safe is stolen from me.

He's the villain in everyone's nightmares. A handsome one, but no less lethal.

Something isn't right about him. But instead of putting as much distance as possible between us, I'm ensnared in his web.

When I don't move or answer, he goes on, "Where I go, death follows. I am a horseman in the apocalypse."

So, not a nickname then.

I remain silent, unsure what I'm supposed to say to that.

Is he serious?

Are the horsemen of the apocalypse real?

"So," he asks, pushing the small black box into my hands. "Open it."

I hate that my hands are trembling, but I can't control it. Both him lying and telling the truth about being Death have deadly outcomes, and I don't know which is worse.

He moves closer to me, clearly having no concept of personal space. "I had it specially made for you."

"Oh!" I force myself to smile. "That's nice of you."

"Open it."

The ribbon comes unraveled at my touch, and it cascades to the floor. Licking my lips, I pull open the lid, and the first thing I see are earrings.

Earrings.

I release all my held breath in relief—that is, until I see what the earrings are actually made of. Gold loops with a single, long, polished, fang hanging from the middle.

Vampire fangs.

"These are…" I glance up at him, losing my voice all together.

"From the bloodsucker who attacked you," he says with a lopsided smile. It's obvious smiling is a foreign concept to him, but he's proud of himself for the gift. I can tell. "He'll never hurt you again."

Call me crazy, but there are butterflies beating their wings wildly in my stomach. The gift touches me so deep that tears spring to my eyes. Or maybe it's his words, *"He'll never hurt you again"* that strike me. When my life has been nothing but rejection and pain from those who were supposed to care about me the most, here Knox is offering me a promise that I'm safe with him. And that means more to me than I think he knows.

What he did might have been fucked up, but he did it for me.

Chest warming, a genuine smile lifts my lips. "Thank you. Truly. That was very thoughtful of you."

"Put them on," he suggests, eagerly.

I hesitate. "Uh…Okay."

I loop them through my ears with him watching me intently. When I fasten the last one, his grin spreads to something out of a horror movie.

"You like them, little dove?" he asks.

I don't know if I'll ever get used to the strange nickname he's given me, but I turn to the dresser's mirror to get a look at my reflection. They don't look too bad. Can't even tell they're vampire fangs at first glance. "I do. They're beautiful. And they mean something, which makes me like them even more."

He nods, and then his mouth opens like he wants to say something more, but he closes it after reconsidering. To my surprise, he spins on his heel and marches back to the door, about to leave.

"Wait, Knox," I call out.

He stops, but when he glances over his shoulder at me, I

realize I'm not sure why I called out to him in the first place. Staring at me, he waits.

"Um…" I scramble for something to keep him around. I decide to go with one of the billion questions I still have about him. "Knox, who is Aris?"

He flies across the room in a blink, closing all the distance between us. Alarm bells are ringing in my head telling me that I've made a grave mistake.

His hand shoots out and grabs me around the throat. I cry out, fear curling around me. He doesn't hold me hard, but with just enough strength so that I know he's in control.

Tilting his head back, Knox studies me as if I'm the most fascinating thing he's ever seen. My heart thunders wildly, desire spinning with panic in the base of my stomach.

One second, he's giving me a gift and ready to kill for me. And the next…

"You intrigue me," he finally says as his gaze continues to roam over me. "You may not be Aris, but there is something more to you. I'm sure of it. I just don't know if you are something I want, or something I ought to kill."

"Keep it up and I'll start to think you're flirting with me," I rasp, and when his fingers curl tighter on my neck, I shudder.

"That's where you're wrong."

I hold back the wince. It's getting harder to draw in a breath. "Let go…of…me…" I croak.

"Darkness have mercy on me, but you're constantly on my fucking mind and I want you out of my thoughts. I'm tired of this!" He's talking more to himself than me, but his words send chills down my spine.

I shove a fist into his chest as a last ditch effort to save myself, and shockingly, he lets me go. Clutching my neck, I gasp, sucking in deep breaths and trying to refill my lungs.

Crazy bastard!

I twist away from him only to find Cassius leaning against the door frame of my room. His arms folded across his chest, one leg across the other at the ankles. How long has he been watching?

"You surprise me every day, Knox," he says with a grin. "I come in to find you here handing out gifts like you're fucking Santa Claus and strangling a woman into liking you." He glances at me and winks. "We'll have to work on that last part, but it is progress."

"What do you want?" Knox rights himself and puts his stoic mask back in place.

"Just a heads up for Eve that we're having a few guests over tonight."

"Guests?" I repeat, still rubbing my sore throat. "Like who?"

"You'll see," is all he says before nodding at Knox to leave with him.

"Wait! You're going to have to tell me more than that," I say, excitement rushing over me. It feels like an eternity since I've seen anyone outside the three Kings, let alone outside this room.

They both pause.

"Dracon wanted to keep you locked up, but I convinced him to let you tag along," Cassius explains. "As long as you follow the rules."

"What sort of rules? And who's visiting?"

"One, you must dress beautifully. You're representing us, our name, our reputation, so you can't embarrass us. And two, no interacting with the guests. Eat the food, keep your distance, and look pretty."

I huff. "So…I'm eye candy."

"And three," he continues, ignoring that, "don't even think of asking these men to *save* you. They might take you home, but they won't be as kind to you as we've been. I promise you that." His blue eyes flash dark for a moment, letting me know he means every word.

"Come, Knox," Cassius says. "Dracon wants to see us."

When Knox strolls out into the hallway, Cassius lingers behind. "I suggest you take off those earrings too. We're not trying to have tension, and it sends the wrong signal for tonight."

I pull them out of my ears. When he smiles, I wonder if what he was saying about tension is true or if he just didn't want Knox's gift on me. "Good girl. Now, go get ready. We'll meet you in the dining room in thirty minutes."

He closes the door, and a flurry of beeps sound to signal the locks being reactivated.

Goddammit, this place is turning into a loony show.

With a heavy sigh, I walk to the closet in search of an appropriate outfit that will fit the King's rules.

CHAPTER SIXTEEN

EVE

Staring in the bathroom mirror, a girl I haven't seen in a long time looks back at me. Dolling myself up for the stage was routine, but ever since I've been stuck in the Tower, things like makeup, hairspray, and body glitter haven't been a priority anymore.

It's nice to get back to those things. It makes me feel more…like me.

I've picked out a dress I *think* says business and fun–or whatever it is the Kings are trying to use me for during this meeting. It's a simple black number with long sleeves that follows every round curve of my body, and the soft fabric falls just above my knees. It seems conservative until you get to the deep V-neck, which reveals a scandalous amount of cleavage. Should get some heads turning, I'd say.

And who knows, maybe if I keep my ears open, I can pick up on something that can help me later. A piece of blackmail, perhaps?

I turn around and glance at my ass in the mirror. Perfect round curves to grab anyone's attention, so it'll do. The men at the club used to love my ass, and a large butt is nothing a girl should be ashamed of. It took me a long time to accept myself the way I am, to love every part of myself and not listen to all the haters.

I grew up bullied at school because of my size, and I hated myself for a long time. I cried most nights, and I did everything to try to fit into the crowd. Crash diets and exercise. School teams. Attended dances and trips. Whatever it took, and it always left me feeling like shit because somehow I was never good enough.

But that's not me anymore. I smile at myself. "That's not who I am."

With a last glance in the mirror, I pucker rosy lips and flutter my bronzed eyelids. The Kings had toiletries picked up for me, including an array of makeup. Nothing really matched in all honesty, but I've been able to make do and keep the colors simple to compliment my pale complexion and eyes.

I slip into heels, which aren't stilettos, but they'll do.

Out in the hallway, the sound of rowdy voices and laughter reaches me, and my stomach twists.

Don't be nervous. I've walked on stage wearing hardly anything hundreds of times, so I can do this.

Shoulders back, I take quick steps toward the main foyer. Guards stand by the elevators, each dressed in a black suit, and I have no doubt they are armed.

I turn the corner to where a male server in a tuxedo stands tall, holding a silver tray with crystal glasses half-filled with an amber liquid. His face is expressionless when he glances at me. I look beyond him into the dimly lit main room where a light classical song plays.

There are at least half a dozen men I don't recognize, and most of them are standing around, listening to

Dracon, by the window. I can't make out what he's saying from where I am.

Well, it's better late than never to make an entrance.

Taking one step at a time, I collect a drink on the way. Lifting the glass, the strong smell of the whiskey has me pausing, and I turn to the waiter and whisper, "Any chance of getting some cola in this?"

He nods, his lips tugging into a smile. "Of course, ma'am."

"Call me Eve," I say, but he's already taken my glass and hurries across the foyer to the kitchen area and wetbar. Moments later, he returns with my glass, filled with cola mixed with the whiskey.

"Thanks," I reply, accepting my drink and taking a long sip to calm my nerves. Then I make my way further into the foyer.

Despite the dimness, every damn eye turns to me. I'm used to leering men from the club, so it doesn't bother me any. And like all those times before, I use their own desires and fantasies to my advantage.

Swinging my hips, I take several more steps into the room, making a show of it. I catch Dracon's heated gaze instantly, and he flashes me a warning through his liquid amber eyes. Cassius's rules come to mind: don't speak or interact with anyone being number two.

Is that for my protection or theirs? I don't know.

I smile back at Dracon and even give him a tiny wave, mostly to annoy him.

A few minutes pass, and I've finished my drink and the server is there in seconds, collecting it from my hand.

"Thank you," I say, to which he bows at the waist. Swanky.

When I turn, someone's standing in front of me. I lift

my attention to the lanky man in a steel-gray suit. He wears no tie, and the top buttons of his shirt are gaping open at his throat. A long, thin face, and no facial hair, but his eyes leave me gasping. They're green and have vertical slits like snakes.

He grins at my reaction, and his tongue slithers out, the tip forked, then pulls it back in. "It's alright," he says, with a slight hiss each time he says the letter S. "Everyone reacts like that the first time. You'd be surprised how uninformed most people are about serpents."

"Y-You're a snake shifter?" I ask, instantly forgetting about the rules.

He reaches a hand toward me, pushing a strand of hair from my face. His finger grazes my cheek, and his touch is icy cold. I pull back, my skin shivering.

"Saanp," he says, drawing his arm back to his side. "We're called Saanp, related back to the original *mythical* shape-shifting cobras, Ichchadhari Naags."

"That's fascinating," I mumble. "I've never met one before." And for good reason. All the romance books I've read talk about powerful wolf and bear shifters, but none with creepy-ass snakes. They are always the villains, even in fiction.

He smiles, and his pupils widen. All I can think of is that I'm eye to eye with a venomous viper ready to strike. I've never encountered one in real life, but I've watched enough documentaries to know you run like the wind when you encounter one.

"We are the most feared in the world. Our bites will kill instantly." His thin lips pull into a taut smile, revealing thin fangs as he leans in. "But we are incredible lovers. Saanp have two penises."

"Wow." I drag out the word, my gaze scanning the

room, knowing I need to get away from this creep. I notice a few of the other visitors also have snake eyes, but there are two guests with eyes black as coal.

Nice business partners the Kings associate with.

"What's your name, baby girl?" the snake man asks, and I can pick up a slight hint of an accent I can't place. But my festering creep factor is going off the charts.

"Well, it was a pleasure meeting you," I say, pretending I didn't hear his question.

Strong hands clasp me around my middle from behind, and I flinch, thinking it's one of his snake buddies.

"There you are," Cassius says, then lowers his lips to my ear, whispering, "For each rule you break, I'll punish you personally."

I force a laugh, shoving my elbow into Cassius's ribs. He barks a half-chuckle, half-grunt.

"He's always the joker," I say as the snake man watches us, then grabs my wrist. His nails are like claws, digging into my flesh, and hauls me right out of Cassius's arms.

"We have unfinished business." The guy's voice deepens, and my adrenaline spikes. Is he kidding? I'm already reaching down to grab my heel. Sure, they're not my stilettos, but beggars can't be choosers. The second he tries to grope me, I'm aiming for the windpipe.

Cassius pushes right past me. His large palm shoves into the snake's face with such a loud smack that it takes him off guard. He staggers back, releasing his grip on my arm.

I stumble, rubbing the skin where his fingernails indented into my skin like half-moons. *What a dick.*

"Listen carefully, lizard breath. Touch her and I'll kill you," he growls, his voice gravelly and deep. The promise of death pours from his glare.

I stiffen and square my shoulders. I'm not scared even if I am shaking at how quickly that escalated. I've seen men fight for me before, but this is very different. Cassius is not a security guard, but a damn demon.

Dracon is there in a flash, slamming a hand against Cassius's chest to push him back, then turns to the snake man.

"I'm sure it's just a misunderstanding," Dracon explains in a diplomatic voice, though there's an underlying darkness beneath his words. "Cassius can be overly protective of his toys."

Toys? I stiffen, glaring at Dracon. Look who's fucking talking–the man who has his possessions mounted all over the walls like trophies.

Cassius whips me around, fury etched on his face as he grabs my arm and drags me into the farthest, dark corner of the room, where we vanish into the shadows.

"What did I say?" he spits my way.

I rip my arm out of his grasp. "I did nothing wrong. He spoke to me first."

"Then you walk away," he murmurs low under his breath.

"Well, I didn't want to be rude. They are *your* guests, after all." I shrug nonchalantly while my wrist throbs from where that prick held me so tight.

"These men are worms. One word from a gorgeous thing like you, and they take that as you coming onto them. They fuck females, then devour them, literally."

Well, shit.

"Are they from another gang?" I ask.

"Cobra Strike." He draws in a sharp breath. "We're trying to form an alliance with them."

"Because of me and Franco? And the vampires?"

"Everything isn't about you, Eve," he says. When I glare at him, he adds, "No, this was something we've been working on *before* you were dropped on our doorstep, so we'd appreciate it if you didn't fuck it up."

Dropped on their doorstep? Was he kidding? "I think what you meant to say was kidnapped."

Cassius pinches the bridge of his nose, growing more annoyed by the second. "It's safer for you just to return to your room. I made a mistake in convincing Dracon to let you join us. And I'm sure he's going to remind me of them the second he can grab me."

"Fine, fine. I won't talk to anyone else. Just tell me what you need me to do from here on out."

"What I *need*, Eve, is for someone to bend you over the table, rip your underwear off, and fuck that smartass attitude out of you."

I arch an eyebrow. "And I guess you're the man for the job?" My head is screaming to not flirt with these monsters because it won't end well for me, but as usual, my body double-crosses me. My clit pulses at the idea.

Stealing a glance over his shoulder, I spy Dracon handing the snake asshole a drink and patting him on the back. Fucking suck up.

"If the Kings of Eden are so untouchable, why even bother with Viper Strike." My thoughts slip out as words.

"Cobra Strike," he corrects under his breath. "They hold power in the south which offers us an opportunity to enter a new business venture."

"Oh?"

"It was Saxon's idea," he says, turning briefly to look at Dracon too.

"Saxon?" Who is that?

Cassius shakes his head frantically. "Forget it," he says

in a rush as if he's just revealed something he shouldn't have to me. But the gears are already turning in my head. Is there another King I haven't met yet? Maybe a boss above Dracon? If he was following his idea, this Saxon guy must be pretty important, right?

Cassius's head whips back to face me. "Be careful, Eve. You may be new to this side of the world we live in, but it's no Disney World. It's Hell on earth."

"And you're the devil," I say plainly.

Nodding, his eyes darken until the blacks of the pupils swallow up the irises. "You bet." Then he marches away from me.

I don't leave the corner right away, but draw in deep breaths.

For the millionth time, I wonder what the fuck I'm doing here. Like Cassius said, I don't belong in their world. They need to just let me go.

Just then, the server walks past me, and I grab another drink.

"I'll bring you some cola for that," he says with a closed lipped smile.

"Nope, I need this one straight." I throw it back.The whiskey feels hot like lava as it rushes down my throat, then I return the glass to the tray. "Thanks," I choke out.

For the next hour, I remain in the room, trying my best to listen in on their conversations but not cause a stir. Though, what I do hear makes no sense to me in any context. That's when I catch Knox staring at me.

He's standing out on the balcony of the living room, his back to the railing, night encasing him as the wind blows his hair. It's his eyes, though, that catch my attention. They seem to have taken on a light glow...

I watch him from across the room for a few moments,

then I take one more look around. Everyone else is in conversation, so I decide to head to my room, where I'll barricade the door my *damn* self. I don't trust any of the men in this penthouse.

I'm halfway across the long room when someone slaps a hand across my ass and squeezes me hard while greedy fingers dive between my crack.

I flinch, completely taken by surprise, and let out a yelp. I snap around, fury pounding through my veins at being groped.

That son of a bitch viper is staring at me with shrewd green eyes, and he's stroking his erection over his pants. "I'm going to enjoy fucking that fat ass of yours, two cocks at once."

In that same breath, someone flies right past me and slams into the snake. The blade in Knox's hand glints in the low lights as he thrusts it toward the man, whose eyes widen.

The Mortem Blade pierces his throat, slicing across his flesh as easily as butter. Green blood splashes, striking me across my face and my chest. I scream just as the guy's body stiffens suddenly from rigor mortis. Then falls over, dead.

Warm, gooey blood drips down my cheeks and chin, and terror seizes me.

Then the whole room bursts into chaos. People are shouting, and everyone is darting around.

I recoil, my back hitting the wall, frantically rubbing the blood off my face. I can feel it sliding down my skin, and I fall to the floor, gasping for air.

Shit! Shit! Shit!

Flashes of the past rushing at me in waves.

Living on the streets. Waking up in the park. My two

friends dead. Butchered. Covered in their blood. Someone had killed them while I slept. Cut them up good, and I fucking slept through it, not hearing a thing.

Not a damn thing.

Over the years, I've learned to accept that I survived and my friends didn't, and to embrace my fear. I'm stronger than this, and yet the memories spring back.

Just breathe. Just breathe.

I'm hugging my knees, pain throbbing in my temples.

Knox's gripping his blade by his side, cursing under his breath, looking mad with himself. He's glaring at the dead man he killed so fast. Guess he lost his chance to torture him like he wanted. Behind him, Dracon tries to put out the monstrous explosion of shouting and flying punches with his other guests.

That's when a shadow falls over me, and I flinch. "Get off me," I yell.

"I'm not going to hurt you," Cassius says, then picks me up and wraps me in his strong arms. "But I need to get you out of here."

My head is still spinning, and I keep wiping at the blood, feeling its stickiness on me. My skin shivers in ripples.

Looking back into the room, Dracon is manically running around, probably trying to salvage the night with Cobra Strike.

But my gaze falls to the dead snake guy where Knox had left him.

And all I can think is that Cassius is right. I'm already in Hell with them.

CHAPTER SEVENTEEN

EVE

$\mathcal{I}$'m sitting on the edge of the bathtub before I know it, while Cassius shuts the door. Still, the sounds of angry shouts from the party boom. God, Dracon is going to be so pissed, but it's not my fault he deals with sleazeballs.

Cassius doesn't seem to notice or care about the noise. He's grabbing a towel and wetting it in the sink.

"I'm fine," I say, though I'm lying through my teeth. I'm still shaking, trying to just process what happened.

I remind myself the supes in this country are ruthless. They'll strike without warning. Add a high-stakes criminal ring into the mix, and that's asking for some deadly trouble.

I grab a nearby rag and frantically wipe my face and chest. It comes back covered in green snake blood. I cringe. And I swear I can still feel the stuff on me, almost wriggling.

Cassius kneels in front of me on the small black bath mat. "You're shaking." He reaches over with the towel and wipes the fabric tenderly across my chin.

He studies my face as he keeps cleaning me with a steady hand. His black suit seems to be molded to his body. He's flawless.

This man…this demon has drawn my attention from the first time I saw him. He has that hard look on his face that tells me he notices everything. Of the three Kings, he's the one who seems most approachable, but it's all smoke and mirrors. He studies me closely, like a predator, waiting for the right time to attack. Biding his time, plotting how to best make his next move.

"Saanp blood can be infectious," he suddenly explains with a rough edge to his voice, as he notices me observing him. "Did you get any in your eyes or mouth?"

I shake my head. "I don't think so."

"Let's clean you up just in case. Saanp venom has neurotoxin effects if it gets into your bloodstream. If you start slurring your words or start falling over, we'll know." He gives me a soft look, as if he cares for me. But I know he doesn't.

"None of that makes me feel better." I swallow the thickness in my throat, not wanting to admit that the stunt back at the party shook me hard.

He collects the damp towel and resumes wiping the snake blood from my face in gentle strokes. "You'll be fine, I promise. And if not, you may need to try more of my blood."

"Right," I say, even if my heart is doing that thing where it flutters at his nearness. "So you can carve your name into my hip again? That was a bastard move."

"What are you going to do about it?" He grins.

Maybe it's the adrenaline in my veins, or the lingering anger at him branding me when I was weak, but I lash out with a fist. I aim for his jaw, but he moves at the last minute and I nail him on the collarbone instead.

He stares down at me. "Feel better now?"

"No, actually. I'd rather mash your balls in a blender."

"Oooh, keep talking dirty to me," he laughs.

Just thinking about the mark has my hip aching. "Why would you do that?"

"When I lick something, I consider it mine."

I glare at him. "Asshole."

He laughs again, the sound light and airy. He's the kind of monster who doesn't live in books or movies, but is flesh and blood.

"Don't pull that shit again. And just for your information, as soon as I get out of here, I'm having it removed. I'm not yours or anyone else's."

"If you say so."

Blowing out a long breath, I try to calm my racing heart. Everything about these Kings sends my pulse into a frenzy. "How can you be so cruel yet kind at the same time?" It's confusing as fuck.

"Take off your dress," he commands, completely ignoring my question, which I suspect is on purpose.

I laugh, loud and fake. "Hell no."

"It's not a good idea to wear something covered in venom."

I look down and find green blood everywhere…

Considering this stuff is toxic, I want it as far from me as possible. Though I also don't want to strip down to just my underwear in front of Cassius, considering I'm not wearing a bra.

He's on his feet and takes my elbow to follow him. "Hands in the air."

My stomach clenches with uncertainty. Then reluctantly, I do as he instructs, and he pulls at my sleeves first, tugging the dress off me fast.

Instantly, I cross my arm over my breasts as I stand there in just my thong.

As he turns to throw the ruined dress on the floor, I snatch a clean towel and wrap it around myself, tucking it under my arms. Despite the coverage, I feel vulnerable and exposed in front of him, two things I rarely feel when half naked.

"I think that party went well." I try to laugh, but it comes out sounding strained. "At least it wasn't boring, right?"

The corner of his mouth edges upward. "Nothing's boring with us."

Understatement of the year.

He resumes cleaning the green blood from my skin. Making his way across my collarbone with the towel, his concentration focused on every stroke. It's not lost on me how much he lingers around my cleavage, even though all the blood there is gone.

"You have beautiful skin," he muses. "Smooth as silk."

"Aha." I'm slightly disturbed by how easily my body responds to his fingertips gliding over my skin. There's heat in his eyes, and my body tightens.

Does he know the effect he has on me? How hard my nipples pinch? How hot I'm growing between my thighs?

He just grins in his twisted, Cheshire cat kind of way, and I hate that look. It's sinister, secretive, and it makes my stomach flip-flop with lust every damn time.

"So tell me, who is the real vixen, Evelyn Dalton?" he asks, which takes me by surprise. "You dance at Kat's Kradle, but no one ends up working there on purpose."

"Eve," I correct automatically. "I don't go by Evelyn anymore."

"Ah, yes. Eve." Nodding, he licks his lips, his interest growing. "I've tasted the darkness in your soul, so what broke you?"

I eye him, wondering just how much I should reveal to this demon. I hate how easily he's able to read me, especially a past that I've been repressing for years.

"Why are you so curious?" I ask.

He shrugs. "I'm a noisy son of a bitch."

I don't know why, but that makes me laugh. It's so blunt, shockingly so, but very much true to him.

"Okay then." Got to appreciate his honesty, right? Sighing, I decide it can't hurt to give him a little bit of Eve Dalton's sorry excuse of a life. At least a skim of the surface. "I was young. I was kicked out of my house and ended up on the streets. Did what I had to, to survive. The end."

He chuckles. "That's all?"

"So, what's your story?" I counter.

His lips tilt upward in a smirk, then he drops the dirty towel behind him. He turns and places his hands on the edge of the tub on either side of me. We're so close now, his breath flutters across my face.

"My life has been long, chaotic, and broken. Something I don't like to discuss and don't wish upon anyone. It's something I've learned to live with to keep any kind of sanity."

I almost laugh out loud if he thinks he's sane, but I go in a different direction. "Sounds deep. Is that how you avoid talking about your past? Making it sound terrifying?"

He laughs, deep and throaty, and I watch his tongue slip out to run along his bottom lip.

There's mystery around him just as much as there is with Dracon and Knox. He threatens me, but tends to me, yet never shares anything about himself.

This literal demon has inner demons too and they're just as terrifying as anything Hell could conjure up. I can see it in his eyes.

Maybe he's right. There may be things I shouldn't know about him. Though, it doesn't make me any less curious.

"Dracon's gonna be pissed about tonight," I state, changing the subject, seeing as Cassius isn't going to share any more about himself. And neither am I.

"Perhaps, but shit goes sideways all the time. It's nothing new."

We stare at each other, and my heart beats louder while my stomach clenches again. What I want to ask him about is who Saxon is–the guy he'd mentioned before. Like, does he live here too? And why haven't I seen him around?

But then Cassius leans in closer, forcing me to shift back.

"W-What are you doing?" I stammer.

"What does it look like?" His hand slides across my back and pulls me toward him. My breasts press against his chest, my body instantly coming alive from his touch.

When a whimper slips past my lips, his gaze drops, and lust swims in his eyes.

I press my palms to his chest, pushing him back. "Cassius," I warn him.

"You can fight it all you want," he begins, voice dropping to a low rumble, "but we both know where this is going."

My throat is suddenly dry, and my heart skips a beat, but I don't respond instantly, so he takes my silence as his answer. One he approves of.

"I thought so," he says. "So let's get it all out there, shall we? I want to fuck you, Eve. After watching you and Dracon in the hallway the other day, the memory has tortured me. I can't get the look of you on your knees out of my head."

What kind of woman does he think I am?

A horny one, apparently.

Well…I guess he isn't wrong there. I've been kidnapped by the Kings of Eden, and when I should be fearing for my life, I'm constantly thinking about their hands on me. Pleasing me in the worst possible ways. I hate myself for it, and yet, I find myself leaning forward.

Despite everything that he's done to me, I crave him.

"I don't think–"

His mouth is on mine, his breaths escalating. My heart beats harder against my rib cage, my inhales raspy and short. I should push him away, but I find myself melting, wanting him. He kisses with strength and aggressiveness, and his tongue plunges into my mouth, dominating and unrelenting.

He's the devil and kisses like a tornado, ripping me to shreds. Completely undoing me at the seams.

"I know you want me," he growls, his lips brushing mine. He watches me the whole time. Tortured blue eyes study my reaction, and at his words, I shudder at the storm of arousal sweeping over me.

When he swallows me back into his kiss again, I return it just as intensely and let him draw my tongue into his mouth. He growls as he enjoys sucking on it.

Pushing himself between my legs, he savagely tears the towel off me.

I gasp, but his hands are already all over my body.

Mostly skin to skin, my breasts are pressed against his

solid chest and all that stands between him claiming me is the thin fabric of my thong.

A loud thump smacks into our wall out in the hallway.

I startle, breaking from our kiss. Dust and plaster falls from the ceiling. We both stare at the door. It's odd to say, but at the moment, I'm thankful for the big giant metal door they had installed.

"It's World War three out there," I rasp, still breathless from his harsh kisses.

When his eyes dip to my breasts, he sighs heavily, the torture clear on his face. Hunger. Need. Indecision.

One last time, his tongue sweeps over my lips and his hand fondles my right breast, squeezing it. I moan, arching my chest toward him, my nipples aching for more.

"Fuck, this is going to kill me," he groans and does the last thing I expect–he pulls away from me. "If I don't get out there, Dracon will rip my head off my shoulders."

Taking my arm, he walks me over to the shower, and pulls open the glass door. He turns on the tap, the water freezing cold at first when it hits my skin, causing me to yelp and jump back. As the temperature gradually gets warmer, I turn to him.

"Are you planning on joining me?" I ask him with a cocked brow. I really don't want this to end and for him to leave. I want him to crave me. To beg for me. To lose control for me.

For a brief moment, he hesitates, considering my offer, but instead of stepping inside the shower with me, he holds onto my jaw and forces me to look up into his possessive blue eyes. "I just know you're going to ruin me."

Warmth settles between my thighs at his promise.

Another thud hits the wall outside, louder this time. Closer.

"Take a shower," he says abruptly, his gaze swinging to the door. "You've got venom in your hair."

"Oh. Okay." I hold back from whimpering at how weak he makes me when I should have my head screwed on.

A war rages on his face, but spinning on his heel, he walks out of my room, back into the fight, with the door locking securely behind him.

More commotion thunders outside my four walls, but all I can think about is how easily I'm falling victim to these dangerous men. That, instead of running from them, they make me feel exhilarated and desperate for more.

Knowing there's nothing else for me to do at the moment, I do as Cassius instructed and step into the hot water. My lips are sore from Cassius's brutish kiss, while my pussy wet and needy.

What was I thinking?

Better question is, what the fuck have I gotten myself into?

CHAPTER EIGHTEEN

In the morning, bags of designer clothes arrive in my room, including—to my complete surprise and delight—bras that actually fit. Could Cassius feeling me up last night really give him what he needed to determine I was a DDD?

Nah.

Today, I opted for a slightly bohemian shirt and faded jeans with a pair of black ankle boots. Not as revealing as what I'm usually wearing, but it's comfortable, which works for me. And, of course, the boots have somewhat of a heel just in case I have to make a quick getaway.

The sound of footsteps draws my attention to my bedroom door opening.

"How are you doing?" Dracon asks, stepping inside, and I lift my gaze to his, hit instantly by a ripple of excitement and dread running down my spine at seeing him. Talk about being conflicted.

"Last night might have been scary for you..." he goes on but pauses. He appears slightly uncomfortable, which confuses me. Especially since he's always so confident in everything he does.

"You think?" I answer, hoping he doesn't notice how easily my body reacts to him. "Anyway, I'm fine. I haven't died of poisoning yet, much to your disappointment, I'm sure."

"If I wanted you dead, Eve, I would've done it the second I met you."

Why does that sound strangely sincere and almost...*kind*?

It's official. I've been with them too long.

"Thank...you?" I'm unsure how to respond to that one. But even with his strange...lapse in personality, I can't forget how he's treated me since I arrived. How close he came to fucking me up against the wall. How helpless he makes me feel. Two times he's done that to me...and both times I melted beneath his touch, his taunting.

My growing dislike of Dracon does nothing to ease the deepening pulse beating between my thighs.

What scares me is that I'll give him what he wants if he pushes me hard enough, and he knows it. He's proved it time and time again.

And that's going to get me into serious shit.

"What you need to understand is that while you're with the Kings of Eden, you will be protected." His brows pinch as he stares at me.

"Protected from who?" I ask.

"Your enemies and ours," he replies simply.

"But who's going to protect me from you three?" That's the real question here, isn't it? They are just as deadly and a hell of a lot more addicting.

He stares at me with something dark and nefarious

glinting in his eyes. When he speaks again, his voice is deeper, huskier. "That one I can't answer."

Yikes. Okay then.

"Well, if you want to start being the good guy, how about you begin by finding Kat. Or even checking in on Kat's Kradle and seeing if the other girls there are safe."

"I'm not the good guy, Eve. I never will be." A smile tugs on his lips as he closes the distance between us in two long strides. "But maybe I can put your mind at ease today."

Silence.

I frown, waiting for him to elaborate. When he doesn't, I ask, "And how's that?"

"Come on. We're going for a drive." Abruptly, he turns and heads for the door.

I'm so stunned that he's suggesting we leave the Tower, that I don't move at first. I can only stare at him, dumbfounded. Grunting, he returns to my side, grabs me by the elbow, and yanks me out of the room.

Annoyance and anger flares awake inside me. I don't know why he thinks he can man-handle me all the time. It's not right. But, like every time before, when I try to fight back and jerk myself away, he only bears down, holding me tight enough to leave bruises on my skin.

"Fuck, Dracon! You're hurting me!"

He pulls me again, making me stumble right into his chest. Pain zigzags up my shoulder, making tears prickle in my eyes. "You will respect me, Eve."

"You get respect when you give respect," I bite back and wrench against his hold. "I'm tired of being treated like your fucking lapdog."

As he half-drags me down the hall to the elevator, he laughs. It's a strange sound coming from him, but it's fleeting. The second the elevator's doors roll closed, his gaze darkens on me.

The air grows hotter, thicker, or maybe it's just me. Being anywhere alone with him is unnerving, but being in such a small space alone with him? It's suffocating. His entire presence seems to fill up every inch of the elevator. I can hardly breathe.

After he punches in another code into the panel and presses the button labeled *Garage*, he whirls around and closes the distance between us.

Oh, fuck. I retreat, my back hitting the wall.

His fingers run under my chin, his thumb teasing me just below my lower lip. "No one challenges me, Eve. No one."

Not until me.

It'd be smarter for me to shrink back and grovel, which I'm sure everyone else does in Dracon's presence, but there's something about him that makes me want to fight back. I've dealt with too many dickheads with overstuffed egos in my life. And I've never been the type of girl to just roll over and show my belly. I'm sure as shit am not going to start now. Even if it may end up killing me.

Dracon's mouth moves so close to mine that I inhale his sexy, woodsy scent. Trying my best to appear indifferent, I stiffen, but his nearness is sending my stomach into a flutter. My inner magic detector is going off the charts. His energy buzzes across my skin, electric and primal. Whatever kind of shifter he is, he's stronger than anything else I've ever met before.

"No matter what you say, no matter what you do, I'll never be yours," I rasp, my arousal flaring and burning within me. His scent alone awakens memories, takes me back to the things he's promised me with his body but never delivered. And right now, I can almost taste his cock in my mouth, sweet and salty, and remember how big he was as I sucked him down deep. Watching him come undone had been icing on the cake.

When it comes to Dracon, I'm going to have to beat him at his own game.

My cheeks flush at the way he watches me, as though he can read my thoughts.

"Oh, that's where you're wrong," he says. "You were mine the moment you entered my home."

Frustration squeezes my lungs, and I fight against my own cravings.

"You are a beautiful creature, Eve. There's no denying that. There's also no denying that your body calls to me, that you like that I take what I want, and that I'm rough with you."

Shit.

"I-I don't know what you're talking about," I whisper, the tremor in my voice obvious.

Studying me, Dracon straightens. He doesn't believe a word I've said—of course he doesn't. The truth is all over me—on my face, in my tone. Hell, he's a shifter so he can probably smell my arousal. That's one of their things, right? I'm pretty sure.

Just then, the elevator chimes, singling out arrival. But when the doors open again to reveal a dark underground garage filled with expensive cars, Dracon doesn't move to leave. His gaze sears into my flesh.

"Listen to me here and now, Eve Dalton. When I fuck you, I will *fuck* you. There will be no sweet. No soft and gentle. No romance. It'll be raw, vicious, and wild. And then, when it's all said and done, you'll turn around and beg me for *more.*"

My body shakes with desire, with fury, and my hands are itching to strike. To wipe the smile off his damn beautiful face. "You're a real bastard."

"I never claimed to be anything else."

He's pushing me until I break. I recognize this now.

When he whirls around and strides into the garage, the haze in my head clears. I bat away the fog that weakens me whenever I'm around him, but it still takes me a while to move my feet again.

The elevator dings once more, and as the doors start to close, I quickly hop out behind him. The chill of the cement structure seeps into my bones, and I immediately wish Dracon had let me grab a coat or something against the cold weather.

Hugging myself, I hurry after him. "W-Where are we going?" I ask as he scans the rows of sleek sports cars, suped up SUVs, and custom-made Rolls-Royces. Maserati, Ferraris, and even a Bentley... So much money in one central location. But that's not what I'm only seeing here. What I'm looking at is another potential exit strategy. If I could just find out what the code to access the elevator is, then I could maybe hijack one of these vehicles and drive off into the sunset, never to see the Kings or Andover City ever again.

"You wanted to drive by Kat's Kradle, did you not?" he questions, glancing at me from over his shoulder.

Excitement picks up my pace until I'm practically running to keep up with his long strides. "Yes! Yes! Of course!" I'm over eager, I know, but I can't help it. The thought of getting to see the girls again—of Mercy and Demi, hell, even Mack—has me giddy.

I hope they are all okay...

"I just have one rule for you," he says abruptly, but I already know what he's going to say.

"Don't run."

"Good girl. You're learning." His gaze lingers over me, watching for my reaction. This man is a predator. Whether it's physically, verbally, or emotionally, Dracon is demanding I submit to him. If I don't, he's going to punish me. And that's what he wants—he *wants* to punish me. So I can't give in, no matter how much he draws on my desires.

I won't submit and I won't give him a reason to punish me. It's going to be a tricky dance, but I'm going to do it. I won't let him break me.

Dracon moves straight for a completely black Bugatti. It's sexy. It has two doors, sleek lines and a ridiculously low body, and the windshield appears to curve around into the side windows like it's one piece. This machine was made to be noticed.

"Wow," I breathe.

"This is my car," he explains and his lips tick up at the corner. "It's called Bugatti La Voiture Noire, simply meaning the black car." He runs his fingers along the top tenderly, unlike the way he touches me.

"Guessin' it cost you a pretty penny," I say.

"Over eighteen million."

I choke on my next breath. "Are you kidding me? You could buy a small island for that." What sort of man spends eighteen million on a car?

When he opens the driver's side door, he just says, "Get in."

I'm suddenly getting hives thinking I'll scratch or break something that'll cost me my life. But he's already sitting in the driver's seat, and well, I am partly curious to see what a machine like this can do. So I sit shotgun among all the black leather and fancy buttons and screens. The only other color is the vibrant blue lights flashing across the dashboard as the engine roars to life.

The seats are buttery soft and race car inspired with a wide center console that curls upward, making it seem as though we're in separate cabins.

Then we're off.

I frantically pull my seat belt on. When I say we're off, Dracon speeds right for the closed exit doors like an adrenaline junkie. Tires squeal and panic flares through my body.

As we peel around a corner to find another row of extravagant cars and the exit doors lifting. A steep incline upward and suddenly we're in what seems to be a tunnel. Yellow lights blink on along the wall, carving a path for us through the darkness.

"There are tunnels under the city?" I ask, noticing more turns veering in different directions from this one.

"I had them built," he explains like it's nothing. "I loathe traffic."

It isn't long before we ascend again and he takes his foot off the gas. Another door slides open upon our approach. Light pours in from outside, my eyes stinging at the brightness.

He speeds forward once more, right into traffic.

"Watch out," I cry out, strangling the door handle.

He takes the turn so sharply, he literally slides the car sideways, tires skidding, forcing himself into the line of vehicles. Everyone else swerves out of the way, one person even driving up on the sidewalk, frantically honking, because no one wants to be in an accident with a sports car like this.

"It's okay," he tells me.

"Really? Because you could have fooled me. This car is worth eighteen million dollars, and you treat it like the Batmobile."

Like everything he does, he even commands control over the road. Instead of responding, he hits a button on the dashboard and something classical starts to play.

Is that Beethoven?

He's crazy.

My pulse is pounding in my temples. Unfurling my fingers from the door handle I'm holding with a death grip, I try to calm my breathing and relax back into my seat.

Outside, people are strolling along the sidewalks, shopping, and sitting at cafes. I miss that life and remind myself I will find it again, that I won't feel like I'm about to die every day. Or put my friends in danger.

The longer we drive, the more my gut twists with thoughts of Kat. It tears me up that she's in danger because of me. I wish more than anything I had killed Franco that night, then none of this would be happening.

"You okay?" Dracon asks me, his hand on my thigh, drawing me out of my thoughts. Warmth travels through me immediately.

I look over at him, nodding.

"You're breathing really heavy," he explains.

I blink numbly. "Just worried about Kat. It's my fault she's in this situation."

"The decisions Franco makes are not because of you. Remember that. We'll make sure he regrets what he's done."

"And what if we're too late? What if he tortures her, kills her?" For a moment, I want to scream with frustration, to punch something hard. Though I resist the urge to put any dents in the car.

"Franco will die," Dracon replies. He's so confident that the promise rolls smoothly off his lips. "My team is searching for his hideouts to track him and your boss down. We will find her."

I wish I could be so certain, like he is.

"He's just another cockroach in this city for me to eradicate. It's unfortunate we weren't able to strike a deal with Cobra Strike, but after their Alpha touched you, it sealed their fate. I'll destroy them, too."

"I ruined your meeting," I begin.

"I should have known better than to let those bastards anywhere near you."

We both fall silent, and in that stillness, Dracon and I have found a sliver of peace amid the war raging between us. There's a first for everything.

We turn down Goldcrest Street in no time, causing my heart to skip a beat. I lean forward in my seat. Kat's Kradle stands out with its red walls and neon sign farther ahead.

As we pull up, the first thing I notice is the lack of cars parked out front. That's okay. There's no way the lot in the back isn't full. It never mattered what time of day it was—Kat's was busy the moment the doors opened.

What takes me off guard is all the windows in the apartments above have their curtains drawn. Is anyone still living here, or have the girls moved out?

Can I blame them for leaving?

Dracon parks out front of the club in one of the many vacant spots.

"It looks closed… Empty," he mutters as he throws open his door and hops out. Urgency churns in my veins to rush upstairs and check who's there. The last time I'd been inside, there had been gunshots and screaming… panic.

"I need to check if anyone is still living here," I say.

"Alright. Let's be quick."

As I jump down from my seat, Dracon comes around to meet me.

"Let's go around the back to the apartments' entrance," I tell him and he nods.

We're several feet down the side alley, when a whizzing sound zips right past my head. So fast and intense, I feel the heat graze my ear.

Thwack!

Something small slams into the stone building feet from us.

What the—

I can't even form the thought in my mind before Dracon is throwing me behind him, shielding me with his body. That's when realization seizes me, along with utter, paralyzing dread.

Gunfire! We're being shot at!

In the next millisecond, Dracon lifts me into his arms and sprints down the alley. My heart tries to break out of my chest as fear stampedes over me. He can run fast as hell, but somehow, two more gunshots bounce off the wall right behind us, just inches from away, and I yelp.

"Sonofabitch!" he bellows.

Next thing I know, he's kicked open the back door to Kat's Kradle and shoulders his way inside. He drops me on my feet, and starts stripping off his clothes in a flash, leaving me stunned and shaky.

"Stay," he roars.

Outside, more shots ring out, and I flinch with each one.

"W-What are you doing?" I gasp. "Who the hell is shooting at us?"

Dracon's suddenly naked, muscles bulging, the nerves

in his neck twitching. Something wild booms in his eyes. Something terrifyingly dark and unlike anything I've seen from him before.

I must be imagining things because he looks like he's getting bigger… How is that possible?

Dracon stares through me, brows pinching, and his shoulders inch up with tension.

"Are you okay?" I ask nervously. "Are you…having a stroke?"

He doesn't respond, but cracks his neck, muttering under his breath. His facial expression twists, his lips warping into a menacing grin.

"Dracon?"

His body twists, bones cracking under his darkening skin. He turns to the open doorway, every inch of him shuddering.

Oh…my…god… He's shifting!

But into what?

My gut squeezes, and I stumble backward.

Something pointy is poking out from behind his shoulder blades, stretching his skin. I cringe, and yet I can't look away. Whatever he is, it's huge.

With a deafening roar, he runs and throws himself outside, his body continuing to change midair.

Black scales cover his skin. Long neck. Claws. Wings stretching outward, blotting out the sun.

He's a full-blown, fucking dragon. An enormous one at that.

Shit, now his name makes sense, doesn't it? But I didn't even know dracon shifters existed, let alone *dragons* at all.

Beating his black wings, he climbs higher into the sky, unleashing a tremendous blaze of fire.

I flinch, swallowing hard, to know I've been pushing my luck with that creature...

Fuck. Fuck. Fuck.

The sight of him leaves me gasping. Dragons in myth all carry the same characteristics, more or less. They're close to unstoppable and known for their fury, their jealousy, and their obsession of collecting things, like gold.

Or magical axes.

It all makes sense now, his personality and control issues...

When more shots boom outside, I throw the door shut, lock it, and sprint upstairs. Frantically, I check every bedroom for the other girls from the club only to find they're all empty. The closets are bare too. They've taken their stuff and run, and I pray they are somewhere safe.

Moving to a window, I carefully peek out just as a black sedan screeches to a halt in the middle of the street. Two men are hanging out the window, holding semi-automatics, and shooting manically into the sky.

Dracon drops from a rooftop like a bolt of lightning, so fast and powerful, I clutch the window frame until my knuckles turn white. Mouth wide, flames blasting, he swoops toward the car despite bullets peppering him.

He grabs hold of one guy with his gaping mouth, biting him right in half.

I scream, leaping away from the window.

My insides feel like they're trembling, but despite my better judgment, I step back to the glass and peer at the streets below. The black car is on fire but Dracon is nowhere in sight.

Three other men in black leather vests are running on foot right past the front of the building, then vanish around the block.

Black Spades. Has to be.

Of course, Franco had his men watch this place in case I returned.

I want to cry out with frustration. My home's been turned into a damn war zone.

I clench my fists by my sides, the ripples of power within me slithering down my spine, a power that comes with rage and swallows me with its darkened embrace. It comes with promises to break the world.

But when an ear-shattering roar shudders the walls all around me, I snap out of my trance. The hairs on my arms stand on end for a different reason.

Dracon.

I sprint down the stairs, my pulse thundering. The stench of something burning hits me. I scramble to the nearest window and frantically push the curtains aside.

Someone drops out of the air just then, landing on a pile of dead bodies. Blood and body parts, some torn to shreds, others burned to a black char.

The image sickens me. Bile rises, and I know I'm going to be sick. It's coming up so fast it hurts. I turn away and instantly hurl my guts out onto the floor.

Wiping my mouth, I jerk up and notice something.

Silence.

Cruel, petrifying silence.

With harsh breaths, I stand still when a glint of black flashes in the alley slit in the curtains. I fly down the rest of the staircase, snatch up his clothes from the floor, and step into the light.

Dracon lands with a thunderous thump, shaking the foundation in his dragon form. His scales glin black with flecks of gold beneath the sun. His wings are tight against his massive body. He is huge and magnificent and terrifying.

I peer up, barely seeing his head, though I see the smoke and fire snorting from his nostrils.

My knees shake. Will I be his next victim? Does he even have control of his animal because earlier he looked anything but in control?

Another thunderous roar, and I cover my ears with how loud it booms. Then, Dracon starts shaking, his dragon seamlessly withdrawing. Wings fold into his back, the torn flesh knitting over them as he shifts back into the human form that I know.

In moments, he stands near the carnage he's created, mumbling something under his breath. His brow twisted in what looks like confusion to me.

I stare at him for a long time, waiting to see what he'll do next. But fifteen minutes pass and he does nothing but talk to himself.

When sirens sing in the air, a new wave of panic washes over me. The cops are coming.

With his clothes in hand, I step out of the safety of the club and into the alley with him.

Right away, he turns to catch me approaching, and his nostrils flare wide as he takes in my scent.

"I'm not the enemy," I say nervously. "But you better put your clothes on before you're arrested for indecent exposure."

His head tilts as he regards me, as if he's still having trouble shaking off the animal side of him.

"The cops are on their way," I go on, hoping he understands that our time is limited if we want to make a clean getaway. "We need to get out of here."

"The enemy is dead," he states.

"Yes, you did a great job of burning them to a crisp." I

toss the clothes at his feet, trying my damndest to keep my eyes fixed on him. Only on him and not the dead bodies everywhere or the blood splattered all over the blacktop.

He only stares at the clothes like he's forgotten how to dress.

Sirens ring through the air, growing louder. They're going to be here any moment.

My heart's thundering. For fuck's sake. Looks like we're doing this the hard way.

Lurching forward, I shove my hand into the pocket of his pants on the ground and grab the car keys.

"Let's go," I say, grabbing him by the wrist.

He grabs his clothes and digs out a small silver flask from somewhere. With shaky hands, he unscrews the lid and holds it to his lips. Then he tilts his head and gulps down something.

I smell the alcohol instantly.

"What are you doing? We gotta go. Now."

Hastily, he wipes his mouth with the back of his hand. He's shaking, almost violently, and I'm starting to wonder if he's not the only one. I'm so scared, my teeth feel like they're chattering.

When his eyes sharpen on me, I see a sliver of the Dracon I know. It's quickly followed up with panic.

The police are so close now, I can hear their sirens echoing from adjacent streets.

"We need to GO!"

This time, Dracon listens, and we're both running back to the car. Him naked, me beyond confused.

He takes the keys from my hand, and by some miracle, we get into the car and take off. Several blocks away, the cops careen past us. I don't even want to imagine what they'll think when they arrive.

It's an image I wish I could forget.

Dracon doesn't say a word on the drive back to the penthouse. And I'm too stunned to do anything but stare absentmindedly outside the window.

Life seemed so much simpler before I got mixed up with the Kings of Eden. And now, part of me is terrified that I'm trapped in this chaos. That those simpler times will forever be just a memory.

*F*uck this.

I know it's all a part of the act we're forced to play. We have to get dressed up to put on a show and rub elbows with the most seedy and dangerous crime lords around. Masked as a charity auction, complete with champagne and black ties and bullshit. Like we don't want to all slit each other's throats if given the chance.

The living doesn't interest me, and I loathe social gatherings like the one Dracon is dragging us to. But he insists we have to talk to the Lord of Night's leader, Marius, to find out about the vamp attack. If it really was his men coming for Eve, well, then we may be in for a war—which is one of the only reasons I'm going to this auction without fighting too much. The idea of inciting a little chaos and bloodshed is enticing.

The second reason is an unexpected one for me. It's Eve.

She's been in her room since her outing to Kat's Kradle with Dracon yesterday, quieter than normal. Dracon gave us the rundown of what happened, including how he lost himself to rage and the dragon. Eve witnessed part of his darkness first hand, so it's no surprise she's a bit shaken up.

Today is a new day, though, and Dracon is back to his walking, talking, asshole human self. He had her dressed like a doll, and I'm starting to wonder if that's how he sees her–like one of the shiny objects he collects and displays in his trophy room. If she ends up staying with us for too long, I'm sure that's where she'll end up. Maybe even stuffed and posed, too.

It's the dragon in him. He's possessive of his treasures.

But even I can't deny that Eve looks radiant tonight. She's in a shimmering gold mermaid-style dress that clings to her perfect hourglass figure, dipping into a low V at her ample cleavage.

Those breasts… I want to bury myself in them until I'm so lost, I can't come back up for air. That'd be the best way to die. Suffocation by triple Ds.

She's painted her face with makeup, and it accents her beautiful face with smokey eyes and blood-red lips. What's even more shocking is that she's wearing the earrings I gave her. I hadn't expected that, but pride swells in my chest at seeing them dangling from her ears. Now she has something from each of us–the mark on her hip from Cassius, the earrings from me, and… a migraine from Dracon.

But that's the kind of gift he likes to give to everyone.

We're all crammed in the back of the limo, the three of us and Eve. After so many escape attempts and the run it with the snakes, Dracon wants to keep her close. At least, that's the excuse he gave when he announced she was coming along. Cassius had offered to stay behind with her, but Dracon shot that idea down before Cassius could even get the full sentence out of his mouth.

"All three of us going to this thing will make a statement," he had claimed when he'd tried explaining his plan.

"Yeah, like we're all in one place to make it easier for them to kill," Cassius huffed, clearly annoyed.

"The opposite, actually. That we aren't afraid of them killing us. That we don't see them as a threat at all."

It's always about power with him and looking like the biggest and baddest monster in the room. I was with Cassius there—it'll be fucking easy for the Lords to pick us all off if we show up together, but I keep my thoughts to myself. I'd be wasting my breath anyway.

Stupid. All of this is fucking stupid.

"Will you stop glaring a hole through me?" Eve warns. "It's making me uncomfortable."

For a second, I think she's talking to me, but when I see her glaring at Cassius, who's sitting across from her, I know I haven't been caught staring...yet.

Cassius flashes her a toothy, wicked grin. "What's wrong, sweetheart? I thought you were used to being ogled."

Wow, even I know that's a dick thing to say.

But Eve doesn't miss a fucking beat. "Only if you have a few hundreds to throw at me."

"Oh, ho!" Cassius laughs, then reaches into his tuxedo pocket for his wallet. "If you're going to flash me your tits, let me just—"

"Enough," Dracon barks from his place on Eve's left. "I don't want to hear another word out of any of you until we get to the convention center."

Cassius sticks his tongue out at him, which he ignores.

I push a finger past the tight collar of my tuxedo and

try to pull it a little looser, but it does nothing to help. These clothes are stiff and restrictive and just another thing I hate about being dragged to this event.

The cab falls silent, and my gaze drifts back to Eve. She's dwarfed by Dracon's massive size, but even though she sits with her chin lifted in fake confidence, I can see the heaviness of something else weighing her down.

I have a feeling her unease stems from more than just what happened yesterday or this superficial auction. She's worried about her friend–or boss, I should say. The one Franco has dangling on a hook somewhere for leverage.

It does seem ridiculous for us to be attending, parading around in gowns and tuxes, when someone she cares for, life is on the line. Even if it is to try and get an upper hand on the Spades and beat them at their own game.

The limo finally pulls up in front of the modern-style convention center with large arched windows and white stone facade. And an usher opens our door. Dracon is the first to get out, then Eve. He offers his hand to her, but she swats it away, which earns an amused chuckle from Cassius as he steps out next.

The moment I climb out and slam the door shut, the limo drives off and the four of us walk towards the entrance, where a large crowd is gathered, moving on slow feet to funnel inside. Dracon presses close to Eve as she shivers from the winter chill, even placing a hand to her lower back to guide her through the sea of bodies. Jealousy flares.

Cassius's constant flirting with her doesn't bother me, but Dracon… Seeing them together makes my skin crawl and anger bubble up. He thinks he deserves her just because of who he is–it's obvious from the way he treats her–and that's the furthest thing from the truth.

None of us deserve her.

Once we pass the threshold, we're escorted with the rest of the group to walk through a series of metal detectors. That's what's causing the delay.

"Wow, they're even checking for weapons," Cassius whispers to us.

"Doesn't surprise me," Dracon replies nonchalantly. "The Lords know who might show up at this event. They want to be the most powerful creatures in the room."

"Good thing we don't need guns and shit. *We* are the weapons."

Speak for yourself. My hand flies to the Mortem Blade's handle. There's no way in hell I'm letting it out of my sight again. Not for a second.

On cue, Dracon's gaze slides over to my belt, spotting it. "I told you to leave that at the apartment," he growls.

"And I told you to fuck off," I bite back.

"Knox," Cassius begins, trying to handle the situation with kid gloves. As always. All it does is aggravate me more. "Come on, man. You're going to screw this up for us. There's no way they're going to let you inside with that."

"Then I'll go home. It's not like I wanted to be here anyway," I retort. *And definitely not dressed like a fucking penguin.*

Eve's hand on my arm stops me, and my gaze drops, shocked she's touching me.

"Stay," she whispers, her green eyes shining brightly under the convention center's crystal chandelier. "I don't belong here either, and I feel a little less out of place with you here."

Her words stun me, and I'm unsure how to respond. Even without all the makeup and the expensive dress and jewels, she's the most radiant thing in the room. To me. But really, she feels as misplaced as I do?

Hesitating, I glance up at Cassius, who's wagging his brows behind Eve, so only I can see.

"Yeah, listen to the girl," he says with a smirk.

The sound of Dracon's throat clearing steals all our attention, and Eve's hand falls away from me. He nods toward a security guard who's pushing his way through the crowd to get to us, and I clench my jaw.

"Don't pick a fight," Dracon warns us. "We need to get to Marius first. Keep things civil, for now."

"Excuse me," the guard says, glancing between us with cautious eyes. One hand resting on the gun at his hip, just in case. As expected, he points to my blade. "You're going to have to either remove that from the building or leave. Weapons of any kind are not permitted at this event."

Fingers gripping the handle tighter, I debate whether or not to just kill this man where he stands. It's a tempting notion... and it *would* get me inside faster. And this boring tux could use a little color...

"Knox..." Dracon warns as if he can see the thoughts forming in my head.

Fucking prick. He always has to ruin my fun.

I don't move for a few seconds. Everyone's eyes are glued to me, waiting. Truthfully, I would rather go home and avoid this circus altogether, but Eve wanting me here is messing with my head. And so is the fact that I even give a fuck.

"Kings!" a friendly and familiar voice calls from behind the security guard. "I didn't expect you all to actually show up."

I know who it is before I see him, and he steps into view a second later. Square jaw shadowed with stubble, stylistic messy dark hair, and stormy blue eyes that are full of secrets–it isn't the first time we've crossed paths with Alec, and I'm sure it won't be the last.

Out of all the Lords of Night, he's really the only one I can stand for more than five minutes. It's probably because the vampire's always been amicable towards us, no matter what the situation is, and that's earned him some respect in my eyes.

Does it mean I trust him? Abso-fucking-lutely not. I know he's loyal to his master, as all the Lords are, and as Marius's right-hand, he's expected to hold him in the highest regard. Then there's also the tiny detail that his master may have sent Ladir and those vampires to fuck with us the other night, therefore breaking our already wobbly alliance… Can't forget that.

"No worries, Wes. I got this group," Alec says and waves the guard to return to his post. He's also dressed in a tuxedo, but his is slim fitted and a deep blue color.

"But sir–" He points to my blade, which hangs clear as day on my hip.

"I said, I got it." Alec's tone becomes more forceful, but the smile never leaves his face. Knowing better than to push back again, the guard leaves.

At least he solved my dilemma.

When we're alone, Alec grabs the end of one of the velvet rope barricades and opens it for us to pass through. Closing it behind us, he gestures for us to follow him into the grand ballroom where guests are drifting in and out, all dressed in their finery.

"Thanks for that," Cassius says to Alec as we step into the huge circular room, decorated in silvers and golds. Everything shines and glitters, screaming opulence and wealth. Waiters dressed in black and white glide through the crowd, holding trays of hors d'oeuvres and bubbly drinks. "Knox and his blade have just been reunited, and he's a bit touchy about leaving it alone."

I slide him a deadpan look.

Alec holds up a hand, silently telling him there's no need for the explanation. "We have no quarrels with you three, as you know. We've always stayed in our respective lanes, so I have no fear of that blade ever leaving its sheath."

Either he's more stupid than I thought *or* he's not afraid I'll use the Mortem Blade because the Lords have already prepared for a battle, expecting the worst. Both are possible.

"No quarrels, huh?" Dracon murmurs as he scans the faces around us, and I know he's hinting at the vampire attack.

Alec stops suddenly and turns to face him. "We did not invite you here to spill blood, Dracon. I was not lying about that."

Nostrils flaring, Dracon stares him down, but instead of pushing, he changes the topic. Alec will never reveal the information we need, not without his master's okay, so talking to him about it is pointless. "Where is Marius?"

"Busy," he says with a dismissive wave of his hand. "You know how it is with these things."

An excuse. He doesn't want us to see Marius. Or Marius doesn't want to be seen.

Dracon must sense that too because he snorts.

Alec laughs loudly. "Comes with the job, doesn't it? Always having to rub elbows and kiss babies."

"Or suck them dry..." Eve mumbles under her breath.

Being a vampire, Alec hears her snappy response, and

his gaze flicks her way. Noticing her for the first time, his brows shoot up, both surprised and intrigued.

"Well, well, well..." He looks her over, his tongue darting past his lips as if he's just come across a T-bone steak, and he hasn't eaten in days. "Who is this delectable morsel you've brought with you?"

Eve squares her shoulders, and the movement presses her tits up against the fabric of the dress. My mouth immediately goes dry. I practically swallow my tongue.

"Eve," she says without a hint of trepidation. She even holds out her hand for him to shake, which turns his smile into a wolfish one. She seems completely unbothered by him being a bloodthirsty creature of the night.

Impressed, Alec slides his hand into hers, but instead of shaking it, he brings it to his lips and presses a kiss on her knuckles. Then, he gently turns her palm up and pauses at the sight of her wrist and the bluish veins there.

"Hmmm..." he muses and peers up at her. "I can smell the magic in your blood, hear its sweet song as it rushes through your veins. But...it's *different*."

She jerks away, touching her hand gingerly. "Thank you?"

Slowly, Alec straightens, but his eyes have darkened a shade from hunger. His movements are stiffer, twitchy. "Well," he drawls, trying to shake himself of the spell of bloodlust, "I hope the Kings warned you about the kind of monsters here. There's no need to hide. We walk in the open."

"I'll be fine," she says with steel in her tone. "Don't you worry about me."

"Worried *for* you, more like," he says under his breath.

She doesn't hear him. Or, at least, she does a good job pretending like she doesn't.

Dracon steps forward, but reaches back for Eve. "Thank you for the escort, Alec. We're going to enjoy ourselves before the auction starts."

He doesn't even wait for a reply before snatching Eve and dragging her further into the room, leaving me and Cassius behind with Alec.

Watching Eve disappear, Alec heaves a sigh and shakes his head. "I never pegged Dracon to be the one to want to settle down. Let alone want a mate."

Cassius's laughter explodes, head thrown back and shoulders bouncing. His hair has been slicked back for the occasion, and even in the suit, the tattoos scrolled across his neck and hands are still visible, making him look like a convict who's turned his life around.

"She's not his mate," I answer in a deadly tone while Cassius cracks up.

"Ah, then a new shiny object? Conversation piece?"

Cassius's laughter halts abruptly, telling me he's been thinking the same thing. We all have.

Alec nods, understanding, without any further explanation. "Well, you're going to have your hands full with that one," he says. "If the magic I smell on her has as much bite as that sharp tongue of hers…"

Something about his words doesn't sit well with me. Alec's interest in Eve appears innocent, but from what I found out from the vamp I tortured, the Lords know about her. They wanted to capture her for themselves.

And bringing her here may be their opportunity to take her from us.

Worry churns in my gut. Dracon may be cocky enough not to ignore the danger, but not me. I know they'll try something the moment the chance presents itself.

We can't leave her alone. Not even for a second. Allies or not.

Anxiety picking up, I push past Cassius and Alec and head in the same direction as Dracon.

"Shit, Knox! Where are you going?" Cassius calls after me, but I don't acknowledge him. My gaze searches the tightly packed bodies for the familiar glimmer of gold.

Do I trust Dracon to keep an eye on her at all times?

No.

Do I think he'll do what it takes to keep her safe?

If it stops him from getting what he wants, no.

I've known Dracon for a long time, and I know he's one selfish bastard. Always about the mission, the goal. To hell with who he has to take out to get there. And if Eve gets in his way… well, I'm not confident she won't be among the casualties.

She's safer with me.

Drinks and appetizers are shoved my way by eager waiters, but I shoulder my way through them, not interested in anything else besides finding Eve. It doesn't take long before the people around me get the hint and step aside, forming a path for me to march through. The entire time, I scan their faces for the one I long to find.

We are not the only big players here tonight. I recognize senators, city councilmen, business tycoons, and famous lawyers in the mix, all of the supernatural variety.

Pixies, shifters, banshees, vampires… free to be themselves among other supes but still stuffed in their white-collared extravagance, bow ties, corsets, and lace.

To me, it's a farce. *Disgusting.*

Once guests start to recognize me, hushed whispers roll through the crowd. The Kings own whatever place we step inside, not only because of our social status and wealth, but because of how unique we are in the supernatural community. With Cassius as a demon, Dracon as the last true Apex alive, and me as one of the four horsemen, we are far from the typical supe found on earth. It's what gave us the idea for our name–Kings of Eden–implying that we've been the rulers since the beginning of time and no one can surpass us.

I finally spot Dracon at the far end of the room, standing beside a large arched window, standing almost a foot taller than anyone else around him. His gaze constantly sweeps the area, searching for someone, and when I see that he's alone, I realize why.

Fear shoots up my spine. Eve's not with him.

Motherfucker. I knew he'd ditch her the moment he got distracted by work. She'll be eaten alive. Literally.

I stomp over to him.

The moment Dracon spots me, his eyes narrow and anger contorts his face. "What are you doing here? You know the plan. I get to Marius, you scout the place and eliminate any threats."

"Where's Eve?" I blurt out.

"She had to go to the restroom," he replies simply, unfazed by my anger, which only pisses me off more.

"You left her *alone?*"

"I have her scent at all times, Knox. If you're worried about her escaping–"

"I'm worried about one of the Lords grabbing her before she even makes it to the toilets," I say. "We know they want her. You shouldn't have let her out of your sight."

I don't stick around to see his reaction. He knows he's fucked up–his silence says it all. Instead, I weave my way back across the floor and out into the hall where the designated restrooms are located.

Ignoring the squealing women who dash back into the ballroom the moment they see me, I stroll into the ladies' room and find Eve immediately, standing at the sinks, rubbing her lips together to fix her lipstick.

Goddammit, she's fucking gorgeous.

Those striking green eyes meet mine in the mirror, and she reels back. "Knox!"

Whipping around, her chest heaves in fear, drawing my gaze to her tits again like a moth to a fucking flame.

"You've got to be aware at all times of what and who are around you, little dove," I mutter. Stalking toward her until I have her caged against the wall.

I inhale her scent, and it does something to me. The citrus and spicy perfume on her is intoxicating, working through my system until it has me thoroughly hooked. Which pisses me off. I don't want to be hooked. I want to be free to search for Aris without any ties.

It isn't her fault, I think distantly. She's not the one to blame for how I feel.

She's smart, snarky, and able to think on her feet.

I want her. And I hate it.

I'm off balance with her around, and a distraction I can't afford.

"Give me your panties," I demand. Loving the way she blanches for a split second before she narrows her eyes at me.

"Why?" she asks.

"Are you seriously going to fucking ask me? Give me your panties."

She chuckles, much to my surprise. "What? Is this some kind of way to pay you back for the earrings?"

I press closer until she shivers against me, and I know it's not from fear. She wants me. Her desire is present and pungent.

That dress…

I made a mistake. I shouldn't be alone with her.

Holding my gaze, Eve stoops, reaching under her dress and drags down the thin lace thong she's wearing. She lifts first one foot, then the other. Righting herself, she stands with the lace hanging off her index finger, dangling it in the open air.

"This is what you want, Knox?" she asks.

Ignoring the panties for a moment, I bend down to rub my nose along the line of her neck. Inhaling her and loving the way she shivers again. Goosebumps rise on her skin. My tongue darts out to taste her; I follow that with a small bite.

To remind her, and myself, who is in control here.

Because for some reason, it doesn't feel like it's me.

Finally, I force myself to shift away and take her panties. I shove them into the inside pocket of my suit jacket, grimacing.

"What else do you want?" I watch her throat work as she swallows hard.

Everything.

I know what I want. I want it all. In a move that is completely not like me, I shift my lips to hers. Capturing her mouth for a kiss and loving the way it seems like I've sucked the air out of her lungs. She gasps at the contact as I work her mouth, teasing her with my teeth and tongue. At the same time, I shift my hand, bunching her dress as I drag it up her legs, and skimming my fingers along the silky soft skin of her thigh.

Dracon had her first. He felt her first, and those

thoughts remain in the back of my mind as I slip my tongue through her lips, at the same time I slide my finger through her folds. Eve is hot and wet. Clenching against me as her legs widen to allow me better access.

My name is a groan.

I swallow that down along with the keening sounds she's making at my touch. I slide a finger inside her, followed by a second, working her despite asking myself why.

Why I feel the need to be here with her?

Fuck. How did I go from thinking this woman was Aris, to needing to possess her?

I've been alone for too long. The guys are a solution to another problem and we rule together, but they are the last people I'd want nestled in the crook of my arm at night. Or looking up at me like they actually want me, no matter what kind of crazy is in my head.

Eve begs me for more. Kisses me like she needs me, and with her arms wrapped around my neck, holding on to me, I know this is where I'm supposed to be.

Her pussy clamps around my fingers, and I use my thumb to work her clit and push her to orgasm.

She falls apart in my arms and no matter how badly I want to bend and taste her, I kiss her roughly once more before forcing myself to take a step back.

I'd stepped over the line I'd drawn for myself and had a fucking amazing time doing it. From the look on Eve's face, she did too.

She gazes up at me through heavily lidded eyes, her tongue swiping across her lower lip like she's memorizing my taste. I like the idea more than I'm willing to admit. That there might be someone out there in this world who wants me for me, darkness and all.

Eve knows who I am, and she's not walking away.

But she has no choice, I hastily push into my mind. Instead, I focus on how good it feels to have her at my side. It can't last, and I know that, but I'll take what I can get for as long as I can.

I shove my hand in my pocket and rub the lace there before glaring at Eve like my thoughts are somehow her fault.

"Come on," I growl at her. Jerking her by the arm, we walk out of the restroom with her frantically adjusts her dress.

"Really? That's all you have to say?"

I hide my smile at her whisper. "I suggest you stay by me or Cassius tonight. Dracon is distracted and there are too many creatures here that want to devour you."

She pales but doesn't reply.

Good. She understands.

It's better for me to keep her scared. I'm too drawn to her. And no other female has done that to me in a long time.

CHAPTER TWENTY

DRACON

Standing by myself at the back of the ballroom, I slide one hand in my pocket and force a mask of boredom onto my face. Really, my insides are vibrating with anticipation.

Marius is here. I know he is. The bastard is just hiding in plain sight as he likes to do. Waiting. Watching. Stalking, like the true predator he is. But I am one too—a better one—and I know that if I wait it out, hide in plain sight, Marius will emerge eventually. Alone. And then I'll corner him.

My gaze glides over the other guests, all enjoying their break away from the humans and chatting freely as they practically drown themselves in alcohol. I find Cassius still chatting with Alec, strategically so, of course. Keeping Marius's right-hand man busy allows me to scope him out and pin him, and Cassius is better at making small talk out of the three of us.

On cue, Cassius glances my way and winks while seamlessly continuing the conversation, never allowing Alec to think anything's wrong.

Then there's Knox.

He's been even more unstable than usual. I'd thought once he tracked down his blade, he'd snap back. Well, maybe not completely, but I never expected him to just shift obsessions. And that's a problem.

When I spot Knox and Eve walking back into the party, my body tenses. Even from this far away, I can see her cheeks are flushed and she's breathing heavier.

Something happened.

Knox has a smug expression on his face as well.

I grind my teeth. It looks like he's found his new obsession. Eve.

And that's going to be a problem.

I've got no claim on the woman and I don't care who Knox finally decides to wet his dick with, but I'm tired of the messes I always end up having to clean up.

Why do I even give a shit? Because his mistakes affect us all, affects the gang and everything we've worked hard to achieve. And that's just something I can't allow.

The flash of movement above captures my attention, and my head snaps up to see the curtain fluttering on one of the second-floor balconies, despite no open windows. In that split second, there's a glimpse of a polished black suit and graying hair.

My lips peel back.

Marius. The leader of the Lords of Night and Master Vampire of all Andover.

Gotcha.

Of course, he'd be scoping out the party from the highest vantage point, a hawk in the sky about to swoop down on his prey.

I steer my way through the crowd, eyes bouncing between the balcony and the ballroom. There has to be a staircase leading to the second floor. I just need to find it and…

There! Underneath the balcony, behind the auction's stage and podium, is a door with a symbol for emergency stairs in case of a fire.

A pleased growl rolls through me. *Fuck yes.*

I shift directions and head for it. A quick glance at where I know Cassius and Alec are confirms they are still wrapped in a deep conversation about who knows what. Perfect time for me to slip away and confront Marius.

Lucky for me, the door isn't alarmed, so it's easy to get through undetected. Sprinting up the steps, I end up in a long hallway with walls covered in expensive abstract artwork. The balcony I saw Marius on is to my immediate right, but it's empty. Makes sense, since I did see him leaving. But he must still be close. Hopefully, my luck will continue, and he'll be alone.

"Dracon."

Shit. Well, so much for luck.

I turn and come face to face with the exact vampire I'd been hunting. He's managed to corner me instead.

Nostrils flaring, I draw in the scents around me. With so much food and drinks and various perfumes and colognes swirling around in one central area, it's harder to get an accurate read, but from what I can tell, he appears to be alone.

Does that mean I'm letting my guard down at all? Absolutely not. Everyone knows vamps are sneaky fuckers, and with my nose hindered at the moment, who knows if there are some of his men hiding in the shadows.

"Marius," I say.

The vampire stands still, hands clasped behind his back as he regards me with a bored smile. "Glad to see you out and about," he says. "I have to admit, I didn't expect to see you here after sending the invitation."

I eye him. Unlike Alec, Marius became an immortal later on in life. Gray peppers his hair and wrinkles crinkle the corners of his eyes. But don't let that fool you. He's pushing five hundred years old–you can see that age and wisdom in his piercing stare–but somehow appears only to be around forty.

Next to me and Knox, he's a baby in comparison.

"Where are the other...*Kings?* Hm?" Marius glances over my shoulder, but I don't turn. Never show your back to an enemy. Even if we have a truce currently, it's always been tentative. When he snorts a laugh, my muscles clench.

He's mocking me, testing me, but I try not to give into my temper. Yet.

"Cassius has Alec by the balls, and Knox...well, you know him," I settle with. "He's uncontrollable."

There's the subtlest of twitches at the corner of his mouth, but I notice it. Marius knows all too well how crazy Knox can be. Before our agreement, the Kings and the Lords were constantly at each other's throats. And the bloodshed…

While the Lords have vast numbers, they were nothing against Death itself, and whenever Knox was unleashed, they didn't stand a chance. It was one of the reasons Marius proposed the truce in the first place–we just live our separate lives, never step on each other's toes, and avoid killing each other, unless extremely necessary.

Marius claps his hands together, the sharp sound making my pulse pick up. "Well, there's a reason you came looking for me, hoping to get me alone, so here I am. What is it you wanted to talk about?"

Straight to the point. I can respect that.

"We were attacked by vampires several days ago," I tell him. "You wouldn't happen to know anything about that, now, would you?"

Marius pauses, eyes lighting up in interest. "Attacked?"

"By vampires, yes. In the industrial park." It's hard to keep the annoyance from my tone.

A long, manicured finger taps the side of his jaw. "Peculiar…"

I clench my teeth, my shoulders stiffening. "I need to hear it from you. Was it your men or not?"

"Sorry, no. Not my men," he answers flippantly.

Right…

"And you haven't heard anything about this at all?" I press. "A bunch of supposed rogue vampires running the city?"

"It is curious, isn't it?" he muses. "And something I'll have to look into immediately."

"I remember at one point you saying you had a record of every vamp in Andover."

"This is true. I do. But this type of thing can be difficult to keep track of, especially with newly made vampires."

I huff. "Are you telling me you can't do your job, Marius?"

A single brow rising, he frowns. "I cannot control every damned soul. Just as you cannot control every shifter. And I don't expect you to."

I open my mouth to argue, but end up shutting it. I guess he's made a good point.

"I can assure you it wasn't us who attacked you that night, Dracon. And I will be looking into this, I promise you that. I'm sure you had no issue eradicating the rogues?"

I nod. "Absolutely."

"Excellent," he goes on. "Then please enjoy your time here tonight. Relax. Spend some money." He chuckles, but I can't hear any real mirth behind it. He's lost in thought about the news I've just dropped on him.

Either he knows we're onto him, or he really has been blindsided by the entire thing and the vampire Knox tortured lied. I'm just not sure which.

Marius may appear like he doesn't want another war, but trusting a person's word in this business will get you killed. I'll discover the truth soon, and if he's lying like I think he is, then all that's left is figuring out the best way to kill him.

CHAPTER TWENTY-ONE

EVE

*E*nemies amid enemies.

That's who surrounds me. I sip champagne from a crystal glass, studying the supes, each dressed more extravagant than the next. They're all mingling, waiting for the auction to begin, though they watch each other cautiously, barking out fake laughs while keeping an eye on each other. Including me.

Especially the vamps. And it has my skin crawling.

Whispers. Side eyes. Glares.

It's clear I stand out and everyone knows it. No one comes near me though, not with the Kings watching over me so diligently. So I play the part and keep to myself.

When in Rome...

I catch Alec's eyes trained on me from across the room. He's predatory in his stare and posture, and ridiculously handsome. This whole convention hall is packed with the most dangerous, most power hungry supes in the city, maybe in the country.

And it amazes me that war hasn't broken out yet.

Knox is being dragged with Dracon across the hall. He

steals one last glance my way. I flip him the finger. His possessiveness today is off the charts. Psycho took my underwear, leaving me feeling even more vulnerable in a room full of sharks.

Doesn't matter. With how preoccupied the Kings are tonight, this is the perfect place to make my final, great escape and go rescue Kat myself. I paid attention to the route we took on our drive here. The place is close to the freeway, and from there I'll hitchhike out of here. I just need a lucky break, then I'm free.

Cassius slides an arm around my waist, as if sensing my thoughts were anywhere but on him. He draws me tightly against him. His fingers dig into my hip, right where he's carved his name into my skin. I wince.

"You doing okay?" he whispers.

"Yep. I don't feel out of place at all." I'm just really hoping this night doesn't end like the one with Cobra Strike.

He barks a laugh, then takes my now empty glass to return it to a tray of a passing server. "Knox hates these shindigs too, but they are Dracon's crack. It's where he makes deals, uncovers who's backstabbed who, and by morning, he'll have an entire strategy mapped out for us for a new venture."

"And you?"

His gaze slides to me. "What about me?"

"What do you think about these types of parties?"

He ponders that for a moment, eyes drifting back to the crowd. "They can be a nice break from the monotony," he says.

"Monotony?" I sputter. "Your lives are anything but."

What, having near death experiences every damn day isn't enough for him?

"You'd think so, but I'm always chasing that next high," he says.

"You're never satisfied," I reply. "That can make life pretty boring."

His lips press into a hard line. "You have no idea."

A moment of silence passes between us, and we switch our attention back to the party.

After some time, I try to resurrect the conversation, wanting to know more about him and the Kings of Eden. "Whatever you three have here, it must be working in your favor too, since you haven't ditched yet."

"Dracon and Knox are family, and you don't betray family." He takes my hand in his and pulls me into a walk around the edge of the mingling crowd. "Let's get some fresh air. It's getting stuffy in here."

We're out on the balcony in no time. It's freezing outside, but tall standing heaters have been placed here and there for guests. He guides me over to one. The spot overlooks a vast golf course, with perfectly manicured shrubs and a man-made pond and fountain.

He draws me against him. "Everyone's asking about you."

"Yeah. And what have you been saying?"

"That you're my latest fuck."

"Yeah, right. You wish you were that lucky," I murmur, while attempting to wrench his hand from around my waist.

"We can make it real," he purrs, holding me even tighter.

"Cassius." A man's voice interrupts us, one that's rolled in a thick Russian accent. I turn to a wide man in a black tuxedo, looking every part James Bond, if he were Russian. He has several scars on his face and a collar of tatts. Two women in skin-tight dresses and pointed ears stand silently behind him. Their eyes track Cassius's every move.

"Dimitri. I didn't know you were in the country." Cassius sounds almost startled. He releases me and walks over to him, as if I'm no longer there.

Strange… I didn't think Cassius could ever be taken off guard by someone before. But it's clear this stranger holds sway. Power ripples off him, even at a distance, and after witnessing Dracon turn into a dragon, it makes me wonder just what other kinds of supernaturals there are out there. I thought I had seen them all.

"Только что вышел из тюрьмы несколько недель назад," the man replies with a snort.

Cassius answers in Russian, and I can't stop staring at the man with eyes so red they might as well be bleeding. Something about his presence sends a dark and ugly feeling down my spine.

Remaining neutral, I watch their animated discussion that sounds like they're arguing. Yet the girls don't seem to be bothered. They must be models; they're tall, thin, and absolutely stunning. None of that bothers me—but what does is that they keep smiling and making flirtatious gestures to Cassius. Winks, licking their lips, blowing him kisses…

A pang of jealousy races through me, the kind that ignites my chest with fire, and I'm not sure why. I scold myself internally. The Kings of Eden mean nothing to me. Every second I've spent with them and survived has been a miracle, and I shouldn't press my luck if I want to end this nightmarish experience with my life. The longer I stay, it's guaranteed they'll break me, make me bleed, and take everything I love.

My objective is easy… get as far from the Kings of Eden as possible.

Still… I can't stop the queasy feeling spinning in my stomach as the girls ogle him. Geez, can they be any more desperate? Luckily, Cassius doesn't seem to care about them at all. He's too wrapped in his conversation with Russian 007 to notice.

Noting a waiter walking past the doorway to the balcony with a tray of drinks, I find my window to slip away unnoticed.

"I'm going to get a drink," I call to Cassius, but he doesn't respond.

I shrug. Better for me.

On quick feet, I stroll inside and follow the waiter, just in case Cassius is watching. A quick scan of the room shows no sign of Dracon or Knox.

Adrenaline shoots through me, and I take my opportunity.

I hurry past the crowds, making a beeline for the front doors, just as I spot Dracon. He's got his back to me, chatting with someone. Knox is nowhere to be seen, and I pray it stays that way.

Backpedaling, I rush right through the crowd, slipping past everyone, ignoring their lingering glances. Darting toward a side door where another waiter disappears into, I take it as my cue to leave Crazy Town. On the other side, I find a carpeted hall, which I sprint down as fast as I can in my dress. I glance over my shoulder, heart racing, but see that one's following me.

There are so many doors in this place, so I try one, and it's unlocked. I come into a huge storage room with no other way out or windows.

Nope, that's not going to work. I hurry back out and

keep trying doors, until I finally stumble into a huge and busy kitchen. I frantically charge right past the cooks and staff, despite them yelling at me to get out, but I have my sights set on the door set all the way in the back.

I burst out of it in seconds.

Night.

Cool air rushing over my face.

Freedom.

I gulp it all down, bunch up the skirt of my dress in my hands, and run. The parking area is in sight, and once there, I'll follow the path toward the freeway.

My hair slaps over my shoulders, as I rush through the darkness down the middle of parked cars.

God, this might just work. Please let this work.

Everything I need to do next to get far away of the Kings tumbles in my mind–I'll need some mode of transportation, maybe then a plane trip. But I'll need money. Cash. They'll be able to track anything else. And what about Kat?

"Whoa, look at you." Cassius's sudden explosive voice startles me.

I halt and swing around, almost tripping over my own feet. He's standing on the hood of a blacked-out Mercedes right next to me, hands stuffed in his pant pockets, and his jaw ticks.

"How the hell? Did you fly here?" My stomach deflates, all the hope now a puddle around my feet.

He tsks me. "I hope you weren't trying to escape again." He's now removing his jacket, which he lies on the roof of the car.

"Oh, no. Of course not. Just needed some air."

His brow arches. "All the way out here? In the parking lot?"

"It's fresher over here."

"Ah ha, I see."

That's when I notice his body seems to be humming... it's the best way to describe it. And it's causing the air around his body to shimmer. Is he about to change into his demon form?

Shaking my head, I say, "How did the reunion go with your big bad Russian friend and his floozies?"

"First, not my friend. I don't have *friends*, really."

I want to come back with something witty and sarcastic like, "That's a damn shame" or "No, really? I never would've guessed," but he starts to roll up the sleeves of his white shirt over muscular forearms, and I lose my words. There's just something about a man doing that simple as hell move that makes their sexy meter skyrocket off the charts. And Cassius was hot as hell to start with, so I'm rendered speechless.

He studies me the whole time.

"And second," he continues. "Those dickfaces were feeding off me. Dimitri is the kingpin of Russia, a dark fae prince, and those bitches behind him were the rusalka." He twitches, a nerve dancing under an eye. "Dimitri thought it would be a good time to drain me just enough for them to ask about some of our recent dealings. You see, he just got out of prison a couple weeks ago, and we've had a shipment of guns stolen since then. There are no coincidences in this business, so I'm convinced the asshole stole from us."

I blink at him, not sure what he's really talking about. "Umm, what are raskies?"

Rolling his eyes at me, he mutters, "Rusalka. They're spirits of young women who've drowned or were murdered in water. They seek to avenge their deaths, and I might have killed their sister on a visit to Russia."

"Shit. No wonder they want to get revenge. How'd you manage to escape them, then?"

"Don't look so surprised. I'm a lot more powerful than you give me credit for. But I'm amused that you were jealous of the rusalka." His eyes narrow on me with an arrogant smirk that I want to rip off his face.

"You wish I was jealous. You can have sex with all three of them, and I wouldn't bat an eye."

"You're fiery when you're possessive. Good. I want you clawing and biting me while I fuck you inside Dimitri's car." His head motions down to the Mercedes he's standing on.

I puff out a breath of air. "You know what'll be even better? You jerking off all over his car. He'll just hate that, so I'm going to leave you to it then. Have fun."

Retreating, I notice he's doing that thing again where the edges of his body are shimmering, like he might just go puff in one second and vanish, or shift. But it's getting worse. His eyes are darkening, his face seeming to contort like he's mid-shift. What the hell is happening to him?

And how can he act so normal while he's physically changing?

"I have it all worked out in my mind, you see." His voice trembles the more he talks, and I'm seriously starting to worry. "You, me…A real *Titanic* moment."

He reaches into his pocket and pulls out something silver that reminds me of a compact mirror. And It has a skull printed on one side.

I stare at him. "Instead of revenge, maybe you should sort out what's going on with your body. You're all…fuzzy at the edges. Your face... Are you turning into your demon?"

"I'm fine," he snaps, his forehead furrowing. But then he rolls his shoulders and tries again in a calmer tone, "I'll fix it quickly."

Fix?

He flips open the silver flat box in his hand and fiddles with something inside it. I can't see what it is while he still stands on top of the car.

Next thing I know, he lifts it up to his nose. One finger presses a nostril flat, and he takes a great snort with the other.

I stiffen.

"Are you kidding me? You're doing drugs?"

He takes another great snort with his other nostril, then wipes the remnants from the surface and rubs it across his gums. Then he snaps the box shut, puts it away, and pinches his nostrils before sniffling. He shakes his whole body and unleashes a tremendous roar.

Lunatic. If he wasn't insane before, now he's going to be worse, isn't he?

Knowing that I should have made a run for it before, maybe now is better. He's doped up, too focused on riding his high, so I round the car, then I take off into a maddening run as far from him as possible.

Strong arms snatch me around my waist, and I'm suddenly off my feet, screaming to be put down. I kick my legs backward to strike him, buck, anything. I need to escape him.

"I thought my name on your hip would've worked, but apparently, you need a reminder of who you belong to."

"Fuck you," I yell. In seconds, he's got me on my feet and spinning around. My ass is against another car as he bends me back onto the hood. He pins me there with his body, caging me in as he pushes a knee between my legs, spreading them, my dress tearing the more he pushes.

Shit!

The acrid smell of whatever he's taking blows in my face on his breath, and I sneer. "Get the hell off me."

"You'll never understand how good crack feels in my body, how much it gets me off. You know it affects the central nervous system, and it's the only thing that helps me heal. It controls my demon." He sucks in a deep breath, and his body shudders again. "It feels like the touch of a god… which is ironic, considering what I am." He laughs crazily.

"Okay, well, you do you and leave me out of it." My mind won't forget his words. *Healing. Controls his demon.* How does that work?

And already, I see the fraying edges on his body fade, his contorting face sliding back to his normal appearance.

"What is going on with you?" My mind swims with confusion.

"That motherfucker, Dimitri knows my weakness with my demon, so he always catches me off guard with the rusalka." His eyes roll back into his head as he smiles again, clearly losing himself to the drugs.

I'm trying to process everything he's said, noting he is now completely back to normal appearance wise, so whatever was going on with him before seems to be fixed.

"Next time, don't be so friendly," I suggest, shoving my hands against his hard chest.

"Easier said than done."

So that's what all the winks and kissy face bullshit was about. On the bright side, I no longer feel jealous. Instead, I want to drive my knees into his precious jewels and make him cry as I run away.

"Fine, you got your high. Now get off me."

He's grinning, the erection in his pants growing. "You know what else crack does to my body?"

With a tremor shaking through me, something else awakens too. A deep, hungry arousal.

The corner of his mouth pulls up, his gaze staying on me, never looking away. His hand brushes the skin along my jaw, and goosebumps rise from the tenderness he's capable of. "You have no idea how beautiful you are, Eve. How much I've craved to eat your pussy, to have you come all over my tongue, to hear you beg me for more."

He leans closer, our noses touching. "I'll bring you unbelievable pleasure. I'll take you to the moon and back as you fall for me. And you *will* fall."

He watches me, his hazy gaze devouring me, He's clearly high, yet he's just as strong as before, just as dominating.

His mouth grazes mine and we're suddenly kissing, me losing my mind just as he promised. That's when I taste something gritty and slightly bitter on my tongue. Wait… is that…

I shove against him, and he breaks away. "What is it, gorgeous?"

"I don't do drugs. Never have and never will. And shit, now it's in my mouth." I lick my teeth, tasting more of the powder.

He grins. "It's not a lot, just enough to give you a tingle. I promise you'll enjoy it."

"You asshole," I growl, fisting his shirt.

The torrent of angry words I want to throw at him vanish when he claims my mouth again, kissing me with need and starvation. Within seconds, the anger in me morphs into moans. He's unrelenting.

This whole hate him, fuck him thing is killing me, and here I am falling prey to him once more. Evidently, I'm weak when it comes to carnal pleasures... that's the only excuse I have.

With his hands on my hips, he pushes me higher up on the hood, but the moment he lets go, I seize the opportunity and scramble across it to escape.

He growls and lunges after me, snatching my ankles, then drags me back to him. A quick flip and I'm on my back again, but with my dress bunched up around my waist.

Oh fuck, Knox has my panties!

His eyes bulge as he looks at my nakedness.

"Eve, if I'd known you were coming to the party bare, I would have lost control and fucked you ten times over already."

"Don't get too excited. Knox stole my underwear." I shove down my dress, but he's pushing my arms away with one hand, the other worming his way between my thighs.

"You have the sweetest little pussy I've ever seen. So wet for me."

"Cassius, don't–"

He shoves open my legs and dives in, his mouth on me in seconds. His long tongue licks the length of my seam. I moan and collapse back on the hood of the car, my back arching. His greedy fingers spread my lips, opening me up, showing him everything.

I'm suffocating with his mouth pressed on me, my breathing growing erratic. He has me drowning in arousal, adrenaline, anticipation, and fear.

All I can think is that I want to murder him... but after

he makes me come because I'm so needy.

Fingers slip in under my ass, and he drags me closer to him. He eats me like a beast. There's nothing delicate about it. It's fast and deliberately messy, like he wants me all over his face. The flat of his tongue runs the length of my pussy, pausing only to dip inside me, flicking, pushing me into a frenzy.

Then he pushes two fingers into me, and I shake with unbearable need.

"You like me finger fucking you, don't you?" he asks in a husky voice.

A growl tears from his throat, and I'm absolutely lost to how much he's enjoying me. How each stroke, each suck, pushes me over the edge.

"Cassius, make me scream. Make it hurt." All I feel is the wanton desire to reach my peak. To orgasm and unleash the arousal that tortures my insides.

Heat engulfs my body and my head swims, but it's more than just arousal. The world around me seems to sway softly, and I feel giddy all over. The rough pad of his thumb circles my clit, and I cry out at the heightened sensation. The muscles in my legs quiver, even while I look around, thinking I shouldn't be enjoying this so much. I should search for something to ground myself, but even I know I'm too far gone.

Like when he'd given me his blood, I've lost control of myself. Why is it that whenever I'm around him, he becomes my drug?

Cassius owns me. He makes me groan, and I dig my fingernails into his shoulders, breaking skin, demanding more. I don't know what's going on with me because it's all happening so fast. One moment, I tried to run, now I'm begging him for more.

It's too late to make sense of anything. My body tightens and my orgasm hits me so hard and fast, I almost black out.

I scream, thrashing against him, and squeeze my thighs around his head. There's no pausing Cassius's licking. He's taking every last drop.

The sensation is intoxicating, thumping through my veins. I'm shaking uncontrollably as the world around me pulses and dances.

Even the stars high above sparkle extra brightly as though somehow Cassius plucked them from the sky and rearranged them.

His hands glide down my legs, and when he comes up for air, he's smiling like a fool. His lips and chin shine with my cum on his face.

My cum is on a King's face.

Next thing I know, he's hoisting me up into his arms, and I wrap my legs around him as his mouth devours my neck. I swear, this guy is pure sin. Everything he touches and kisses leaves me breathless.

"I'm going to fuck you now," he pants in my ear, carrying me across the parking area. "Are you ready?"

"Yes, I want it." I'm still floating, and I feel so light.

He chuckles then sets me on my feet. "Don't go anywhere," he commands.

I teeter, a strange sensation of fire claiming my body while arousal has my nipples hard and wetness sliding down the inside of my thighs.

We're next to the blacked-out Mercedes again, and I roll my eyes. "Seriously, Cassius."

He grabs hold of the back door and rips it right off the car with the sheer force of his demon strength.

I gasp.

A sharp car alarm goes off.

"Whoa." I step back, startled by what I just witnessed.

Cassius tosses the door aside and frantically unlocks the front door before getting in and fiddles with something in the driver's seat. In seconds, the sound flatlines.

He tears off his shirt. Muscles ripple across his broad chest, biceps big enough to hang from. The guy is an Adonis covered in ink. He's beautiful and tempting.

"Now, where were we?" He reaches out and grabs my arm, dragging me over to him. He takes hold of the deep V of my dress and tugs with ferocity. A great rip fills the silence.

I cry out, my body lurching forward, and he catches me, but the damage is done. My dress hangs open, my breasts flashing him.

"You asshole."

"I want to see all of you. Now come here." His dark tone is commanding. He collects me into his arms savagely. Then, his face is on my neck, his lips dragging over my jawline and cheek.

His tongue darts out, and he licks my lips. "You've evaded me long enough."

I open my mouth, but he steals my response with a punishing kiss.

His hands find my ass and he squeezes, then they lower to the back of my thighs, and he lifts me into his arms. I exhale loudly as he lays me on the back seat of the Mercedes. I'm spread open for him, again, and my stomach flutters with desire.

"I want you to look at me when I fuck you, and I need to see those delicious tits."

"You talk too fucking much."

Chuckling, he unbuckles his belt and unzips himself, then lowers his pants.

I swallow hard when I see his cock. Of course, he's huge and thick. Guess it matches his gigantic ego.

"Don't look so scared. I promise you, you'll love it."

"Make me believe it," I tease.

He replies but laying his body over me, his erection stroking my folds, and his touch leaves me engulfed in heat. I'm moaning, adrenaline soaring through me before he even enters me.

That's how desperate he's gotten me. He's invading every inch of space I have, leaving me weak for him.

He lowers his head and sucks on a pebbled nipple as he pushes into me. I groan, my body tensing. Okay, I knew he was big, but shit, it's taking a bit of effort to make him fit.

My eyes meet his as he lets go of my nipple with a pop. "Just breathe. Let me in, Eve."

Exhaling, letting my muscles relax, he eases into me, pushing, filling me. I demanded pain, and he's stretching me to that point.

Fingers digging into his arms, I hold on to him as he pushes in and out of me, slow at first, finding his rhythm. I lift my hips for easier access. His pace picks up, though, plowing into me, and with each thrust, I cry out. My body rocks back and forth with the force.

Everything about the way he fucks is possessive and primal. Before I think of catching my breath, he's pounding into me, shaking the whole damn car.

There's no rhythm now, just a maddening fuck where he speeds up, then slows, and takes me even harder. He fucks me violently, like his life's depending on it.

Fire ignites between us, the kind that swallows me, and promises to never let go.

He never ends, giving me everything I crave. Tomorrow, my legs will hurt. I feel it already, but I don't care. "I fucking love this," I groan, my body tensing. The way he shows no mercy, our bodies slapping together, has my brain fogging over.

He gives me a sly grin and suddenly pulls out.

"Hey, you better not be pulling that shit and not finishing, or I will hunt you down."

His laughter is music to my ears, and he takes my hand to get me out of the car. "I promise you, sweetheart, I'm not going anywhere. I'm just close, and I need to be ready."

"Ready?"

"Bend over for me. Hands on the trunk." He's turning me around and slaps my ass.

I moan at the sensation. And yeah, I know I'm completely messed up to just follow his instructions and let him boss me around. Maybe I'm just too horny, too lost, to say no to Cassius. Even when he and the Kings promise me nothing but darkness, I still give in.

Leaning forward with my hands on the trunk of the car, I part my legs.

"Good girl." He steps up behind me, shoving whatever's left of my dress up to my waist. His cock is against my pussy instantly, and he thrusts into me. There's no buildup this time, he's just claiming me hard, pounding into me.

"I'm going to ruin you for anyone else. Just like you've ruined me," he snarls.

My attempt at a response comes out as moans while he thrusts into me quicker, harder. My breasts will be permanently indented into this car with the way his fucking me. I can barely hold myself up. I'm quivering as my second orgasm rolls over me just as fast.

It tears me to bits. I cry out, my body arching against

the car.

Cassius howls, and I can feel his cock twitching inside me. He instantly pulls out and steps up to the back seat of the Mercedes.

He roars like a bear, palming his cock as he explodes all over the fine leather upholstery.

Barely catching my breath and still soaring on my high, I lean against the back of the car, staring at him in amazement. This guy is a vengeful bastard.

"Dimitri is going to murder you." I mutter, tugging my torn dress across my chest, my legs wobbly.

He bursts out laughing. "Who gives a fuck? I sure as fuck am not afraid of him."

"You're a sociopath," I say.

He glances over his shoulder at me, his face twisted as he's still ejaculating all over the inside of the car. When he's finished, he fixes his pants and rubs his nose with the back of his hand. It reminds me of the drugs, and I frown.

Then, Cassius does the most unexpected thing. He walks over to me and cups the side of my face with the gentlest touch. He brushes his lips across mine for a feathery light kiss. "You should know, Eve, that I've experimented with some pretty hard drugs while on earth, but you are the most lethal thing for me."

My breathing quickens because I know he means every word, and I feel the familiar thump in my chest that he's impacted me more than I want to admit to myself. But it's going to backfire on me somehow. I know it will.

I mean, I just had sex in the back of a Russian Kingpin's car with a deranged demon, who's then defaced the interior leather seats with a ridiculous amount of sperm.

If this doesn't come back and bite me in the ass, I don't know what will.

CHAPTER TWENTY-TWO

EVE

Sitting down to a friendly dinner with two Kings is like I've just stepped into a damn alternate dimension. A day after the auction, and all time has passed in a blur.

I'm still feeling unbalanced from it all. The attention, being finger fucked by Knox, my attempted escape...

Or maybe that's the after effects of the drugs Cassius had me taste from his mouth, or... the sex. Who's to say?

These men are killers, murderers... yet I find them irresistible, even knowing everything they've done. I'm starting to think I have a death wish or something.

Now Cassius and Dracon sit across the table from me, shoveling food into their mouths, like any normal men having normal dinner. However, this is anything but normal. It's completely fucked up.

They're dangerous, and they're acting like the Chinese takeout is a matter of life and death.

They're also silent as the grave, which somehow seems worse.

No one wants to talk about the auction. Cassius doesn't

want to talk about what happened between us, at least not in front of Dracon. It makes me wonder if he has any idea what happened between me and Cassius, or if it's supposed to be a secret.

Dracon does seem to get testy when it comes to me, but Cassius hadn't said anything to me about not letting him find out.

I hate being left in the dark like this.

The door slams, and I feel it all the way here, jerking in my seat. A few moments later, Knox storms into the room. My heart leaps all the way into my throat. He's roughed up badly, bloody and covered in bruises.

He grabs the chair next to mine, pulling it across the floor with a screech, then sits and reaches for a box of chicken and broccoli.

Is…no one going to ask what happened to him? I glance around the table barely, keeping my eyes from popping out of my head, but neither of the other Kings even look up at Knox.

This must be normal dinner etiquette, I decide. Not sure I'll ever get used to it.

I don't want to get used to it. I want out of this and the more time that goes by, the more I have to realize…there may never be a way out.

This might be my life until they decide it's done.

Blood oozes down from a gash on the side of Knox's face, practically dripping into his food. He keeps his gaze downcast, with the chopsticks looking like twigs in his massive hands.

He still has my panties.

I know because he's still wearing his tux from the auction—now torn and bloody—and occasionally, I catch him reaching for his pocket where I know he's stashed it.

A flash of heat curls in my stomach.

I'm such a hussy.

A knock sounds, and all four of us twist around to the kitchen's entrance, where a beautiful young woman stands with a tense smile, wearing a pencil skirt and modest blouse. She's tall and skinny with the curliest dark hair, looking so damn innocent that I wonder if she wandered in here to the Kings' lair by accident.

Until she moves further into the room and places a stack of manila folders on the table between the men.

"I'm sorry it's late," she begins, her voice soft and lacking substance. "I've got the papers you wanted—"

Dracon snatches them and looks over all the scribbles across the front.

"My fault…" she mumbles with a deep frown. "Sorry."

I don't even know who this girl is, but sympathy tugs at my heart for her.

"Hey, what's your name?" I ask, offering her a gentle smile. "I haven't seen you around here before."

"This is Taliah," Cassius offers before she can answer herself. "She's our personal assistant."

Scooping up all the folders, Dracon snaps his fingers for the other two Kings, and the three of them shift out of the room like shadows, following the trail Dracon takes.

And leaving me alone with Taliah.

She seems to have to stick around until she's dismissed, and stares at her shoes, which makes me feel super awkward.

I offer her a smile because she reminds me a little bit of Mercy. Timid, passive.

"Do you want to sit down and join me?" I gesture toward the empty seat at my other side, pointedly trying to ignore the trail of blood that Knox left behind.

Taliah shakes her head before saying, "The Kings wouldn't like me sharing their food. They have strict rules in place."

Wow, the girl can't even *eat?* That's pretty fucked up.

"I don't care." I burst out laughing at the horrified look on her face. She's probably wondering if I'm crazy too.

Too bad I don't have an answer for her.

"You…s-speak as though they've given you a-authority," Taliah stutters.

I shrug. "In a manner of speaking. And even if they haven't, it doesn't matter to me. I've got more than enough food, and I can't eat it all on my own. You look like you'd enjoy some, so please. Join me."

I can use the company, too, although I keep that thought to myself. If the Kings have left me alone with their assistant, then they better be prepared for me to make friends. End of story.

I'm a friendly person because it's always been a necessity. And like it or not, I miss Kat's Kradle. I miss the girls like crazy.

At least I seem to have convinced Taliah to sit, and she joins me at the table. Blanching slightly when I drag over a plate and pile food in front of her. I offer an easy smile in her direction instead. The one I've carefully cultivated to put people at ease.

"How long have you worked for the Kings?" I ask.

She stiffens at the mention of them, which I find odd, but eventually relaxes enough for some of the lines around her mouth to smooth. "About five years now. Not terribly long."

Not long? Is she kidding me right now? "Hey, I've got to commend you on that," I tell her. "It takes someone with a spine of steel to deal with them."

And just like that, I've lost my appetite. But watching Taliah eat eases some of the tension inside me.

"Tell me about it," she mutters. "I started right out of college. Needed the money to pay off my loans."

"They've got the money to pay you well for what you do. And you deserve it. I wouldn't want to be at their beck and call."

No, I'm just at their mercy in an entirely different way. Or maybe not. Maybe Taliah's personal assistant duties extended to other activities as well. I narrow my eyes at her, reassessing her, scanning from the top of her head to the scuffed tips of her All-Stars.

I must be a little crazier than I first thought. Because the thought of this meek woman with her expressive blue eyes beneath one of the Kings, with her hair fanning out on the pillow, has me slightly enraged.

Only slightly, though. So, there may be hope for me yet.

"You get used to it after a bit," she tells me. Her smile is a little warmer this time.

I hadn't seen a hint of her in this place until today.

"Get used to it?" I ask.

"Yeah. You learn to just keep your head down and give in. It keeps everyone happy. It's efficient," she finishes.

"Honey, no." There's nothing that makes me angrier than a woman bowing to a man without fighting back.

Taliah might be good at her job, but she's got no spark. I wonder if she's always been this way, or if the guys extinguished it for her over the years of her employment.

"You've got to stand up for yourself. You can still do your job while you hold to your convictions. It's all about respecting yourself," I continue. I toss my chopsticks aside like it will somehow help me make my point.

"You're on their good side," she insists, leaning closer. "It's different for you."

Now I'm laughing outright because the poor little thing has no idea. "I am definitely not on their good side. I've been trying to break out of this place since they brought me here. But I know about men, and I know about having to be strong for your job." Boy, do I ever. "People are going to try to walk all over you and if you let them, then it never ends."

"I appreciate what you're trying to do." Her voice drops an octave. Is she afraid of being overheard?

Admittedly, Dracon does seem to have some pretty sensitive hearing. Let him come in and give me a spanking. See what I'll do if he tries.

I'll probably bend over and take it like a champ, and I keep *that* to myself.

"They're not so bad," Taliah insists. Her fingers tighten on her chopsticks. "They can actually be pretty decent."

I scoff and say, "Oh, come on. You really expect me to believe they're upstanding citizens? I've been here for days, and I've seen things that have scarred me. After five years, I bet you're ready to bleach your eyes."

Her laughter is a welcome thing. Oh yeah, she definitely reminds me of Mercy. Sometimes it just takes a little bit for a person to warm up. Sometimes people just click. I can tell that if we had some more time, we'd be close girlfriends.

"There have been some crazy times." She blows out a breath. "Some crazy things."

I lean forward with my chin balanced on my palm. Classic *tell me more* posture.

Eventually, after looking around to make sure none of

the Kings are around, she scoots closer. "Cassius went to rehab. For his drug addiction," she whispers.

I'd seen it firsthand. "I believe it," I whisper back.

"He ended up dating his life coach. It only lasted a few months." Taliah breaks off, shaking her head until hair falls in front of her face. "I'm not sure what happened, but he killed her."

A cold void opens up inside of me. "He what?"

"He killed her, and I had to clean up the body."

This is not the gossip I expected to hear. Never in my wildest dreams would I think Taliah capable of hiding a body. It's not like I know her well, but she's scrawny and mousy. Now she's an accessory to murder?

"That's why you stay here," I manage to get out. "They've got dirt on you and are blackmailing you into doing their dirty work."

And if they've got her, they've got other people ready to do the same. Will they be there to take care of my body once the Kings are done with me?

One has to wonder.

I've got to make sure I get out before we get to that point.

It might be a good idea to get Taliah on my side, too, in case I need her help to escape. Although with the brand on my hip I'm not sure how I'll ever be able to manage it. The Kings will track me down no matter where I go.

I force a grin on my face to put Taliah at ease after my outburst. It's bad enough she already looks guilty for over-sharing. She doesn't need my judgment as well. It's a risk to reach out and pat her shoulder, a small gesture of reassurance.

"It's okay," I say softly. "You had no choice. You had to follow what they ordered you to do."

Because I highly doubt they'd asked.

Relief flashes across her face and dies in an instant as Dracon returns. He dismisses her with a growl, staring her down as she scurries away from the table and out of the room without so much as a goodbye.

"You." He points at me and my blood goes cold.

"What do you want? She was hungry," I toss out.

Then he says my least favorite phrase. *"We need to talk."*

CHAPTER TWENTY-THREE

DRACON

I didn't like leaving Taliah and Eve together, but we needed to discuss what Taliah had discovered. I could hear them talking, but their voices were lowered to an octave I can't actively listen to. What are they talking about? Whatever it was, the moment I enter the room, they both look fucking guilty.

Especially Eve.

I know she doesn't want to be here; she's made that clear, and she'll use any excuse to get out. But Taliah knows better than to divulge our secrets.

However, the awkward hunch of her shoulders and the way her fingers twitch have me glaring at her. I growl and jerk my chin toward the door in a clear indication for her to leave. Our assistant runs out with a small squeak, leaving me alone with Eve.

"We need to talk," I say, pointing at her. We agreed that I would be the one to tell Eve the truth. Though Cassius looked like he was going to punch me, and Knox just kept flipping his Motem Blade with a look on his face that called for my death.

I didn't fucking care. I'm the fucking Apex, so Cassius and Knox went to prepare for tomorrow.

"Why? Because I'm a prisoner, I can't make friends?" she snaps.

"What makes you think you're a prisoner?" I ask her, in a tone designed to piss her off.

She hates me. I know, and if the roles were reversed... I shudder to think what I'd do.

Eve pushes up from the table and crosses the room toward me with a finger outstretched like she can actually do me physical harm. Her lips are drawn in a harsh line. And I know what those lips can do. I know how good they feel wrapped around my cock and despite having to meet the Spades tomorrow to get to Kat, and what I'd seen in that folder from Taliah, my gaze heats.

"What's the matter, little one?" I fucking love pushing her. "Do you not like the food?"

"The food is not the issue, and you know it, Dracon. It's you and the others keeping me here against my will. Let me go."

I snap my arm out and grab her throat, walking her backwards until she hits the kitchen island. Her hands wrapped around my wrist with her nails clawing and drawing blood.

"Do you have any idea what kind of trouble you've found yourself in? Do you know what I'm trying to do to keep you alive? To keep you from ending up with your finger or *head* in a box?"

Eve shakes her head, gasping. "I don't give a shit. I never asked for this. I just wanted to live my life on my terms and dance. But you assholes...it doesn't matter," she says frustrated, as her scent invades my lungs.

I push in closer to her, releasing her neck, and bending

to run my nose along her jawline to her ear. "What else?" I press.

With her increased breathing and the way she's shifting, I know she's turned on, even if she hates me. I can read her body. Smell her arousal whenever we're alone.

"You're all overbearing and ridiculous, psycho. You're controlling, egotistical, arrogant—"

I step back suddenly, needing distance. And she grips the island for balance, her eyes wide.

"Keep going," I urge, trying to maintain my control.

Since the day I shifted in front of her, I've been trying to be better. When I asked her if she was ok when we got back to the penthouse, she just nodded and went to her room. I knew I fucked up, but I thought it was best to give her space. Pushing her to talk then when she was so shaken up would've made things worse. Especially since I'm not the best at talking about…feelings and shit.

I had to protect her from the Spades. That was my goal, and I did what I had to do to keep her alive. At least she hasn't judged me on my past or shifting.

Yet.

I'm sure it's coming.

"I want to walk out that door and never see any of you again."

This time, when I look into her emerald eyes that don't hide anything, I see the truth.

Fuck. She means it.

And that infuriates me.

After all the trouble we've gone through for her, to protect her… Losing the deal with Cobra Strike, our rocky standing with the Lords of Night… She's still ungrateful as ever.

If Saxon were here…

I pause, thinking about my old friend, and the familiar twang of sorrow and guilt returns. I've been shoving memories of him down because of this very reason, but with Eve here, I can't help but wonder what he'd do if he were still alive to meet her.

Knowing him, he'd probably tell me to get my head out of my ass and admit to myself that I like her here with us. Even as annoying as she can be sometimes, I want to keep her.

Then, he'd tease me relentlessly about it. The fucker.

But none of that matters now because he's dead and he's never coming back.

I'd failed him. And I had promised myself I wouldn't fail Eve too.

So, as she glares at me with such disdain and wants to leave, my temper ignites. Why can't she see that what I'm doing is for her? I don't understand.

Maybe she just doesn't fucking care.

"Fine," I ground out, reaching for her. She tries to move, but I'm faster. "Let's go."

"I didn't mean—" she starts.

I don't give a shit what she meant because once the anger rises, I'm not shoving it back in the little box. My normally tight leash of control snaps, and I drag her behind me to one of the living room windows. I smash my fist against it twice with all my strength, and the glass shatters, covering the sound of her sharp inhale.

But I'm not done.

Eve is screeching and struggling against my hold as I pull her out the window with me. Free falling.

She screams her head off like I'm about to fucking kill her instead of trying to a prove a point.

Maybe I should though. It would make things easier.

Right before we hit the ground, I partially shift, my wings snapping out. And I catch an updraft, soaring over the buildings and dragging her weight up against my chest.

Aw, poor Eve. She's shaking, her arms and legs wrapped tightly around my body. Her head is buried against my chest, and her screams have turned into quiet whimpers of terror in the back of her throat. I guess she's afraid of heights, or maybe that I'll let go.

"You want freedom?" I ask her, bringing my mouth right next to her ear, so she can hear me above the rush of wind. "Here. This is what I can offer you."

I'm not sure how Cassius and Knox feel about her outside of their curiosity… No, that's a lie. I do. I know the three of us are possessive bastards and only our need for each other keeps us from ripping the others to shreds in order to claim her.

This curvaceous blonde vixen.

We want her. So there is no freedom for her outside of what we can allow. As I take her higher above the skyline of Andover City, I hope it proves that point.

She's at our mercy, but we'll keep her safe. If she lets us.

Eventually, I pull my head back so that I can look at her, and much to my surprise, she's staring at me. This time I can't read her face. She's examining me, for some reason, and the whimpers have stopped.

I'm not sure why, but it's fucking with me.

So instead, I smirk at her. "See something you like?"

She shifts her focus to my wings. "Have you ever fucked like this?"

Have I…okay, that was not what I was expecting her to say at all. For a long moment, I'm speechless. "Fucked as a dragon? Can't say I have. Fucked from a great height? Why do you want to know?"

When I told her we needed to talk, this was not what I had in mind. This isn't even close to what I'd wanted to pick her brain about. Yet here we are, flying above the city. The night sky is open and infinite, and the cool wind is cradling us, and we're talking about fucking.

I never meant to kiss her. The urge struck me a moment before I crashed my lips on hers, swallowing whatever she wanted to say. Probably nothing I'd want to hear anyway, or just more questions for me to consider.

I hate to admit it, but I love the way she tastes. I sweep my tongue against hers at the same moment I flap my wings to have us both upright. Making it easier for me to nip my way down her neck toward those magnificent tits.

She unhooks one of her arms from around my neck to run her hand up my spine to find the soft spot beneath my wings, kneading along the ridge where skin meets leathery hide.

"More," I groan against her mouth.

There's something about this woman that I can't resist, and I've never felt it so brutally, so intensely, as I do now. I kiss my way back up her neck to just beneath her ear. Loving the way she shivers for me as she continues to massage that spot near my wings.

Eve twists her head to capture my lips, the height not seeming to bother her anymore. She's hiding it if it does.

No, she's taken the power back from me in a way only she can manage as she shifts her hips over the solid line of my cock in my pants.

She knows how to kiss every molecule of air out of my body before I'm even aware that I've submitted to her.

I deepen our kiss, her lips parting for my tongue.

"No more waiting." My words are a growl. "You're mine. *Mine.*"

"Fuck you," she bites back. Then this seductress rolls her hips against me and I practically come undone with the need to claim her. Physically. Immediately.

I rip her dress from her body, followed by her underwear, and the fabrics blow away from us in the wind. Leaving her absolutely bare ass naked in my arms. My grin turns wicked the longer I stare at her.

Goosebumps decorate her creamy skin, and her defiance melts into a moan as I trail my fingers over her pebbled flesh, pausing at her hardened nipples. My cock strains for more especially when she shifts against me. I can practically feel the wetness of her pussy grinding along my dick, making us both crazy with the need to claim each other.

"I hate you, Dracon," she mutters through kisses. As she hastily moves to undo my zipper while I hold her tight and my wings keep us aloft and safe. "I fucking hate you and your Kings and everything about you."

I'm okay with that. Angry, hate sex is my favorite kind.

The second she has my pants pushed down, my dick finds her entrance, and I slam upward. Her spine arches as I move inside her. The only sound she makes is a strangled gasp at the intrusion. That's the way it's supposed to be.

I hold her green eyes, sinking all the way inside of her before I start my brutal rhythm. Consumed by her. By the need to brand her insides.

I know she sees the dragon burning through me as I fuck her, neither one of us caring.

Her eyes blaze as the desire between us continues to grow. Her nails dig into my shoulders and down my back, drawing blood, marking me. I bend to bite her and hold her in place while I build the rhythm. Driving deeper and making her breath catch with each thrust. But I want more from her, so I wiggle my hand between us and find her clit with my thumb and slowly rub circles until her grunts turn to moans of pleasure.

She's mine to own, to take, to bend to my will.

And so far, I've been holding back. She's on the verge of coming undone, and I feel my body tightening, my balls squeezing.

Driving into her. Kissing her hard, punishingly, and I pinch her clit. She explodes in my arms, and fuck, I want to give her so much more.

She's even more stunning when she cums in person, with her head thrown back, her mouth open, and body shuddering in ecstasy.

I get lost watching her lose control and feel my climax building, shooting electric pulses down my spine and straight into my balls. I roar as my orgasm bursts through me, and I slam into her hard, all the way to the hilt. I pulse as she quivers in my arms, flooding her with my seed.

Her sweet pussy squeezes me, greedily sucking on what I have to offer, swallowing my cum. It floods her, while my cock swells, stretching her tight, bringing me unrelenting pleasure.

Her head juts forward, eyes widening, the green in them blazing. "W-What am I feeling?" she breathes the words, her body still shuddering. She moans, sensing my bulbous knot locking in her sweet cunt.

I struggle to find my words right away. Fierceness coils in my chest as I keep streaming my seed into her.

I growl, losing myself to the flame of white heat pummeling through me, and I can tell my desire influences her as well. Her eyes dilate, moans slipping from her mouth as she curves her spine from the sensation rising within her.

This is primal, animalistic fucking and attraction. My body claiming her, and she doesn't know it yet, but right now, she needs only what I can give her. And she'll beg me for more after this.

My wings beat around us, keeping us in the air, and this moment is everything.

She still stares at me, completely stunned and confused.

I lean closer and lick the curve of her neck, inhaling her intoxicating scent—pure sex.

I could fuck her for hours. Bring her orgasm after orgasm.

"Dracon," she moans my name, sounding slightly alarmed.

"It's okay," I assure her. "What you're feeling is my cock engorging inside you. I knot when I fuck. It's a primal instinct, one where my inner beast needs to ensure my seed floods your womb. And if you were a shifter like me and our bodies were compatible, it would ensure you'd carry my baby."

"WHAT! A baby?" I've freaked her a bit with that word. "Fuck, I didn't even know knotting was a thing."

She has no idea what she's doing to me, looking so adorably cute and shocked, while her cunt tightens around me, milking me.

"Not all shifters knot." I growl from the desire that leaves me vulnerable to her.

My eyes roll back as the pulse of seed punches out of me. My kind produces extreme quantities of cum.

Her body is wrapped around me, her heels digging into my back to hold on, but I've got her in my arms. She's not going anywhere, and with each breath, her scent intensifies, driving me wild.

A purr slides up my throat, a lustful purr that calms my

rageful monster. "We will be like this for a bit longer," I tell her.

Her eyes widen once more. "H-How much longer?"

"Hour, maybe less. All depends on how long it takes for the swelling to go down, so I can pull out."

She blinks and I can tell she has a dozen more questions, and it has me smiling. "Take a deep breath and relax. That will help," I exhale the words as I shudder with the final explosion of cum filling her. Tingling spreads over my groin, tightening. "I'll take care of you."

Her hips shift, and I hold her closer, deciding it's time to take this down to earth.

"Hold on, we're heading down."

She clutches me tighter, her naked body so delicious and all mine. The wind swirls past us as I descend slowly, not wanting to scare or harm her, seeing we are connected. I head for the rooftop of the penthouse, where there's a small viewing area with couches set up for entertaining guests.

Wings beating, I land with us, my feet touching the floor right next to the pool, and draw my wings back into me, the sensation accompanied by a slight sting across my shoulder blades. Then it's gone.

"You have a pool?" she murmurs, hanging onto me, staring at the rippling water over my shoulder.

"Yes, and I'd be happy to bring you up here anytime for a swim, as long as you're naked," I say as I walk us over to a wicker couch and sink into the cushioned seat, aiding Eve in adjusting her legs to kneel on either side of me. Every move she makes strokes my cock and does the opposite of helping it go down. So I cup her ass and settle her in my lap.

"Well, this is kind of awkward," she says, glancing down

between our bodies. I look down and linger on her gorgeous, full breasts, her nipples hard and calling to me. "I guess there's no such thing as a quickie for you." Her grin is captivating, even when she uses humor to avoid feeling vulnerable.

"Not at all. I can, but I don't want to. This is natural and beautiful. And I want my cock inside you, so this is the best of all worlds. I'm deep in you, and you can't run away from me."

I shoot her an evil grin, to which she sticks her tongue out at me. I'm laughing for a change. She has this way of bringing needs out of me that I haven't experienced in eons. A desire to see her smile, make her scream for me, hold her close so I know she's safe.

What the fuck has she done to me?

"Well, I can feel you in there, and every time we move, it twitches."

I want to reach over and smooth out the furrow on her brow, but I hold back, trying to maintain some of my control. I hadn't planned on this going past fucking, and yet it had. She's still a liability, even if my head is fucking broken when it comes to her.

"Once we separate, you will need a long shower because my cum will be everywhere," I say to distract myself from my thoughts.

She arches a brow, but she'll learn soon enough what it's like to be with a shifter who knots. "Oh, okay," she murmurs, uncertain.

I don't know when it all changed. When I went from showing her who had the power to giving it to her. I've lost control. And having her sweet, naked body wrapped around mine is fogging my brain, making me think that this woman belongs in my home in a different way.

Despite fucking her brains out, her earlier words are in the front of my mind. She wants to leave us, which only makes me want to stay buried in her forever and never let her go.

"What's up?" she says, interrupting me. "You've gone all tense and growly."

It's not a conversation I want to have while we're locked together, so instead, I say, "I have good news. We found Franco's compound and I'm waiting for confirmation that Kat's there."

"Holy shit, yes! Where are they? Let's go get her." She's bouncing around on my lap, her delicious cunt rubbing my cock, stirring my arousal.

"Tomorrow," I explain, grasping her hips to keep her steady. "We're heading out first thing."

Her eyes are huge. Is she going to start crying?

"I give you my word," I say. "We'll save your friend."

She hugs me suddenly, her face buried into the curve of my neck. Her breathing is heavy, her body tense.

"Thank you," she whispers, her voice croaky. "You have no idea how much this means to me."

Enough to stay?

I rub her back, holding her tightly to me, wanting her to be a part of me.

I always considered my actions irremediable. I've done horrible things, spilled too much blood. I'm not a hero in any sense of the word, and the ugliness of this world has destroyed me. My own family rejected me, tortured me, and that shit changed me.

But then she came into my world.

A woman who is more vulnerable than she lets on, and I'd ruin anyone who hurts her. I've been working on controlling my desire for this woman, to force her out of my thoughts, to eliminate her.

Except, after fucking her, I realize the truth.

I've lost myself to her. And whether she likes it or not, I'm making her mine now.

My new sweet little treasure has no idea what's coming her way.

"All clear," Dracon mutters under his breath, rearing back from around the corner of Franco's warehouse.

Last time I was hauled into one of his facilities, I landed in a world of trouble. And yet, here I am, about to confront the prick again… hopefully for the last time.

His hideout sits on the outskirts of the city in the middle of nowhere. No houses or cars on the dusty road, not even birds. Just fields of overgrown grass surround us and the sun beating down on our shoulders.

And then this eyesore. A massive warehouse that looks brand spanking new and several black Audis out the front. Not suspicious at all.

Franco's guards have all been eliminated by Dracon's men from around the property. And now it's time to save Kat.

"Time to move in," Cassius says, settling his hands on my waist, the touch sending a shot of flutters through me. My night with him at the auction still hasn't left my mind, and even a small touch from him sends my body into a horny mess. He literally lifts me from the corner of the building and carries me beneath the window that is high above us. "Your time to shine, sweetheart."

"I'm ready," I murmur, swallowing hard and glancing up to where Knox is holding open the high window for me as he stands on two stacked, wooden crates.

"Any day now," he whispers.

That's the only reason I'm on this mission with them. The only way they'd allow me to attend.

I'm the bait, you see. I go in and distract Franco, lower his defenses, hoping he doesn't kill me instantly, while the Kings slip inside and surround him. Then we save Kat. What kind of death they have in store for Franco... don't know, don't care, whatever it is doesn't bother me. I just want the fuckhead dead.

A solid plan, and yet here I'm slightly hyperventilating too. If I've learned anything about the gangs in this city, it's that everything ends with suffering and blood.

Dracon places a hand on my cheek and pulls my attention to him. My heart pounds, my insides alert at his touch.

Today we're a team about to face an adversary, and yet, flashes of his hunger, him fucking me in the sky and knotting inside me, crash through my mind. The climax he brought out of me taunts me, and I want it so badly again and again. But it's more than that. Something has shifted between us that I can't quite put my finger on.

"Dracon," I breathe, torn about my feelings. Torn at how he treats me sometimes, torn that I crave him, torn that he looks at me like I'm his world.

These are all things I shouldn't be thinking of when we're in enemy territory. I exhale loudly.

"You've got this," he tells me. "Just don't do anything stupid that puts you in danger. I want you alive," he explains with sincerity in his voice. "We'll be right behind you in the shadows."

"I got it." I clear my throat quietly as he lowers his hand.

Cassius whispers in my ear, "Just as we practiced, okay, Eve? Distract him and take him as far from Kat as possible."

I nod. "I was made for this job," I tease, and he smiles with his eyes.

Then he lifts me up high, and I grab hold of the window frame, Dracon pushing me higher by my legs with ease.

Knox is holding the long window open. He watches me with that killer expression he wears when he's torturing someone. He's excited to go ballistic on these men, to have fun, I can tell. "Once you drop inside, go left, then stick to the wall until it comes to the front of the warehouse," he explains.

"Okay." My knuckles are white with the pressure I place on the window ledge.

"They hurt you, I'll skin them alive," he explains nonchalantly, like that's a normal thing to say to someone. I don't complain because, like I said, he's on my side this time.

With another shove from Dracon and Cassius, I throw a leg over the frame and look inside, the place is littered with shelving units. It's dimly lit in the back where I am, but from my location, the front entrance is in view. Roller doors are up, sunlight pouring in, and I count five men, but I don't see Franco.

"Hurry up," Cassius hisses.

Right. I drag myself over and look down. It's a bit of a drop, but not anything I'll die from.

So I let go.

Landing on my feet, I bend my knees to catch myself.

When I take a quick look up, Knox isn't watching, so he missed me sticking the landing. His loss.

I turn left and dart into the shadows as per my instructions, scanning every aisle between the stacked shelves. I pass several henchmen keeping guard in the shadows, most facing away from me, one tapping on his phone, another scratching his balls.

Nimbly, I sprint forward, not making a sound, my black clothes and hat concealing me.

Three quarters of the way down the warehouse, I pause, check around me to confirm it's clear, and pull out the cell phone Cassius gave me for the mission. Turning away to conceal the light from the screen, I send him details fast on where the goons are located and how many I've seen so far.

Then I'm off again when a female's voice cries out. "Please, please. Just let me go."

I freeze on the spot. I know that voice. It's Kat.

Dread creeps up from my gut, the hairs on my nape rising. Her pleas aren't coming from my right.

I shudder at the sound of her crying out, and my blood turns to ice.

Of course, I need to keep going straight ahead, but what if Franco is with her? What if I find a way to rescue her without anyone knowing?

I pivot and sprint down a narrow aisle between high shelves stacked with wooden crates. And I'm brought out to a wide passage that divides the room into two enormous spaces. I peer out and there are the guys by the open doors to my left, and to my right, only darkness.

"Johnny!" someone yells from the front of the warehouse. I look to see a burly man with a rifle over his shoulder marching in my direction. "Can you get a hold of Tony? The fucking weasel isn't answering my messages."

Panic slams into me, and I throw myself against the nearest shelf, squeezing in between two crates. It's tight, and my ass wasn't made for fitting into tight spaces.

"Nah," Johnny answers, and he strolls right past where I'm hiding. "Seth isn't picking up either."

They're mumbling something when the first guy barks, "Find out what the fuck's going on."

Shit. Tucking the phone in under my shirt, I blindly send Cassius a heads-up text of men coming his way.

Four more guys emerge from the shadows of the warehouse, and after a few moments of hearing their voices fade, I sneak out. I peer around the corner, and that's when I spot the edge of a cage sticking out from behind a metal shelving unit at the front of the warehouse. And from it comes whimpers. Kat's whimpers.

My insides curdle. *I'll get you out. Won't be long now.*

A man saunters into the warehouse like he owns it. A huge burly man, wearing a three-piece pin-stripped suit, shoulders squared, and an eyepatch. His good eye scanning the area in one quick sweep.

Franco.

My pulse is on fire, my hands curl into fists. He'll die today.

Showtime.

Do anything to distract him, I remind myself. Does stabbing him in his good eye count?

Taking a deep breath, I shake myself and step out of my hiding spot, strolling toward Franco, putting force into my steps on purpose, and do my best to look as scared as possible.

Which isn't hard, considering nerves already dance

through my body. I sense the weight of the knife in my boot too, because I'm not insane enough to do this unprepared again.

He snaps his head up at my approach.

His good eye widens in surprise, which makes me grin, to know I did that to him.

He growls. "I was wondering how long it would take before I'd see you again." He runs a finger under his eyepatch, the corners of his mouth tugging down into a terrifying smile. "We have unfinished business, you and me."

"Well you did invite me, and I couldn't be rude and not attend."

That's when a flash of movement bursts from my side, and next thing I know, I'm locked in one of Franco's henchman's arms, a thick arm tight around my throat. I tense up, but I don't fight.

He roughly walks me over to Franco, who grabs me by the hair and wrenches me out of the other man's arms. I bump into his huge torso from the force. Solid as steel, the guy is a beast.

"Where are the Kings?" he spits the words in my face, and unease settles in my gut.

I take a side glance at the cage Kat's sitting in, her cheeks covered in tears. She's bloody and filthy, and fury pummels through my veins at her state. She sees me and whimpers louder.

Franco tugs my hair harder, and I cry out, turning my attention to him. I let out a frustrated sigh and stare into his creepy, dark eyes—well, eye.

"Those pricks. Who the hell knows?" I lie. "They're probably somewhere fucking themselves. I escaped the first moment they looked away. Then, I followed one of your men from the city here because I know you've got Kat. And I'm here to rescue her."

He barks a laugh, the sound booming through the warehouse.

"You are a very stupid girl," he says. "But I'm also no fool."

"Then you'll hear me out. I have a deal you won't be able to pass up," I purr, which is a feat, considering my scalp is screaming in pain.

"You have nothing I want. But I will kill you today."

"How about you stop pulling my hair like a girl and hear me out?"

His upper lip curls away from his perfect line of white teeth. He releases me, but with the same move, his fist connects with my gut.

I let out a grunted breath and stumble back, clutching my stomach, agony carving through me. I might have cried out, but it's hard to tell as the pain strikes deep before and my knees give way.

"Talk," he bellows.

My heart pangs, and I try to work through the throbbing pain. Why does it hurt so much to get struck in the gut?

"Me for Kat," I gasp, lifting my gaze to the ass. That's when I notice more guards appear from the shadows. How many of them are there? "Let her go, and you've got me."

"I already have you." He snorts, while the goons laugh as Franco roughly drags me back to my feet by my shoulder. "My boss will be here any moment, so your timing is run out."

Wait! Did he say, boss? What the fuck does that mean? Everyone knows Franco is the head of the Black Spades.

Maybe I can use this to my advantage and distract him. Bruise the ego.

"So, the big honcho himself isn't the boss. I'm surprised. Don't tell me you're just a puppet like the rest of the men you order around?"

With a piercing glare, he grabs a black handgun from his belt and points the barrel in my face. "Why shouldn't I kill you right now?"

Fuck. Bad idea.

Okay, don't taunt the lunatic mobster, Eve.

"B-Because I can g-give you insider information on the Kings." I hate that my voice shakes. "I've been trapped at their place long enough to have picked up things. I know the ins and outs. Which gangs they're doing deals with. Where they hide their merchandise. I'll spill everything to give you an advantage. Let my friend go, and I'm yours." I'm lying through my teeth about knowing so much, but I need to reel him in.

Free Kat.

The Kings will come for me.

Then we kill Franco.

He looks at me, his good eye full of interest.

"So, we have a deal?" I press him and clench my jaw. Behind me, Kat doesn't make a sound, but I sense her watching us.

Nerves curl around my spine and the urge to look around for the Kings grows with each passing second. Are they even here yet or dealing with the henchmen outside?

Crack!

Something explodes at the entrance of the warehouse, and I jump in my skin.

An explosion of red smoke billows in front of the door. What the hell is going on? It better be the Kings.

Power ripples down my arms.

I stumble back a few steps, unsure what I'm staring at as I frantically peer into the smoke, waiting for something to leap out, to do something.

Franco drops to one knee, his head low.

What the hell?

His men follow suit. They look like they are paying respect to something... someone.

The back of my heels hit the cage, and I swing around to see Kat locked up. She's gripping the metal wire, her fingers poking out through the holes. When I spot the one missing—just a bloody stump—bile scalds the back of my throat.

"Eve, let me out, please." She's pleading, crying. The fear in her voice strangles me.

I crouch down. "I will, I promise. No way will I leave you here."

A thunderous growl booms and I spin back around, facing the entrance of the warehouse. Something's emerging from the smoke.

My breath catches, and my feet are glued to the floor.

Something steps out that looks nothing like a man.

A rider atop a monstrous red horse emerges, holding a flaming sword. With fiery pupils, he's dressed in red armor.

Terror bores down into my bones at what I'm seeing.

I grip my stomach, staring in disbelief.

The horse abruptly rears on hind legs, appearing larger than life and snorting red flames.

I might have just screamed.

"I knew it!" Knox suddenly bellows from behind me, his voice sharp and commanding.

I snap around, startled. He's storming out of the shadows, scaring me half to death.

"What the hell is going on?" I cry.

He doesn't even notice me as he shoots past. He's fuming, his face flushed with rage, and swinging his Mortem Blade at the monster.

"I knew you'd fucking return for me, Aris. And I'm ready this time, motherfucker!"

KNOX

The rest of the room fades away. The noise, the screaming, the fight raging around on either side of me and a fat Franco somewhere. I square off against Aris, my brother. I've been waiting for this moment for-fucking-ever, and it's high time I stop running.

My blade, his head.

It's a date.

He dismounts from his red charger like some kind of knight in the same crimson armor he'd worn the last time I'd seen him. Tossing the reins aside, he faces me with his helmet on, and even though most of his face is covered, I know he's fucking grinning at me.

I grind my teeth.

He's the reason I'm on this planet. He's the reason my scythe was broken and my horse was lost to me. Because of him, my life has been completely flipped on its head.

I'm not sure why he's here and although rage courses through my veins instead of blood at the sight of him, it's a blessing. This is the one fucking thing in my life that's gone right, because him appearing saves me from trying to track him down.

A sharp crack of his palm sends the horse running back into the smoke and shadows where it first came. Aris slowly removes his helmet, revealing his dark hair, neatly trimmed facial hair, and fiery red pupils. They bore into me.

He cocks his head to the side as if to say this isn't the meeting he expected. Which is a bold face lie. "Brother," he muses with a short laugh. "What in the cosmos are you doing here?"

Skidding to a stop, my chest heaves as I stare him down. "Don't give me that shit, Aris. You came looking for *me*."

His laughter booms, ricocheting off of the walls around us. "Knox, really? Come on now. Not everything is about you."

A muscle in my jaw pops from clenching my jaw so tight.

"I haven't seen you in over a millennia, and now you think I've come all this way...for what? Christmas dinner?"

His attention shifts from me to who's behind me, and it takes me a second to realize he's looking at Eve. My entire body numbs, and I grip my blade even tighter. Fury unlike anything I've ever felt before whirls through me.

Aris's gaze tracks back to me, and when it rests on my blade, a sickening smile creeps across his thin lips.

"Ah, I see you found your scythe," he muses, but then another clip of laughter escapes. "Or, at least, a tiny piece of it."

"It still has enough power to kill you," I snap and twist the thing in my grasp for good measure.

"It sure can." Aris watches its every move. My scythe—now the Mortem Blade—can not only take out living souls.

It is the only known object that can kill us too. Permanently.

Which means that I am Death over *all*. And Aris hates that I have that power over him. He always has.

He tries to look around me to get another glimpse of Eve, but I sidestep, blocking his view again. His lips pinch, his aggravation growing.

"Why are you even here? Except to get in my fucking way," he barks, holding his arms out wide. "As I told you before, this has nothing to do with you, so you need to step aside."

I'm not falling for his lies. "It has everything to do with me."

Aris pauses, glancing around the room and taking in the scene. "Wait a minute," he starts as he begins to put the puzzle pieces together. "Don't tell me you're involved with these *mortals*." He spits the word like it disgusts him. "Criminals? Money? Gangs? You're not really part of their little club, are you?"

Everything he says only fuels the blaze inside me. Maybe it's because as horsemen, our powers are always stronger when we're together, but I feel like I'm about to burst at any second.

"You are!" he shouts, throwing his head back in a fit of laughter again. "It's official. You've lost what little is left of your sanity."

"I'm a King of Eden," I say and stare him down. "A King!"

"A king can die." As if he no longer sees me as a threat, he extinguishes his flaming sword with a flick of his wrist and sheaths the handle on his belt. For some reason, that enrages me even more. Fire erupts behind my ribs.

He thinks I'm a joke.

He strolls forward, trying to get around me, but I whip out my sword, blocking him from taking another step closer to her. One touch, and he'll keel over dead, like the rest of the mortals he turns his nose up at.

Lazily, his gaze slides up the blade to meet mine again. "You really want to do this again?" he asks.

I grin. "I thought you'd never ask."

His eyes flicker reddish orange like burning embers. Then, he gives the subtlest of nods right, snapping my attention that way.

Another wave of Franco's men come rushing at me, gunshots raging.

"Knox! Watch out!" Eve's voice catches my ear, but I'm not fast enough in this human body to dodge every bullet. Two bury themselves into my shoulder and thigh, and the pain is so sharp, it takes me aback.

Fuck, that shit stings!

Knowing I can't just ignore the new wave of Spades, I rush toward them, blade out. That was his goal, wasn't it? To keep me distracted.

Aris simply steps back, watching the show as I cut down as many men as I can before they can shoot more holes in me. With Dracon and Cassius still fighting outside, I'm on my own in here, but I refuse to let Aris walk out of here alive.

My blade slices easily through the sea of bodies. Left, right, over and over. Another bullet sinks into my stomach, making me stumble and gasp. I may not be able to die from gunshots, but they can still slow me down.

I use the burning pain as energy to keep me going, and gradually, I make my way over to my asshole brother.

Plunging my knife into the final Spade's chest, I roar

my death cry. Blood coats me, soaking into my hair and clothes, seeping into my eyes, and running off my chin.

"Aris!" I bellow, blind in my rage. "Come over here and fucking fight me yourself!"

It's his turn to die. I'll see him on his knees in front of me, one way or another.

The taste of blood sings on my tongue, along with a hunger for death in my heart.

Aris continues to stare at me with a bored expression, and all it does is infuriate me more. This isn't the showdown I'd been expecting, the one I'd rehearsed for decades–centuries–in my head.

I'm supposed to be getting my revenge. This is meant to be my retribution!

Breathing hard, I wait for Aris to grab his sword again and plunge into battle, but he doesn't even reach for it. Only sighs, tsking me and shaking his head. Like I'm nothing more than a nuisance in his way.

"Look, Brother, if you want to play house with the mortals, go right ahead. I won't stop you," he says and strides across the warehouse, stepping over the dead Spades without even glancing down. I chase his every move, waiting for the outburst, the war cry or charge. But it never comes.

"I didn't stir up all this destruction or meddle in living affairs for you." Aris peers over my shoulder, and when I follow his gaze, I find Eve kneeling on the ground beside her boss in the cage.

Confused, I glance between the both of them. "I...don't understand."

"Don't you see, Brother? I've come for her," he explains further, and my heart falters.

Her?

All this…has been for *her*? Eve? My little dove?

A fierce wave of protectiveness comes over me, and my entire body shakes from the force of it. I raise the Mortem Blade higher, daring him to even *think* about taking her from me. I'll cleave his head off so fast, he won't even know what's happened.

But still, Aris is unfazed by my threats and the danger he's in. Instead, a prideful smile flickers across his lips as he keeps gazing upon Eve. "She's my offspring, you see. She's the Daughter of Chaos."

Daughter?

With his words, my mind fractures into pieces.

He's lying!

He *has* to be lying! Has to be!

I watch as Eve's eyes widen in horror, and in that instant, I think back to everything I've witnessed with her—the wildness of her powers, the untamable strength, and how I was able to see it manifest while I was in spirit form.

Or how she'd been able to use my blade without the Death magic killing her…

Only horsemen can wield it and die from it.

Only horsemen.

Oh no…

I've always only had two goals:

Keep Eve safe.

Murder Aris.

But those things aren't aligning anymore. Now, they're on opposite ends of the spectrum.

No. Fuck, no!

My little dove has become my enemy.

STOLEN PARADISE

KINGS OF EDEN, BOOK 2

With my life already at stake, my world has just taken a turn for the worst... It turns out that the Kings of Eden are so much more than I ever bargained for.

Read the captivating dark paranormal romance sequel, Stolen Paradise.

Grab your copy today by clicking here.

PLAYING WITH HELLFIRE

SIN DEMONS COMPLETE SERIES

Demons are real.

They say never enter into a deal with them, but what if I had no choice?

What if they are three of the most gorgeous men I've seen my entire life?

And what if my lesson to learn here is that no matter how attracted I am to them, how much I yearn to kiss them, I'm in danger.

But my life's never been the easiest. I've bounced from house to house, living in foster care, with no true place to call home. And there's an ancient darkness that follows me around where I go.

They may be demons, but I'm no angel, and this darkness craves the Hell they give.

Or maybe I've just been damned from the start.

Available on Amazon

ABOUT MILA YOUNG

Best-selling author, Mila Young tackles everything with the zeal and bravado of the fairytale heroes she grew up reading about. She slays monsters, real and imaginary, like there's no tomorrow. By day she rocks a keyboard as a marketing extraordinaire. At night she battles with her mighty pen-sword, creating fairytale retellings, and sexy ever after tales. In her spare time, she loves pretending she's a mighty warrior, walks on the beach with her dogs, cuddling up with her cats, and devouring every fantasy tale she can get her pinkies on.

Ready to read more and more from Mila Young?www.subscribepage.com/milayoung

www.milayoungbooks.com
For more information...
milayoungauthor@gmail.com

ABOUT HARPER A. BROOKS

Harper A. Brooks lives in a small town on the New Jersey shore. Even though classic authors have always filled her bookshelves, she finds her writing muse drawn to the dark, magical, and romantic. But when she isn't creating entire worlds with sexy shifters or legendary love stories, you can find her either with a good cup of coffee in hand or at home snuggling with her furry, four-legged son, Sammy.

RONE AWARD WINNER
USA TODAY BESTSELLING AUTHOR
INTERNATIONAL BESTSELLING AUTHOR

Want to read more from Harper A. Brooks?
Subscribe to Harper's newsletter and get *Halfling for Hire* for free! http://BookHip.com/MCBDCN

www.ingramcontent.com/pod-product-compliance
Lightning Source LLC
Chambersburg PA
CBHW050752190726
48285CB00005B/1631